D1570841

STREET OF LOST BROTHERS

STREET OF LOST BROTHERS

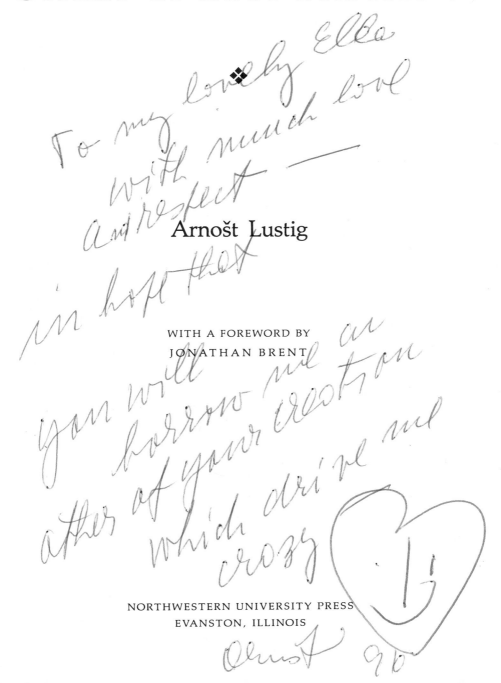

Arnošt Lustig

WITH A FOREWORD BY
JONATHAN BRENT

NORTHWESTERN UNIVERSITY PRESS
EVANSTON, ILLINOIS

Northwestern University Press
Evanston, Illinois 60201

"Morning till Evening" was first published in *Formations* 5:3. "Infinity" was first published in *The New England Review*. "A Man the Size of a Postage Stamp" was first published in *The Kenyon Review*. "Red Oleanders" was first published in *The World and I*.

"Morning till Evening," "Infinity," and "Red Oleanders" were translated by Vera Borkovec. "A Man the Size of a Postage Stamp" and "Night" were translated by Jeanne Němcová. "First before the Gates" and "Clock Like a Windmill" were translated by Josef Lustig.

Printed in the United States of America

95 94 93 92 91 90   5 4 3 2 1

The paper used in this publication meets the minimum requirements of American National Standard for Information Sciences—Permanence of Paper for Printed Library Materials, ANSI Z39.48-1984

Library of Congress Cataloging-in-Publication Data

Lustig, Arnošt.
    [Selections. English. 1990]
    Street of lost brothers / Arnošt Lustig; with a foreword by
Jonathan Brent.
        p.   cm.
    Contents: Morning till evening — Infinity — A man the size of a
postage stamp — Night — First before the gates — Clock like a
windmill — Red oleanders.
    ISBN 0-8101-0959-X (alk. paper). — ISBN 0-8101-0960-3 (pbk.:
alk. paper)
    1. Lustig, Arnošt—Translations, English. I. Title.
PG5038.L85A2 1990
891.8'635—dc20   90-46131
                                                        CIP

Four things disquiet man: war, misery, pain, and death.

CONTENTS

❖

FOREWORD

❖

Kurtz gazed into the heart of darkness and pronounced the words: "The horror! The horror!" This utterance by Joseph Conrad's devil/saint has haunted the literature of our bedeviled century. During the Nazi catastrophe, the nature of this evil seemed to assume a specific appearance in all the outward signs of German power and the details of German actions. In the Nazi uniform, Kurtz's horror was incarnated; in the Nazi death camps, evil achieved its ultimate and fascinating ends.

Many subsequent writers have attempted to repeat Kurtz's act of vision. Tadeusz Borowski, in *This Way for the Gas, Ladies and Gentlemen*, has described in Dantesque detail his personal descent into the pit.

We climb inside [the cattle cars unloading at Auschwitz]. In the corners amid human excrement and abandoned wristwatches lie squashed, trampled infants, naked little monsters with enormous heads and bloated bellies. We carry them out like chickens, holding several in each hand.

The morbid procession streams on and on. . . . I can still see corpses dragged from the train, trampled infants, cripples piled on top of the dead, wave after wave.

Elie Wiesel has recorded similar scenes in *Night:*

> Not far from us, flames were leaping up from a ditch, gigantic
> flames. They were burning something. A lorry drew up at the pit
> and delivered its load—little children. Babies! Yes, I saw it—saw
> it with my own eyes...those children in the flames....I was face
> to face with the Angel of Death.

To Borowski and Wiesel the evil lies in what they see, feel, smell,
touch, hear. "I saw it with my own eyes," Wiesel insists. Who can deny
these images? Who can disregard the evil they signify? The "wave after
wave" of infants and trampled corpses gives its measure. But evil in
itself is not a quantitative phenomenon. In the terrifying visions of
Wiesel, Borowski, and so many others, we glimpse the reality of what
the Nazi evil has done, but not necessarily what that evil was or is.

There is an undeniable voyeuristic interest in scenes of Nazi brutality.
The imagination dwells on them. They possess lurid fascination. They
are evil, of course, and so we condemn them; but they are also slightly
pornographic. Voyeuristically excited by the descriptions, we simultaneously experience great moral satisfaction in abhorring them. Toward
these images we can feel absolute revulsion, absolute indignation. But
evil itself is perhaps more complicated. After all, we are told that the
serpent, whom God created, was more subtle than any beast of the
field.

Evil does not wear a uniform; nor does it consist in fire, excrement,
or tortured flesh. Arnošt Lustig, perhaps alone among the writers to
depict the Nazi world, recognizes that the true horror is always precisely
what you do not see, what you *never* see. The encounter with evil in
Lustig's fiction is always an encounter with what eludes the eye.

If one cannot see evil—or for that matter truth, justice, or goodness—
in Lustig's stories, one can imagine it. And it is through the process of
the imagination that his characters attain a knowledge of evil or a
perception of truth. Revelation, for Lustig, comes from within oneself,
not from without.

The stories in *Street of Lost Brothers* depict the imagination in its attempts at grasping unimaginable reality. Each story leads to a different, subtly attenuated encounter with this world. Not simply a fixed faculty of mind, the imagination in Lustig's fiction is a working together of thought, feeling, perception, memory, and fantasy. Broadly, however, he depicts two types of imaginative process: one that conceives of life in absolute and totalistic systems; the other, diametrically opposed, that conceives of life in terms of relative and fragmentary experience. The first could be labeled the Nazi imagination; the second something like the liberal imagination, as Lionel Trilling once defined it. In *Street of Lost Brothers*, as in all of Lustig's fiction, these two radically opposed ways of seeing the world clash.

The second type of imagination informs the opening of the first story of this collection, as Emanuel Mautner greets his wife:

"I'm back," he said.
"Yes," said the woman.
Emanuel Mautner, taking off his coat, whistled the melody of a song from the Italian front. He stood there, thin, with soft black hair. His narrow, nut-brown face camouflaged the fatigue of nighttime.

This fleeting scene of Emanuel Mautner's return home and conversation with his wife draws us into the world of partial illumination, fragmented time and space which characterize daily experience. The melody of the song he whistles is from the Italian front of World War I. When he says, "I'm back," he is both back at the Italian front at which presumably he fought some thirty years before and back home with his wife in Prague. The complexion of his face obscures the inner fatigue. The doorway Emanuel Mautner enters opens onto the past as well as the present, the seen as well as the unseen.

Their son was murdered on a Nazi death march in 1945. Now, Mr. Mautner goes each day—or pretends to go at his wife's direction—to a bureau to inquire whether his son might not yet return. Emanuel knows his son will not return, but his wife clings to the illusion and hope. Before the war, he had worked for two brothers in their umbrella factory.

He no longer knew where they were or where they emigrated to. He didn't know that the brothers had left during the last possible days in 1939, just before the fifteenth of March. On the sixteenth, when the Germans had already invaded the country, Emanuel went to work and the clerk told him the two brothers were out.

Later, Emanuel reflects:

The two brothers—what did they look like? He tried to re-member their voices or the sounds inside their voices when business was good. . . .

He looked at the wooden umbrella on the facade of the house in Carpenter Street facing Peters Square. It was displayed on the wall between the first and third floors. . . . The children of future parents would wonder about the origin of the wooden umbrella on the building. . . .

Maybe they were living somewhere far away in an unknown place and would never come back. . . . Maybe they were selling umbrellas somewhere in New Zealand. Or they joined one of the armies that helped defeat Nazi Germany. He imagined men who defended the lives they were in charge of, armies that didn't fail, officers who died rather than jeopardize the lives of their troops.

As Emanuel walks down the street of the lost brothers, his mind draws together past and present and searches toward a future. Memory mixes with desire until an image forms which reveals more of Emanuel's character than the brothers' unknown fate. The ability to unite disparate, small details of both the self and world, of the self *with* the world, the seen with the unseen, enables Emanuel eventually to know and accept his son's death. Emanuel is able to move from past to present to future, while his wife remains trapped in what he refers to as "our memories of a better past."

As he leaves the street of the lost brothers, Emanuel wonders what time it is. For his wife it is always time past; for those building the new social order it is time future. But for Emanuel the echo of the past merges with awareness of the present and the expectations of the future. What is lost has a dual existence. This is the meaning of the boy's revelation in the story "Infinity," when the women in the adjoining camp at Auschwitz begin their nightly singing.

> The singing filled the night with double voices. Double darkness. Double eyes. Double blood. Double snow, and far above the snow clouds, in a double star-filled sky. Double memory. Double hope and illusion. It filled it with all the things that man possesses only once in his life and loses.

The doubleness of this world is the double horizon of man, thrown forward toward the future while embedded in the past. The realization of this double structure is itself fundamentally opposed by the Nazi order.

While the women's voices elicit a vision of the doubleness of man's existence, Captain Johann Wolfram von und zu Wulkow, in "First Before the Gates," observes the world through a monocle. This single eye allows Captain Wulkow, "with his silvery hair and polite, reserved manner, . . . a German count who spoke fluent French, English, and Latin," to "leave the city as a warrior, without looking back." Later, the Captain recollects the wife of his commander with whom he had once been in love: "It was the past, a bridge where a man shouldn't turn his head backward. But he did, in secret, for himself." To not look back demands an act of will. The captain consciously cuts himself off from his past, his desire, and his individuality.

Lustig's portrayal of the interior life of this aristocratic German captain must rank as one of the most penetrating in all of contemporary literature's attempts at seeing into "the other." It is here that the one-

eyed, monologic Nazi imagination is most fully represented in its opposition to the world's plenitude.

Captain Johann Wolfram von und zu Wulkow, a German count
with beautiful manners, commands a military camp overlooking Prague
during the last days of the war, just before the outbreak of the Prague
uprising. It was said that the captain "talked without shouting, read
poetry, and listened to music." This subtle man of the highest culture,
who is capable of observing to himself that Prague was "Rainer Maria
Rilke's city, the place he described as a 'miserable town of suborned
existences,'" finds before him one evening the young boy, Otto Kubarsky.
Otto wets his bed, often as many as three times a week. Orphaned
during the war, he is cared for by his grandmother, a washerwoman in
the railroad station. The boy is fascinated by the noble German, by the
arms of the soldiers, and by the Nazi tanks "like the Königstiger, the
King Tiger, the Panther—the best tank of the war."

The captain observes young Kubarsky and reflects "about what the
military camp of the victors meant to a child of a close enemy tribe.
Captain Wulkow thought then of history, of what makes it greater than
man." The captain's poetic temperament is evinced in his evocation of
the child's mind, but just as he dismisses his recollection of his commander's wife, he instantly subordinates the concrete image of the child
to the abstraction "of what makes [history] greater than man." In this
seemingly innocent inner action of mind lies the evil which eventually
will realize itself in the satanic spectacles of Borowski and Wiesel. Later,
the captain reflects that "only the strongest, most ruthless will survive
this time, this place, this world . . . not the most civilized."

The captain thinks about history. Otto Kubarsky's grandmother
thinks about her former neighbors, Emanuel Bloch and his ninety-eight-
year-old mother, who had been murdered in retaliation for the killing
of Reinhard Heydrich:

> They were part of her thoughts when she was scrubbing the floor,
> the restrooms, and the cloakrooms at the railroad station, and
> when sweeping the hall around the bumpers of the railroad cars. . . .

In her mind she saw Mr. Emanuel Bloch drink water from the faucet in the hall or go to the common restroom with his hands folded as in prayer. Was it true that Mr. Emanuel Bloch and his mother prayed facing east? Was he dead like his mother, like her husband and her daughter? Who ate at his table now? Who sat in his chair, slept in his bed?

The captain's imagination produces categorical assertions and abstractions; the grandmother's imagination leads her to a concrete image and a question. The Nazi captain thinks in endless monologue; the grandmother in dialogue with the dead. The captain's world, for all his ability to quote Rilke and translate from Latin into French and English, is nonrelational, abstract, a closed system of premises and conclusions. The grandmother's world is concrete, associative, highly individualized, penetrated by details, questions, and possibilities. The captain's monologue produces the death camps and boundless ambition of the Reich; the grandmother's dialogue produces an action of mind that can withstand, albeit with great suffering, the Nazi terror.

The old lady considers the fate of a single man and his mother. She discovers Mr. Bloch's discarded prayer book and although she is not Jewish teaches herself some of the prayers. She comes to identify with him so that her life becomes a double life. She, like Mr. Mautner and the narrator of "Infinity," enters the horizon of dialogic time.

The captain, too, thinks of the past. But for the Nazi imagination, the past is impersonal, collective. "The captain thought about their Teutonic past. That age didn't seem so far off. Nor did it seem difficult for him to look forward a thousand years." Past, present, and future stand in linear relation to each other so that a thousand years in the future is as clear to the captain as a moment just past. No questions, accidents, or unseemly possibilities interfere with his vision. Only certainties array themselves before his monocled inner eye.

Smiling slightly, he . . . felt how one thing was connected to another. History didn't just follow. It is the result of individuality and resolve and conduct in unstable times. History made Captain Wulkow tell the soldiers to bring a small barrel of rum for those who were not on duty.

History makes Captain Wulkow order rum. Mr. Emanuel Bloch causes the grandmother eventually to find her way to the Nazi camp to plead for the life of her grandson. History, again, causes the captain to order that both boy and old woman be tied to the gun barrel of a tank which tomorrow would be driven through Prague to suppress the growing insurrection.

A stunning image occurs in the story, "Clock like a Windmill." During the first days of the Prague Uprising, a group of frightened Czech citizens takes refuge in the Town Hall. Two clocks surmount the building: one, in the tower itself, has Arabic numbers; the other, located in the gable under the tower, has Hebrew letters, rather than numbers, and the hands move counterclockwise "like leaves in a Hebrew book." These two clocks are still to be found keeping time above Prague's town hall. A woman in the group imagines that she "could feel the tensions created by the two clocks, so near each other but in perpetual opposition." For those in the cellar, time moves forward and backward simultaneously. For the Nazis who come upon them, time moves straight toward victory. The radical opposition in Lustig's fiction centers on this difference.

Nazi time is epic time. The literary scholar Gary Saul Morson has distinguished, in contradistinction to the genre of the epic, a genre he has termed the prosaic. This distinction serves well to illuminate another dimension of the Nazi menace as Lustig protrays it. As much as it was social, political, economic, and military, the Nazi order also constituted a particular genre of imagination. We find this confirmed in the smallest details of Lustig's picture of the Nazi regime. In "A Man the Size of a Postage Stamp," Feldwebel Karl Oberg, the leader of the camp band, hums the tune to "Entry of the Gladiators." He tells the camp commandant's simpleminded son, who can remember only three of the four elements of the universe, that the fifth element "is us"—the Nazi spirit. He also muses that simpletons like this boy should either be given a mercy death or castrated.

The Nazi's grand dreams of the Teutonic Knights are counterposed by Henryk Bley's dream of the Persian city of Susa where Queen Esther had once rescued her people from destruction.

Henryk Bley stared at the toes of his shoes. He tried to concentrate on Easter Monday, or on a distant picture of the city of Susa, in Persia, where he'd been once. The muddle of the village came closer and then faded away—fragments of an image. There was also a man in a regal robe, embroidered with pearls, gold, and rubies, who'd wanted to exterminate them some hundred and fifty generations ago but had decided not to at the urging of the queen, one of his wives—maybe a little whore in the king's harem—but certainly someone clever, brave, and most probably just.

The picture comes in fragments, the town is a muddle, Queen Esther possibly nothing but a little whore. How different from the image of the legendary Teutonic Knights: "lethal as wolves, keen as hawks, proud as eagles. . . . born of song, blood, and the land, of honor, light, and voices, as hard as tungsten steel, lithe as a leaping panther, mighty as an ocean." Henryk Bley is eventually murdered along with the orphaned children he seeks to protect, even as he attempts to complete the story of Purim for the children.

Lustig offers no consoling fantasy of escape. The imagination is no shield from physical threat. The Nazis, however, cannot fully destroy the innate ability of the mind to discern the truth of what they attempted to do. The narrator of "Infinity" dreams that he is an SS officer in charge of the gas chambers. When the commandant asks how his work is coming, in the dream he replies that although he tramples thousands of ants every day, he can't destroy the breed of ants. The imagination urges us toward vision. Those who do not destroy it in themselves eventually will see.

Henryk Bley and the children are gassed in a van painted like an ambulance. But the commandant's simpleminded son, who Feldwebel Oberg has brought along to educate in becoming a man, is troubled by his visions.

The commandant's son heard the first noises in the back of the van. It was as if sacks of potatoes were falling on the floor, or as if those sacks had ripped open and the potatoes had rolled out, or as if the teacher and the children were fighting. That was when it occurred to him that the exhaust pipes looked like the trunks of old, sick, dying elephants in some unknown jungle. Drops of sweat stood out on his childish, almost girlish forehead.

The boy says nothing, but he knows. Later, while the van is being unloaded and washed, Feldwebel Oberg throws a stone in the swamp. The rings it makes gradually widen and disappear.

"That's the difference between right and wrong," the feldwebel said. "There's no difference in them when you don't want to see. You see?"

    .   .   .

"No," the boy replied.

The boy's "no" cannot be dissipated by reason. The boy rides home in the back of the van.

In the fiction of Arnošt Lustig, evil may end in what is done to the flesh, but it begins in what happens to the imagination. The Nazi world may possess great culture, may identify with a noble past, and may look forward to a heroic future, but it lacks the truth of ordinary experience in the world. "It's unbelievable," Corporal Maurach reflects, "how much depends on ears, noses, and chins, on the color of eyes, hair, and on the mouth." Lustig's stories show us how much does not.

Lustig's moral vision goes far beyond the immediate setting of the Nazi death camps to the inner world of every man and woman. Just as the caretaker in "Clock Like a Windmill" must wind up the two clocks on the tower every Monday, each of Lustig's characters—Nazi, Jew, Pole, or Czech—must wind up his own clock and is responsible for keeping his own time. Will he live in the monologic, epic time of the Thousand Year Reich? Or in the dialogic time of concrete, prosaic experience? Absolute time and bloody apocalypse? Or relative time and fragmentary illumination? Every man and woman is responsible. Not history. Every situation in life forces this choice upon us.

The horror for Lustig is not in the carnage of war or the unspeakable violations of the Nazis. As reprehensible as these are, the horror into which Kurtz first peered and western civilization plunged lies within the subtle calibrations of daily thought and feeling.

Jonathan Brent

MORNING TILL EVENING

1

I'm back," he said.

"Yes," said the woman.

Emanuel Mautner, taking off his coat, whistled the melody of a song from the Italian front. He stood there, thin, with soft black hair. His narrow, nut-brown face camouflaged the fatigue of nighttime.

"How about something to eat?"

"Were you there?"

Emanuel Mautner dropped his eyes. Her glance—as at night with the unfathomable sound of broken branches and the leafless stumps of wood— filled the echo of what she would only suggest. He was glad there was plenty of light coming through both windows of the kitchen.

"Did you look everywhere? All the time you were at the railway station?"

"Now Emily," he tried once more.

He looked at the table, the blue tablecloth, which he had bought before the war, marked with imprints of plates and glasses. The stove was cold. The dishes from yesterday were in the sink.

"Did you talk to anyone?"

The skin on Emanuel Mautner's cheeks furrowed up to his eyes. He held out his coat for her. (When he was leaving that morning, at nine, she had promised to sew on the torn coat tag. The velvet collar was ripped.) She sent him to the railway station and the other places where efforts were being made to locate missing persons.

It occurred to him that they could move from here, from this apartment, this house, this street. Maybe he should prepare Emily for the thought of a retirement home somewhere far away. For a moment he pictured the company they would keep: old women with dyed hair or wigs, wearing heavy make-up like they do in the theater or in the circus.

"Button up, mamitschko," he said.

Emily stood there in her robe, a washable fabric, with nothing under it. She looked at him remotely. He smiled at her. She had blue eyes, tired from the previous night's sleep. Her complexion was smooth and pallid.

"You know what you are."

Emanuel Mautner looked at the floor and slipped into the corner of the kitchen by the window. His cheeks twitched; then the corners of his mouth lifted. He felt an old pang. She had hinted at his origin, as though echoing what had been said daily since the war and Miroslav left.

"You ought to button up," he repeated.

"What happened when you spoke to the building supervisor?"

"They will repair the elevator."

"I can imagine what you told her. What would you be talking about if you couldn't bring me into it?"

He felt a desire to caress her, but he reprimanded himself. For thirteen years he hadn't touched her. When her headaches started, he convinced himself that things were better this way. He smiled a little bit again. The bright daylight whitened him now.

Emily looked at the torn coat tag and then at Emanuel. In his eyes she noticed a moment of retreat. He looked like a bird whose vision has lost the trees or the sky above and the earth and rivers below. She waited to see what he would say. Maybe he would talk about Italy, which he knew during World War I at the river Piave, or about applesauce and coffee, whose prices had soared again because of the frosts in Colombia.

Maybe he would invite her to the Zoological Garden, to watch endangered species like condors, Mongolian horses, or Chinese bears.

He wouldn't let her see the mailman for the same reason he'd given up one newspaper and his subscription to *The Jewish Gazette.* He also terminated his membership in the stamp collectors' society. He even made several trips to a secondhand bookstore to sell their books dealing with the war and, later, Miroslav's book about the famed Lafayette Escadrille, the American volunteer who joined the French Army as a pilot before America entered World War I in 1917.

"Come on, mamitschko," he said, "let me button your robe."

She tore herself away. He wanted to hold her so she wouldn't fall, but her back hit the edge of the stove. Emily pursed her lips slightly. In her mind there circled a planet whose axis revolved without her instructions. It made her pretty and at the same time diminished her beauty.

The sleeping pills had dropped from her pocket. He bent over and picked them up.

He had just gone to the corner drugstore. He continued to buy sleeping pills, not only for the holidays and the end of the year. (Sometimes he played cards for small sums no one would worry about, and this helped him to forget during the hours spent awake.)

"I don't believe a word you say," she told him.

She flushed out a moth that flew up and then perched, its transparent wings fanning on the shade of the kitchen lamp. Emanuel straightened himself. He tried to guess whether she had found out what he and the superintendent had been talking about.

"I'd give anything, darling, to know he's still alive," he whispered, but to be sure, inaudibly, "even if I were never to see him again." In his mind he saw a picture that he'd never confided to his wife.

2

There was a highway leading from the downtown of Landsberg to an adjoining town, Kaufering, known during World War II for its eleven prison camps, some large, others pocket-sized. It was a cold winter day in 1945;

there was snow on the ground. The heavy white flakes glistened at night. They covered the mud, the swamps, the rocks and fields. Miroslav walked with the last row of prisoners. By morning he couldn't continue, and in stopping he moved from the path into a ditch. The column moved on. Some had fallen in the snow before him.

Miroslav knew the order of the two gunmen who walked at the rear. He saw the two escort men at a distance of twenty steps, then heard the bang of their pistols, dry, as though they were firecrackers.

An alder tree grew from the ditch Miroslav sat in. In the dark, his hands could feel the hard bark of its trunk. The tree creaked about close to him. He was glad it wasn't a man. But when he attempted to lean his back against the tree to rest his head, the trunk seemed to move away.

Miroslav knew he was going to freeze. He knew that before freezing one has a sense of warmth, as children do when falling asleep. The breath of the snowstorm began to brush against him. The snow seemed soft.

Suddenly the windy night turned quiet. Before the gunmen could see him, he grew torpid. That was the last he was aware of, no longer conscious of the men who stood over him, neither when they were approaching, nor when they stopped.

First they tried to summon a response by kicking him.

"My nose is frozen," said the first one.

"This will take care of itself before you can blink an eye," the other said.

They tried to awaken him once again. There was no response. They heard only the cracking of bones.

"As they say within the city limits of Landsberg," said the first, "it isn't enought to aim. You must hit. Not all who snore are asleep."

"There are fewer of them," said the second one. "But it seems there are more all the time."

They didn't hear what echoed in Miroslav—Emily's embrace, a mother carrying her frozen son in her blue eyes. Nor could they see the movement of Miroslav's lips, a kiss intended for his father.

Miroslav didn't hear when the first gunmen instructed, "Don't shoot. Save two rounds. He is frozen already."

"We won't lose this war because of one bullet," the second gunmen said. He needed to restore circulation to his fingers before the shot. He took off his gloves.

"As the saying goes in Kaufering: When the apple's ready, it will drop," said the first soldier.

The blast of two gunshots, fired in succession, split the air. The boy's body twitched as though someone were trying to wake him, but no one did. The column moved on. The smell of gunpowder dissolved in the freezing air. The stars didn't move.

3

"Why are you looking at me like that?" Emily asked. "What happened?"

"Nothing," Emanuel Mautner said. "I'll have to be going again."

"You haven't had breakfast."

"I'm not hungry. I'll eat when I return."

"I know you weren't there." A little while later she added: "So many smart people have left. It could have been different."

"You shouldn't blame yourself, mamitschko."

"Don't call me mamitschko. Swear that you were there."

He raised his hand. His fingers were steady.

"Put that hand down for God's sake!"

He avoided her glance. He heard the alder groves falling in his mind—sparks heard in the crisp, biting air of the Polish wasteland. He was looking at Emily, at her head and hair, at her throat and flat breasts. She stood with her shoulders stooped, head almost on her chest because of her dropped chin. In a split second, he recalled the story of how his son had spent his first night with a woman, just before he was to leave Theresienstadt in the fall of 1944 for the East. From there they went into Germany. Some said that Miroslav hadn't been shot, but had his frozen legs amputated.

"You've always been able to rely on me."

"You should be going to work."

"I will shortly."

"Come back as soon as you can."

"It's a nice day," he said.

"Don't leave me alone."

"I like this kind of light, don't you?"

4

An hour and a half later, Emanuel Mautner found himself on Ridders Street watching a grocer arrange a crate of Meissen apples according to size. The apples were bright red and round with well-defined stems and smelled of fruitful lands.

For a moment he imagined that he was strong and careless like people who don't need to worry. Light makes them stronger and, maybe, weaker at the same time. He thought of Emily.

The biggest apples were on the bottom, the smaller in the middle, and the smallest on top, forming a pyramid.

"Would you like to buy some?" the grocer asked. He had his crates stacked so they looked like stockades. "This fruit is all from the same tree."

"No, thank you. Maybe on my way back," Emanuel Mautner told him. The apples reminded him of Miroslav's red cheeks.

The grocer was removing the apples that were damaged or beginning to rot and discarding them into a little bin under the counter. "You should buy while there are still some left," he muttered casually. "Those who wait too long miss the boat."

Emanuel Mautner slowed his pace and looked into the shops and into the apartment windows with curtains. At an inn by the roadside, daily patrons were drinking lemonade, beer, and coffee at their tables.

In a conspiratorial tone he said, "Of course, mamitschko, I know and you know, too." And then he added, "I don't have time to criticize anyone." He smiled. "Joy and sorrow are sisters." Earlier in his life he would measure each year from spring to spring. Each day by every night. He liked the daylight as much as the darkness. As a traveling salesman for the umbrella company on Carpenter Street, he took his vacation with his family in August. Three people: blond and blue-eyed Emily, fair-haired and blue-eyed Miroslav, and himself. Every year they talked about going skiing, but were content with Miroslav's ice skating and sledding in the winter at home.

"Dis si pasce di sper anza, muore di lame. He who lives on hope dies fasting," he said again, somewhat loudly. "It's hard to get money out of an empty pocket." The streetcars, numbers 10, 15, and 23, rang their bells, sounding at once into the streets, and screeching their brakes.

When Miroslav was a child, they had met a man on this same street who talked to himself in the way Emanuel found himself doing now. The man would tell stories about himself until he either laughed or cried. Emanuel had explained to Miroslav that some people went crazy from being alone and advised him to stay out of the man's way.

"I'm here with you, mamitschko," he said now.

No one paid any attention. He delivered the last parcel at the corner of Peters Street and Peters Square. He ran errands for the workshop electricians. He could come and go; it was understood he was to make deliveries on the neighboring blocks Goldsmith, Carpenter, and Spinner Streets.

Across from the workshop, before the war, two brothers had owned the umbrella factory he had traveled for. He no longer knew where they were or where they emigrated to. He didn't know that the brothers had left during the last possible days in 1939, just before the fifteenth of March. On the sixteenth, when the Germans had already invaded the country, Emanuel went to work and the clerk told him the two brothers were out. At first he thought that the clerk meant on an errand; maybe they had stopped for some cappuccino in the Arco Café, or at the Café Roxy on the first floor at Long Street.

"Where do people vanish to all of a sudden?" he asked aloud.

Many people had left. Those who remained were the shreds of families without fathers or mothers, parents without children, or brothers without sisters.

He thought how "hope" was an old word whose meaning was taught to him by the Italians. He imagined the word as an old woman who knows about fate. Or the soldiers in Italy who compared luck and hope to an aging whore.

After the war, Emily had gone to a palmist. For two crowns the Gypsy told her that Leo would unite with Virgo and that the number forty would be important. There would be a train for Emily, the palmist read, but she must not entrust her passage to any engineer who had derailed once before—even if that were his first and only mistake.

Miroslav left in 1942 for Theresienstadt; they expected him to return in 1945. He left Theresienstadt in September of 1944 with a transport headed for the East. The number forty was on all of his documents.

The Gypsy also told them that the Revolutionary National Council of the Second District in Prague had found Emily a job as a cashier in the box office of the Anchor movie house.

Emanuel Mautner passed the Anchor movie house at the beginning of the Avenue of the Revolution. It was a year since he and Emily had gone to see a movie. The last one was called *Steam Over the Pot*. The newsreel showed an Italian Saint Bernard receiving a medal for faithfulness from the War Ministry; for twelve years after the war, the dog went to the bus station and waited for his master. He was a rust-colored salivating dog with weeping eyes.

Maybe he'd made a mistake with Emily by not meeting with those who had a similar fate. Why does everybody think his fate will be exceptional?

Emanuel crossed the square looking in both directions so he wouldn't get hit.

"I can't do it, mamitschko," he said as loudly as he could. "There is no sense in doing it. Let's start again, mamitschko. Come on. You understand why I'm not doing it anymore, don't you?"

In the main hall of the central station, Emanuel Mautner inhaled the sweet clouds of smoke. He followed the yellow signs with black letters—schedules of stations and trains, timetables of departures and arrivals. On the other side of the hall, two strong women were washing the stone floor. Although it was the middle of the day, the hall was illuminated with big yellow lamps hanging from the ceiling. Emanuel stood in the way of a railway employee who was riding on an electric cart.

"What train are you looking for?" the employee asked. "An express?"

Since Emanuel didn't answer, the man in the uniform volunteered some information. "There are several changes. Summertime and wintertime. Some trains have been added."

"I'm not sure it's an express," Emanuel said.

"The locals usually go through Main Station and a few of them go to Prague-Center."

Emanuel thought that the blue eyes of the employee in the spotted uniform saw him as a lost man—as a scarecrow with his wrinkled yellow tie and torn black umbrella under his arm.

"A train from Germany," Emanuel Mautner told the man. "Kaufering II—does that mean anything to you?"

"Kaufering II. Sure it means something to me," the man answered. "Like Buchenwald or Dachau or Landsberg, right? Did you say 'Kaufering II'? I drove freight cars to Theresienstadt in 1943. The Little Fortress and the Big Fortress. Then I went there in May of '45 when the typhoid epidemic broke out. I drove Czech and Russian doctors there. And three German ones."

The railway employee noticed the dark circles under the small man's eyes. He thought how people like this lived during the night, like some insects so preoccupied with sustenance that they don't notice their wrinkled condition. The daylight doesn't make them well. Then he noticed the throbbing veins in Emanuel's temples and forehead.

The railway employee spoke again. "The interstate and express trains have been arriving at the Main Station—which used to be the Wilson Station—for the last nine months."

The employee looked one last time at the slight man with the umbrella. Emanuel was dressed in a pinstriped woolen suit, as though it were not the end of summer. At the same time, the railway employee thought that this man's thin, straight Jewish nose, greasy skin, stooped shoulders, and diffident eyes reminded him of a moth or a mayfly that lives for two days as if born by mistake.

The railway employee saw that the little man was blinking as though he had cinders in his eyes.

"Haven't we seen each other before?"

Emanuel Mautner shrugged his shoulders. He headed for the door to the main hallway. Behind him he heard the departing electric cart, loaded with baggage and mailbags.

At the corner of Goldsmith Street—next to the Imperial Hotel, which housed the Union's Recreational Center—a girl to whom Emanuel used to deliver parcels bathed in the sunshine. She called to him from the first floor window, reminding him to listen to the radio in the evening. "A lovely day, isn't it, Mr. Mautner?"

Again he passed the house of the lost brothers. His memories were an invisible tissue made of multicolored silk, Indian bamboo, and local imitations of rain and dreams.

The two brothers—what did they look like? He tried to remember their voices or the sound inside their voices when business was good. He had begun selling for them in small towns, moving up to more important positions, until he became sales representative for Prague.

He looked at the wooden umbrella on the facade of the house in Carpenter Street facing Peters Square. It was displayed on the wall between the first and third floors. There was nothing next to it. The children of future parents would wonder about the origin of the wooden umbrella on the building. It had been raining the day the two brothers left the country.

Maybe they were living somewhere far away in an unknown place and would never come back. People who emigrated to who knows where. Maybe they were selling umbrellas somewhere in New Zealand. Or they joined one of the armies that helped defeat Nazi Germany. He imagined men who defended the lives they were in charge of, armies that didn't fail, officers who died rather than jeopardize the lives of their troops.

He passed through the street with another look at the wooden umbrella. He wondered what time it was.

5

"Why aren't you eating?" Emily asked.

"Look. I brought some money."

"Did you have a lot to do?"

"Only some envelopes to deliver and one box and a roll of copper wire."

"Would you like more soup?"

"This is really good soup, mamitschko. Did you water the plants?"

"Why aren't you eating?"

"I have a little heartburn. It looks like we're going to have a long warm spell. We still have time. They are predicting snow for the winter. The snow is good, really, because there isn't enough water."

"How do you know?"

"It was on the radio. They know all about the Ice Age and about the next five winters."

Emanuel Mautner wiped his lips. He wanted to clear the table, but he felt Emily's glance and then something frightened her, as she abruptly swept the bills from his pay envelope off the table with her hand. The bills fell to the floor.

"What are you doing, mamitschko?" When she looked at him he added, "Don't worry, nothing's happened. I'll pick them up myself."

Emanuel bent down to pick up the bills. He put them back into the pay envelope. "Everything's OK, mamitschko. That young bookkeeper in the shop gave me some ten-heller red stamps with a picture of Albert Einstein when he taught in Prague."

"What do you need stamps for? What will the people say?"

"She had some extras."

When he'd collected the bills, she said, "What's new?"

"In the shop? Nothing. It's better when there's no news." He smiled. "They explained that England exported her criminals to Australia. Now the new generations have to pay for the sins of their fathers."

He was squatting on the floor. Emily watched her husband as though he were part of a night's dream. But her dreams weren't just summer storms with their thunder; the lightning was like a fiery serpent penetrating the streams of falling waters.

"Button your dress, mamitschko."

Did she know the contents of the telegram from the postwar Center for Repatriation in Vienna? Emanuel Mautner thought he had hidden it from her. *Castelles Strasse 57 Stop*, the telegram read. *They are supposed to be missing.*

Emily was not far from the night when she dreamt they arrived in Kaufering II in the dark while the disinfection carriage waited for them. In the canteen near the former Frauenbunkers, people ordered beer and sandwiches. The nearby stand sold souvenirs, bookmarks, and postcards. Where the camp had been before, the ground was blackened. The man who sold flowers kept lying to them or changing the conditions of the sale. The only hotel to sleep in was in Landsberg or Kaufering I, where warehouses and apartment buildings were built on mass graves. Emanuel Mautner tried to entertain her all the way, as though they were going to a variety show. The gravedigger was in a hurry, even though they had paid him for a full day's work. He was trying to convince the mother of another son that the crust of civilization is thin. The gravedigger folded Miroslav's body as though it were frozen or as though it had no legs. He did it as if stacking wooden logs.

The gravedigger in her dream covered the pit with the broken earth that had given him so much trouble. With soft earth, he could work faster. Sometimes he came upon huge holes in the ground that were capable of hiding a battleship. But could he be sure that under all that dirt, all the way down, Miroslav really lay there?

"No one reproached you for being out so long?" she said.

Emanuel Mautner placed the envelope on the table. "I don't take it that way, mamitschko. Fortunately, no one checks my time."

She thought about the part of Emanuel Mautner that was guilty as well as the part that was innocent. Was it because of his dark hair, the curve of his nose, or the olive tone of his skin that he looked like the

Spanish grandee to whose ancestors he was related? Or was it that sign of his race or purity performed on a Jewish man once in his life, the rite she didn't allow Miroslav to have? Why then wasn't she able to save Miroslav by herself, with his bright blue eyes, straight nose, and fair hair?

She looked through the kitchen windows into the bright sunny light and at the reflections of light on the windows across from them.

"Did they give you a raise on their own?"

"I didn't ask for one. It sure made me happy."

"Sometimes I think they'll let you go."

"You're too trusting."

"They need people everywhere these days."

He handed her the envelope with his pay. "Will you take care of it?"

The corners of his mouth moved up. It was only half a smile. *Tempi passati.* He knew she would be afraid to kill a fly. They were both swallowed up by the bright sun; the kitchen was full of light.

6

Dusk poured in—an end to a day. The kitchen windows faced the courtyard. Across the street, from the entrance of the inn to the garrison in number 23, a man's voice was shouting to the woman in a window.

The water in the kettle was boiling; Emanuel Mautner made tea. He threw a vial of sleeping pills into Emily's cup. He poured water into the cups, making sure not to confuse the two. He looked at Emily's light hair, her blue eyes. Afraid that she could read his thoughts, he blushed, grateful for the dusk.

"I'm afraid I'm going to have dreams again," Emily said.

He held the gas valve of the stove between his thumb and forefinger and lowered the heat by turning the knob until the flame quieted. Whenever he turned the valve, the same thought came to him: how lovely she once was, not so long ago. Only thirteen years. He was still holding the gas valve on the range between his fingers. Then the flame died down.

Her silence sounded like the flight of a bird whose wings are tired but still has a long way to fall before shattering on the ground. It embraced her silence, her voice, thousands of silences and voices he'd never heard. His fingers let go of the gas valve.

"We've grown old together."

"I don't want you to look at me like that," Emily said.

That sound was flowing through her voice again, just as in the mornings, the burning remains of smoldering wood—her unfathomable voice of trees and broken twigs, a dry crack that cut the wind and frost that carried the sounds afar.

He imagined birds perched in big cages and how he used to sell Latin American umbrellas with handles that resembled lion's claws or cock's heads.

He brought the cup with the dissolved sleeping pills. "Drink it while it's hot."

"I can't drink it so hot. I'll burn my tongue." Then she added, "I don't feel anything." It seemed to her that the tea had the taste of soft clay. She inhaled a couple of times to get rid of the taste.

Emanuel Mautner took a sip of his tea, then waited until the first signs of fatigue formed in her eyes. Sleepiness fell silently on the apple shade of Emily's cheek, and on the dark, almost transparent semicircles of muscatel spots under her moist eyes. All of a sudden, her eyes seemed small. He wondered where her eyes disappeared to during sleep. He was thinking about the idea he dreamt about so often, how good it would be if they would die, to have it all over with. Unconsciously, he didn't want to make it gas, and he was afraid to die first, also. He felt dead tired and deeply ashamed.

He started coughing. He was not at all sure he hadn't mixed up the cups. Both contained sleeping pills, but there were more in hers.

Someone across the street lit a candle in a window. It looked like a slender sun praying in the windowsill; the rosy clouds drifted from east to west until the sky grew dark. Then the candle went out.

He watched Emily falling asleep. Later, when he himself was half-asleep, it seemed to him that she sat up next to him on the bed.

"Go and open the door," she said.

Emanuel Mautner rose and walked through the hall. He passed the wardrobe and the coatrack by the door. There was the chest they'd bought during the war—for storage and to have their traveling things ready all the time. Next to it, there were suitcases stacked in the hall. He unlocked the security lock, loosened the chain, and opened the door.

Outside stood a young man who had visited them right after the end of the war, on the morning of Tuesday, May 19, 1945. The slanting scars across his forehead made it look as though his skull were separating under the skin. He wore honey-colored corduroy pants, a dark blue flannel jacket, and a red kerchief around his neck. He asked, had Miroslav also returned home? This "also" confused Emanuel Mautner. Might they have parted somewhere on the corner, by the garrison or just across the street from the Ideal Hotel? Emanuel Mautner's heart stood still. Could it mean that Miroslav was only delayed somewhere?

"No," Emanuel Mautner answered; he couldn't breathe. "Miroslav hasn't come yet. When was the last time you saw my son?"

"In Theresienstadt, in 1944," the young man answered. "We were sent East on different transports."

"Of course." Emanuel Mautner understood at once, though not understanding anything.

The boy then began a story about a girl with whom he and Miroslav had spent their last night in Theresienstadt in September 1944. Emanuel Mautner remained silent then, not wanting to spoil the young man's homecoming.

"It's been a long while," Emanuel Mautner said now.

"I hope you have forgiven me for confusing you then."

"You look well."

"How are you?"

"What do you do?"

"It's not bad. I'm an aeronautical engineer. I wanted to be a pilot, just like your son, but that didn't work out. They told me I don't have the best vision. Unless I would be satisfied being a navigator. How are you doing, Mr. Mautner?"

"How do you manage to make it so well?" Emanuel Mautner countered with a smile. "Do you have an apartment of your own? If you hadn't been in a hurry then you could have had the bedroom of a German untersharführer who occupied a Jewish apartment, number sixteen next door."

Emanuel Mautner led the young man into the hallway. "My wife is home. Be careful. *Di salto in salto.* She draws rather rash conclusions from everything."

Emily was stretched out on the bed. She rubbed her eyes.

"Was that you ringing just now?" Emily turned to the young man. "We always ring three times."

"You haven't changed, Mrs. Mautner," the young man said.

"None of us is getting any younger," Emanuel Mautner added. "So we live in our memories of a better past." And before Emily could say anything, "We must have sent him a hundred and fifty parcels during the war. Isn't it so? We still have some postal receipts."

"They must be somewhere—I haven't thrown out a thing," Emily said.

"Don't even ask how much it cost," Emanuel said. "All of Emily's dowry, her jewelry and our savings. It was fortunate that I could work; they raised my commission before Miroslav left. We were lucky to send one parcel a month, including things bought on the black market." And again, before Emily could add anything, "Tell Emily about where you and Miroslav spent the last night before leaving Theresienstadt with a transport to the East."

"In good company," answered the young man. "She was a half-German Jewess. Twenty-two. Pretty, strong. Her name was Inge. She had pink cheeks, dark eyes, and black hair. She looked healthy. Someone told us that she had TB. We all ended up falling in love with her, although some of us only after we looked back on it. She loved your son the most, I would say."

The young man didn't say that Miroslav received few of the parcels they sent him and always shared the ones that did come. And that this half-German and half-Jewish girl Inge, the last name unknown or forgotten, was sent to Theresienstadt directly from the streets, with a police note in her papers, being *vollblütdirne aus Café Ammarkt*, a full-blooded prostitute from a notorious café.

When she heard about it for the first time it was obvious that it pleased Emily, just as it pleased Emanuel Mautner, but now, like her husband then, she felt embarrassed.

"I hope the girl survived," she said.

"No one's heard of her," the young man answered. "The only thing of hers that survived was her parting gift to us." He smiled.

"We're never too old to learn," Emanuel Mautner said. "*Non si e mal vecchio per imparare.*" He was thinking: is it true that a liar should have a good memory?

"Stop by again," Emanuel told him. "Let us know beforehand so we'll be home."

8

Emanuel Mautner tossed about in bed. His throat and forehead were wet. So were his groin and armpits.

He imagined the room with the dozen boys, all the same age as Miroslav, and how the girl was able to make each one feel as if he were the only one. Inge. He heard the echo of a sound as though someone were ringing a bell. He always disconnected the bell from seven in the evening until eight in the morning.

He thought again about his son's first moments with a mature woman. He tried to breathe softly in order not to wake Emily. He dried himself with the blanket. He was thankful for the girl. He tried to imagine her face and her hair and whether she was allowed to use lipstick in the camp. What did she look like?

"What's the matter?" Emily asked, half-asleep. She still held the cup in her hand.

"Didn't you hear the bell, mamitschko?"

"Can't you be at peace with yourself, at least at night?"

"I thought I heard the bell."

"I sleep as though I'm on water. I would know if it rang. Wipe your nose."

The cup from Emily's hand fell to the floor, breaking into pieces, the sound of shattering china.

"It's still night, mamitschko."

"I have to sleep," Emily repeated.

He watched her fall asleep again. He felt her dying soul. He wished to breathe life into her. He felt that with her soul his soul would die, too. The freshness of youth dissolved from Emily's face. The wind outside howled, sounding like the branches from trees, and whispers between boys and girls, men and women; or like the peeling paint of distant pictures—signs that one no longer understands; like ashes crumbled by frost, or reeds in Polish or German swamps; or faraway lakes filled with human bodies that disappeared from foreign maps. Only an echo contained the color of ladies' umbrellas and gentlemen's canes with ornamental mother-of-pearl or silver handles.

The night was flowing through the darkness. Everything Emanuel Mautner saw before him looked like hot rain, smothering chips of alder wood—layers that flowed downstream, ashes thrown from trucks into rivers during the war before they were lost in the oceans. He thought about the strange tides between people, like an ocean of fish that struggle to eat one another, only to be caught by fishermen and gulped down; there were acquaintances with strangers, the dead, the living, the real, the imagined, and those in the past with those yet to be born. He felt a force that passed him in the night with a motion that went from nowhere to nowhere, beyond man's control, that you could touch only the way the stars touch each other. He remembered days when Emily was beautiful, when she became his wife, before he could compare her with the unknown girl in Theresienstadt.

The fool who mumbled to himself when Miroslav was still a child flashed into his mind. He asked himself whether the man only wanted to be happy. A thin bald man in greasy shirt and shorts, unkempt and unshaven, with sparse rotting teeth. Sometimes he ran around Goldsmith, Carpenter, and Peters Streets singing an aria from *Aida*. Where are all those people who have disappeared from Germany, like Inge and the fool from their street?

The image of the girl Miroslav slept with remained with him. The wind from the street sounded like cobwebs, like broken gossamer nets, a lullaby, frozen snowflakes.

Someone was returning from the night shift out on Carpenter Street. Emanuel heard the downstairs entrance gate slam and then the door of the inn. In front of the Ideal Hotel, a brief strain of a woman's laughter broke out, followed by a man's voice saying how difficult it was to bring up daughters. Is it right that the eldest daughter receives money and the youngest beauty? Is it true that when a woman behaves well, she will have a baby boy? Then everything was quiet.

Emanuel Mautner kept returning to the girl, to Miroslav, to the fool in the street, who had to rely on his own world because the surrounding planet of men had failed him and he had failed it, and to how Emily, tired from sleep extracted from sleeping pills, could remain so beautiful, at least in the dark. He thought how those who were together remained alone. Again he wished to live longer than Emily, even if by one day or a few hours, so that he would be able to bury her with his own hands. He felt the throbbing of his veins in his temples. Then he saw an image of the Landsberg camp and contours that he had been trying to avoid the entire time, which, against his will, completed what he'd seen so many times in the same way.

9

Slowly he began caressing Emily. He stroked her forehead with his palm. He touched the edge of her hair, which was done in a tight twist. It wasn't the first time she had fallen asleep without undressing. The murmur of her double sleep, which he had provided for her, swept past his greasy forehead.

"I didn't wash or undress yesterday either, mamitschko." He knew that she had drunk all of the sleeping pills.

"I will carry you over, mamitschko," he whispered. "It's not comfortable. Come on. I'll unbutton it for you."

He was relieved when he felt movement in her. "It's a shame we haven't gone out together in such a long time."

Emily blinked and ran her hand across her forehead. "Why do you keep waking me?" she asked. Then she added, "No one has ever confirmed it for us." She was dreaming about ships suddenly taken by a storm and never heard of again. But the wives and mothers of the sailors, nevertheless, believed their husbands and sons lived somewhere, forgotten and safe.

Emanuel Mautner carried Emily in his arms. She was easy to carry, almost like a child. Only he knew. In the darkness her skin looked like weathered wood, exposed through the years to heat, to frost-beating sun and prolonged rain. He remembered again how young and fresh she used to be and how her parents wanted only the best for her. It seemed to him that her heart beat like that of a caged bird, trembling with fear even in sleep. He held her with one arm under her knees and the other around her neck, but even so, her legs and head felt limp.

"I have to change your clothes, mamitschko."

"I wouldn't leave anyone behind."

He put her down carefully. He folded her underwear, her dress, and her robe on the armchair next to the bed. He dressed her in a white batiste nightgown that covered her up to her neck. Then, he lay next to her. He first put his cheek to her shoulder, then to her breast. It seemed to him that her small, almost unwomanly breast smelled of geraniums. He felt her dry coarse skin. He stroked her with his palm and pressed his lips to her chest.

"Where are they?" she asked. "Where are they all?"

"Sleep, mamitschko."

"I don't understand you. What do you want to do with your own hands?"

He turned on the radio, which looked like a big white seashell. He remembered the girl on Goldsmith Street who had reminded him to listen tonight. While the lamps of the radio warmed up, he thought of Miroslav. Emily opened her pale blue eyes and looked at him. The wind streamed in through the window and the starlight skimmed over her blanket, passing over her face and disappearing into the hall. It was the light of dead and living stars. Both of them heard the words of the song on the radio:

> *While the red orchids bloom*
> *Our flower will bloom for everyone . . .*

"I have to sleep," Emily said.

"Sure, mamitschko."

The nightly news came on the radio for a minute. The newscaster was talking about an eruption of a Pacific Ocean volcano next to some faraway Australian island. He reported that silent volcanoes thousands of miles apart talked to each other.

"Let it play if you want," Emily said.

"Remind me in the morning of what I wanted to tell you. We'll go out somewhere."

He put his cheek on the pillow next to Emily. Through the window, the winds, flowing from the Ideal Hotel to the inn at the garrison, from the Avenue of the Revolution to Peters Square, carrying the song and words, seemed like a funnel through which everything flowed into him. He held Emily around the shoulders, as though they weren't lying down but standing and about to go out, with their arms around each other the way they used to hold each other. Then he waited for her to fall asleep. He huddled up beside his wife as though he were lying and walking and guarding, killing his and her loneliness at the same time. He lowered the arm that held her around the shoulders. He felt her heartbeat, her rattling breath. He felt the layer of freckled skin. For a moment he felt removed from everything, like a distant star in a nightless sky.

"I'm not dreaming of anything," Emanuel Mautner whispered when he was sure Emily was asleep. He thought about the soul of words never uttered and the soul of unchallenged memories—and about the things one never knows. Did he want to know now? What good would it do Emily to know?

She didn't answer. Her palm was touching his hand. The music on the radio was already wordless.

"After all, no twig is only green," he said in Italian. He felt younger.

Emanuel Mautner felt like a ship that had sailed through the fog in waters full of unexploded and forgotten mines, past rocks and whirlpools. He felt like a volcano of the sea, which erupts each night to spit out an island touching the surface, penetrating it. He closed his eyes. They walked through a garden where men were firm, where mothers and fathers were not afraid of daylight or volcanoes or the voices of silence; where all the flowers, trees, and grass looked different from those they had known before. Their long undeclared war had ended; daily strength had been taken, and in its place, this nocturnal truce had formed. The sun rose and set, and the winds and rain came and went again. The shadows were soft and indicated only by beginnings and endings. Time was no longer their master, and night and day filled its waiting.

"Mamitschko," Emanuel Mautner said softly, so as not to wake her.

In silence, the sound of pistol shots faded like dry firecrackers.

He kept repeating to Emily that it was all right, that everything was good because no one could live with joy alone, and they didn't have to die for suffering either. The wind's melody carried the voices of Miroslav and of the German-Jewish girl who was his son's friend on the last night before he was shipped East. It separated smell and strength, kisses and tears, as well as anguish and doubt, the life that was, the life that continues, and the life that would like to be.

Emanuel Mautner held Emily in his embrace without waking her. He wished her a dreamless night. He felt like a twig grafted onto a dying branch. He wanted to penetrate Emily so that neither of them would feel like a fallow field or a dead tree. It was the strength born of weakness, like the flight of birds.

And then, very much later, when the white shell of the radio receiver, with its strange names of cities and countries, had turned silent but the station panel continued to send its green lights into the depths of the bedroom, he turned to her once more and said, "Good night, my love."

INFINITY

❖

During the night I dreamed that I was an SS officer and was in charge of the gas chamber selection. In the dream, the lager commandant asked me how I was doing. I answered that I felt as if every day I trampled underfoot thousands—tens of thousands—of ants on the flat stone, but it didn't seem to lead anywhere. I cannot destroy the breed of ants. The ants will go on living even when I trample a hundred times more under my feet. Then the commandant changed into a voice. It could speak, and listen, and it was omnipresent. I have had similar dreams in the camps many times already. Once I dreamed an octopus was reaching for me and every tentacled arm pulled me toward its mouth and I tried to resist. But it had the ability to speak and announced to me that the average life span in Auschwitz-Birkenau is fifteen minutes. During the course of the day I forget the dreams, but as I prepare for each night of sleep I fear what I will dream of.

We got the upper bunk for the three of us: Harry Cohen, Ervin Portman, and myself. We did not have blankets. They were taken to the laundry in the Delousing Station because they were so full of lice and infested with typhus bacteria. We pressed against each other to make the most of our bodies' warmth. Portman was quietly repeating the number tattooed on his forearm, as he usually did before going to sleep, so that he would remember it if someone woke him up in the middle of the night. He preferred to lie on his left side so that he could see the number, in case Rottenführer Schiese-Dietz came to make his night selection.

Before sounding the taps, Rottenführer Schiese-Dietz had made the rounds with his whip. It had a long handle like the whips used by coachmen driving teams of horses. The whip itself, twice the length of the handle, was braided leather made from human skin, fastened at the end with a double golden ring (cast from gold teeth) into which a Jewish jeweler in the camp workshop had engraved his initial. You could never be sure when Rottenführer Schiese-Dietz would get the idea to come to the barracks. He'd learned to crack the whip like a lion tamer. It sounded like gunfire. If the tip of the whip happened to touch someone it would slice the skin. A little while ago, satisfied that the barracks were quiet and that he'd seen nothing unusual anywhere, he had returned to the SS quarters and played the piano. He could play Bach, Schumann, or Mozart from memory, proud that he remembered so well everything he had learned. He had a different whip before, from somewhere in Saudi Arabia or from some German enterprise exporting whips to the near Orient, to make camels go faster. He was told that a camel never forgets a blow, even a baby camel, and that they sometimes run away in the middle of the desert. This couldn't happen here. People never escaped. There was nowhere to go. He had worn out his camel switch by using it too often and too hard, to beat out of people their habit of asking futile questions about boredom, or why they were living or why they were born or, most often, why their lives were so miserable. It was up to his whip to show them why they were still alive, and what had to be accomplished and why they were dissatisfied with their lives.

Somewhere in the night, a German voice called out: "*Laufschritt! Laufschritt!*" On the double! On the double! And again silence spread over the camp. Everywhere was mud. It was good at least to be under a roof.

A half hour later, Portman asked me, "Why aren't you asleep?"

"I'm cold," I said.

"Quit lying. What are you waiting for?" asked Portman.

"They'll begin soon," I blurted out.

"Get some sense into your head," Portman reprimanded me.

He must have known what I was waiting for, and he was right. I was waiting. I knew that he must have been waiting too, if he was not asleep. Maybe he waited for the same reasons I did and maybe at the same time it was because he wanted to refute what I wanted to verify for myself once it began. I felt a secret shame and didn't know exactly why. It encompassed many other shames, and all were present in one question: how and why were we born as we were born? And probably Harry Cohen was also waiting, although he said, "You shouldn't wait for it. It gets on your nerves. It isn't half as encouraging as it would seem."

"You'd better sleep," said Portman. "Be glad that we can sleep and they're not driving us to do some loading or unloading. In the mud it's obnoxious. It goes right through my rags." He trembled. "You keep wiggling. Who can put up with that?"

I did not answer. I did not want to be talking to Portman when they began. There were the usual noises in the bunks. Someone was quietly praying and somebody else told him to shut up and leave him alone and let him sleep in peace. And close to them, someone had a dispute with his Creator. The Creator didn't answer but the man had madness in his voice.

The wrangle finally stopped. Harry Cohen got a bit of gossip from his neighbor: that morning, the grüppenführer in the office of the Gestapo had been found dead, shot by his own hand.

Harry Cohen put his arm under his head. "That Chinaman who once said that the more a man knows, the luckier he is, was wrong," he whispered. "It's just the opposite. The more you know, the more your world is filled with misfortune. Shit. I think I'm already dead. Don't let me oversleep. Do you know how long it's been since I've had a dream?"

"It's better to wait for the swallow to come back in the spring than to wait for *them*," said Portman.

He stretched out his arms. He had long arms. He believed that was a sign of luck, and that, when necessary, he could reach farther and easier than Harry Cohen or I. His ears stuck out and he was convinced that this was a sign of someone who was satisfied with his lot; he was always sleepy and tired, but at the same time he had great willpower, although not the best talent for choosing friends. He did not have much patience. It was good that Harry Cohen did. In his former existence, Harry Cohen had had a lot of good luck, both in cards and in love, and was very successful in business undertakings. Portman considered my kind of patience morbid. He could not understand how I could go on waiting.

But Portman still wasn't asleep. Maybe he could still hear the rotten-führer cracking his whip. Maybe he could imagine that golden ring, cast from teeth that were knocked out of corpses and sometimes, just for the gold, out of the living. Most of the gold went into sealed railroad cars to the underground safes of the Berlin State Bank, but quite a bit of it slipped through the fingers of the SS men. Sometimes he dreamed about his little sister, up the chimney four months ago already. Her skin was very fair, with a touch of pink or peach; she was so white he could still see in his mind the blue veins beneath her skin. Her soft skin smelled like spices, maybe like flowers. Her fingers—not rough or damaged by manual labor— were long for a child of eight, and she also had long, dainty feet. Perhaps Portman envied the dead just as you would envy the living. Yesterday he had mumbled something in his sleep about Samson, and no one wanted to remind him of it. On Monday he dreamed that he had gotten typhus, on Tuesday that he had diarrhea and couldn't stop it, and Wednesday morning he realized that it had been both a dream and a reality. It wasn't hard to figure out what brought Samson's name to his lips. Samson was definitely the last resort.

"The rabbis know what they're talking about when they say that Noah was wrong to send out a pair of doves to bring the news that the flood had subsided. Maybe it drove him mad," Harry Cohen said. "To go mad— that's not the worst there is. The worst is when you know it. This afternoon when we were coming back from the soccer field, they were picking out women who had no shoes and those who were sick. The deaf and dumb are gone already and so is that shipment of war invalids from Vienna."

"Did you think they would be feeding them white bread and milk here?" asked Portman.

"Half of the people that they added to make up the count for the transport were healthy and strong—something was going on," added

Harry Cohen. "They're in a hurry now. But why do they want to get rid of the women first?"

"The Nazis don't like women," said Portman. "They're dead set in their beliefs that women are the source of all evil, just as we are. I heard Rottenführer shouting at the women in the laundry that they like to screw, especially when they were menstruating, so that they could infect everyone with syphilis and other infectious diseases. He yelled at them that here they would lose all their bad blood. He told them that he knew a woman could not wash laundry properly when she had her period and then he threatened to send them all to the bath and burn them with their dirty rags. And then he said point blank that he would shoot down any woman who got closer than three steps to him or dared to touch him."

"There are places where the men believe that if you glance at a menstruating woman your bones will go soft and you'll lose the ability to have children," said Harry Cohen.

"I hope it happens fast," I added. "At least without having to stand in the snow and mud." I liked Harry for never complaining about anything. Whenever they beat him he never moaned a minute after. Maybe he believed human dignity lies in never speaking of pain, especially afterward. In Prague he left an Aryan girl, Maruschka. Sometimes at night, when he was looking at the stars, his big lips would have a tender smile like the Mona Lisa's. Once the rottenführer caught him with that tender smile and beat him to chase it away. Cohen opened his mouth, but didn't complain.

"Why don't you both go to sleep?" Portman said.

I couldn't sleep. I waited for them to begin. Maybe they wouldn't.

When the killing came so close that he couldn't pretend not to see it, Portman would always get nervous. The blood would rise to his brain, and he would take it out on me. I could imagine that he was putting the blame on both the living and the dead, on people who had already gone through it, as well as those who were still waiting. I did not confide in him that for the last few nights I had been seized by a vision of crashing stars that in a fraction of a second would crush the whole camp and the planet on which the Germans had built this camp with our hands. It was a strange wish and it actually had something to do with Samson—only it was not just a matter of a few columns holding up the roof of an ancient palace. My vision encompassed the destruction of everything and everybody: the crushing of the earth, down to the very last pebble. It embraced the transformation of the planet into stardust—together with all and with everything, down to the last crow and the last ant. It was a very disturbing yet comforting obsession, and I knew it would depart with the first sleep or when the women from the adjoining camp would begin. It was safe as long as the Germans only killed new transports and picked out the sick and those people who were guilty of being old, of having gray hair or wearing glasses. The old-timers still held on to some hope or illusion, which turned into a new truth when the Germans started killing even the healthiest and strongest, those who could still work for them.

I did not want to miss it when the women from the adjoining camp began. It was always the beginning of something else as well. The beginning and the continuation of something that had no end even when it was over.

There were two women's camps. One was for Jewish women from Hungary and Slovakia and the other was for both Jewish and non-Jewish women from other occupied countries. They worked in the hospital ward, in the showers where water actually flowed from the sprinklers, and in the delousing station where they exterminated lice and insects with Cyclon B. The latter came from the same cans as those which were used in the underground showers next to the disrobing stations and the crematoria from number one to number five, and was used in fourteen-hour cycles, necessary for the proper extermination of vermin. The women also worked in cleaning stations, laundries and kitchens, and in the warehouses where shoes, gems, underwear, hair, orthopedic devices, and costume jewelry were stored. These women also had opportunities to work through all seasons as performers in the whorehouse or in the concert hall. Polish and Ukrainian henchmen and guards and German criminals wearing purple triangles took their opportunities in the brothel, although they had to pay two Reichmarks from their wages or other remuneration for the services. One mark was for the whore, and the other went into a special account which the commander of Auschwitz I, II, and III had been ordered from above to keep aside.

In the family camp B2b, which was burnt to ashes during the night of March eighth, there were kindergartens and nursery schools, and their teachers, before being killed, had rehearsed theatrical productions and gymnastic performances which the SS would come to watch.

Would they begin? They really ought to begin. If they were planning to, they should begin now.

As far as Portman was concerned, I had not been behaving like a normal person for the last few days. It was not the first time he had caught me waiting for them to begin. He knew why I had stared at the wooden ceiling with my eyes open, why I stared at the open, glassless window under the roof where I could see the stars or the moon or snow or smoke, waiting all the time. Sometimes my teeth would chatter with the cold and Portman would hear it and it would upset him because we lay so close to get heat from each other. He would blame me for not sleeping because I waited for the women to begin. He was mad at the women for what the camp had done to them instead of being mad at the camp. He thought that the women were crazy. Their faces had become coarse and some had hair growing on their cheeks, which made them look old.

Sometimes Portman would get furious, though at the same time he was afraid to vent his fury. That made him stutter, although maybe it was because he could not speak out loud. Yesterday, for some unknown reason, he had broken a tooth and thought he would die of it. Harry Cohen mentioned that people who had such widely spaced teeth as Portman did would always have to look for their good fortune far away from home. Well, as long as he was here, he was far enough from home, but what good fortune could he have when his teeth were crumbling, even though they had not sent him to the showers yet? Sometimes he became speechless when I waited for the women, but not now. He also feared he had tuberculosis. He believed that he would pull through if he could make it through the next month, unless Rottenführer Schiese-Dietz would spoil everything with his next selection, needing one more for the showers. It was already the twenty-seventh of October. He told himself that October was not a good month for those who have TB, and he fixed his mind on November. Portman sometimes blamed it all on his mother, whom he had never known because she left when Portman was born. Sometimes the thought came to him that it would be rather ironic if his mother had not been Jewish. He also believed that he could get rid of his suspicion of tuberculosis if he could take one gulp of milk.

It was strange that the image of women was associated in my mind with the image of milk, but I preferred not to mention this to Portman. My back drew the heat from Portman's belly and I pressed my stomach and chest against Harry Cohen's back. That afternoon I had given Portman a piece of my bread and blood sausage because I knew what he was afraid of. He gulped it down at once. Now he had the hiccups.

Everything was permeated by the smoke that rose toward the sky during the day and during the night, smoke from the dead who would not have a grave. I remembered what Rabbi Gans once told us in the Vinohrady synagogue: that when they were in the Sinai desert, Moses had ordered his successor, Joshua, to bury him in the ground so that no one would find his grave. The Germans were now doing it on a grand scale.

Portman hiccupped again. "I washed my rags in the latrine and the rottenführer came there and whipped me out of the hole. He yelled at me in his Bavarian German: 'Höre doch auf, Mensch!' He told me to stop it or he'd take the handle of his whip and press me out through the hole in the planks to see if I could swim."

"They should have started," I said.

Portman yawned. "It's better if they stay quiet. It won't help the dead. And the living should stick with common sense. You don't want them to run into bayonets, do you?" Then he added, "It brings them bad luck, just like the night air. Don't they know that? It's making their brains soft. Or they've gone crazy already. They sound like men. I don't miss it. And most of them don't have periods anymore even if they're sixteen."

Harry Cohen was feeling his chest, his body, the last thing that he owned. He was at rock bottom. He had used up his last bit of willpower and self-control to pretend otherwise. He did not say that here in Auschwitz-Birkenau everything, even breathing the wind, a draft, or still air, brought people bad luck. The good luck of one always meant the bad luck of another. Everyone who lived, lived at the expense of someone who lived no more. It was not his fault. It was the Germans' organized way of killing. There were batches that were sent up the chimney for punishment, and the rest were picked to feed the crematoria according to numbers. And so there would be no cheating, these numbers were tattooed on each person's forearm. People could live in the camp only until it was their turn to go to the showers or into the furnaces and crematoria, because even the best German engineers could not figure out how to burn them all at once. The Germans loved order and kept better discipline than the Frenchmen, Englishmen, Italians, Czechs, Belgians, and other nationalities which the Germans deported to this camp for liquidation. Even those Germans who had no more than a seventh-grade education, like Rottenführer Schiese-Dietz, managed to command order, even when the situations got very confusing.

Harry Cohen lay with his mouth shut not only to avoid wasting energy talking, but in order to breathe through his nose so as not to inhale the germs of typhus and tuberculosis. Neither his former nor his future elegance were of any use to him here. Every memory of the past that could be uplifting was at the same time depressing. Everything that could heal could also wound. Once in Theresienstadt, Faiga Tannenbaum-Novakova ruminated about the omnipotence of the devil. The devil now seemed like an amateur compared to what the German Nazis had dreamt up in Auschwitz-Birkenau and its subsidiaries. Harry Cohen felt the skin in the middle of his chest with the balls of his fingers, trying to ascertain how much there was; it was thinner than wrapping paper, and he wondered how long it could last. He was probably thinking of all those things the tired, frightened minds were thinking, all those who hadn't yet managed to fall asleep.

"They're burning the old Hungarian women who came Monday," said Portman. "The Polish and Romanian railway engineers who brought them were completely drunk because the women stank so much. Somebody said he'd never seen women so full of lice. When the old women stripped at last, because they did not understand what they were supposed to do—since most of them did not understand a word of German, just like the Italians or Frenchmen—the barbers asked for double disinfection before they started cutting their hair."

His words became lost in the thick air of the barracks. Words were the first thing to become silent and lose their meaning. There were no innocent or inexperienced people among us. We had all been there too long, even a single day or a single night. None of the people believed any longer that they were going to take a bath, even if they actually went to baths to be deloused and disinfected before the journey. Nor did they believe that the Germans would send them to work in one of their dominions because they were experienced tailors, goldsmiths, black-smiths, or automobile mechanics—or that they could find work in the German armaments industry. Everyone knew where he was going if the order was to take the road to the left or turn on the road to the right. The road to the right led out of the camp, into a room which had doors without door handles, and they knew that no one who entered the room came out alive. No one was fooled by the notices about cleanliness and health, by the cursing and light banter of the Nazis.

"The dental technicians had a hell of a job prying the gold teeth out of those old women," Portman added. "As usual, they searched everywhere, up and down, back and front, to see if they didn't have some hidden gold, bank notes, or diamonds. Most of them had used them already at home. A couple of them were beaten just because nothing could be found on them in any of the places that women tend to hide things."

The words faded again. They were lost in the rotation of the earth— which did not fall between the two crashing stars as I had wished—and in the thickness and smell of emaciated bodies, covered with sweat, but at the same time getting numb, because it was already the end of October and it was cold, made more so by the wind. Most of the men were quiet. This silence sounded like the dried-up language of the dumb, like the very last silence of the earth as it will one day be heard by the last human generation, even without Auschwitz-Birkenau, when the sun will approach with its enormous ball of fire, and all that is human will turn into fire, ashes and ice, before the planet earth turns into an infinite night, like this night, but much more desolate, much more silent, and much more cold. In my imagination it came sooner.

For the third time Portman said, "I'll bet anything, including your bread and blood sausage, that they will beat it out of them five minutes after they've begun."

Harry Cohen did not say anything. He was, as always in the rare moments of quiet, concerned with the number of possibilities every situation seemed to offer, while really offering only one. It encompassed all possible endings.

"It's not worth it," Portman repeated. "They should be glad that they had time to undress. They wouldn't even have to bother dressing again."

Women over forty, just like girls under fifteen, usually went into the furnace right away, directly from the ramp, or by the first or second selection. They had to wait only if the dressing rooms and the crematoria did not have time to process them all. Although it was cold now—not like during the summer heat—the Germans were afraid that the corpses might decompose and epidemics would start, and so the old women had waited since Monday afternoon. Their lice-infested underwear, clothes, and shoes were burned. And so they had to wait naked, some for hours, some for days and nights, in the wind, rain, and snow, and no one bothered to give them water or anything to eat. About two hundred thousand Hungarian Jewish women had come here since the summer. It was said that in Hungary there remained, until the beginning of 1944, about eight hundred thousand Jewish men, women, and children, and the Germans had now decided to liquidate them quickly, just in case Hungary changed sides in the war.

In a few hours the Hungarian women stopped asking what happened to their husbands, their children, and their families. They wanted to go into the showers and get it over with. When the women were undressed and their belongings taken away, they had no poison they could take, nor knives with which to slit their wrists.

"What's today? It must be Friday. Right, it's Friday," said Portman.

"Or maybe it's already Saturday," said Harry Cohen. "And it will begin all over again. But actually, why should it?"

No one had a watch. A watch was the first thing the Germans stole from you in Auschwitz-Birkenau. The first day here, Harry Cohen made up his mind that he should lie and tell them that he was a trained watchmaker in order to get a cushy job, but fortunately he did not do it.

"You were probably born like a rabbit, with open eyes," Portman grumbled in my direction. "Or do you sleep with your eyes open?"

I didn't say anything. I was waiting for the women to begin. Portman probably debated with himself whether he should continue his talk about food. He knew as well as anyone that talking about food made one hungry. Someone would tell him to shut up. Once, when Portman served as Rottenführer Schiese-Dietz's orderly, he got outside the camp and carried back an image of deep and silent woods that only here and there were fenced with barbed wire. These were endless woods, pines, firs, and sometimes deciduous trees, full of game and silence. The SS men went out to hunt, but they did not shoot deer, does, and hares—they shot people.

Outside, the flames cut through the night and the snow. The sparks flew out of the darkness. The wind howled. Now and then you could hear the crows across the evening sky. They were evil omens. They were flying to the left. That, according to Portman, was the worst. If they flew to the right, that meant he should be cautious. And he could make a wish, as when you see a falling star. All sorts of superstitions came back, and many of them resembled crows. Crows were always an omen of death, of the worst there is. In the night I could imagine the curved flight path of the crows. Portman believed that they talked to each other. But according to him, they talked only because some farmer and some village children had slit open their tongues. The crows held court and they sentenced individuals from their ranks; and a male and a female carried out the sentence together, pecking the culprit to death either in flight or on the ground. But Portman would reverse this sometimes and insist that crows are capable of helping the weakest ones in the flock, the young ones and the weary. A squadron of crows will send out a patrol from its midst to save the weak, the falling or ailing ones. And they know how to warn others of danger.

Already on Monday, before it got dark, Portman, Harry Cohen, and I saw the old Jewish women who spoke Hungarian or Yiddish. We knew what awaited them. We hoped it would be quick. But our wishes did not matter. I also wished that the crows would fly somewhere else with their cawing and hoped they would fly in a straight line without detours. Their sounds reminded me of the worst things: of humiliation, hunger, cold, of illness, weakness, and helplessness. I envied them— their life, their flight, their freedom. I couldn't understand how they could live a hundred and fifty years. But it occurred to me that they could collect endless secrets in that time. I thought of all that they had lived through and wondered where they could take it in their flight.

Portman talked only about the living. He pretended that he had never seen the dead in the camp, as if there weren't any dead here, not to mention the dying. He did not see them. He did not look. Or maybe he looked elsewhere. He forced his hungry red eyes not to see, his brain not to comprehend, as if he had heard about the dead only secondhand.

I wasn't even thinking about the selection that Rottenführer Schiese-Dietz had come to perform. He made the prisoners walk over the long stable-chimney that ran horizontally about knee-high all the way through the barracks ever since the days of the Austro-Hungarian empire when the cavalry was garrisoned here. The prisoners had to walk over the chimney bricks naked, so that the overseers could quickly discern their healthy or sickly condition. Men whose penises had turned black, who were skin and bone, or those with exalted feverish eyes went at a trot down the whole length of the chimney; and only the healthy ones, when the thumbs-up sign was given, could jump off and go back to their bunks. The others who did not get the thumbs-up were selected to continue to the end of the chimney and then through the back entrance down a plank to be loaded onto a truck that took them to the showers. If someone's penis got hard as he was running down the square chimney, either from excitement, from fear or cold, or from some nervous disorder, he had to run to the end of the chimney down the plank, into a car, and into the disrobing rooms, where Germans would make short shrift of his Jewish lust as well as of him, in the surest possible way.

In the women's barracks there had been today—like every day including Saturday and Sunday—two, three, perhaps even five routine selections. For the Germans, it was both a necessity and a pastime. Naked women, in the presence of two or three well-built and elegant SS men, would run or walk along the chimney as if on a stage, waiting for the sign of the thumb. Women with sagging or dried-up breasts, the skinniest ones who had turned old overnight or all of a sudden, women weakened by menopause and with fear of illness or nervousness in their eyes, women without husbands and children, swollen or again thinner than dying mares, women with male traits and beards which they had no time to pluck out, women who were bleeding in the groin but could not clean themselves up, or just women who were splattered with mud and dust—they all waited for the sign of the thumb. Up, horizontally, down. Down and horizontally. The SS would take turns. They had enough women so that among the three hundred and thirty-three, each one could choose his own figures. Each time it was ten or twenty women who got the sign to walk or run to the back entrance at the back of the truck.

"Now," said Harry Cohen all of a sudden, just one second before I wanted to come out with it.

"I know," I said. "I can hear them."

"They're like swans," said Portman. "Women are always faithful beyond the grave to someone, just like swans. Or maybe like geese. But they're wrong if they think they're laying golden eggs in the darkness. How will this help them? I bet they haven't eaten. Are you telling me that you both knew they'd begin, as if nothing had broken them?" Sometimes, after the selection, the women would sing. They would wait for darkness to cover the camp, when everything except the fires had died down. No one could guess how long it would go on. Sometimes the guards sicced dogs on them, and sometimes the guards would fire a few volleys from a machine gun from the door to silence them. Sometimes a few shots were enough, sometimes a few magazines. It was always only a question of time. But before that there was the question whether they would begin, or whether they would give up even this, the very last thing they had. And now they began. It evoked a horror that most people could no longer sense. It gave a new birth to something that had perished long ago. They filled the void that spreads from space, like waves over a calm surface rippled by a wind out of nowhere. It was like a stone that had been given a voice.

"The heat from the chimneys gets on some people's brains," said Portman. "They must all be mad, or they wouldn't be asking for it. Do they want to drive everybody crazy?"

I could not yet identify the words of the melody, but I felt how they filled the space of the camp and of the whole night, the space of the world and beyond, extending into infinity, the incomprehensible void, which they filled with their voices, with their melody that was only beginning to take shape. I imagined a labyrinth, bodies, voices, wooden bunks in the dark, a maze from which the women tried to find a way out—like all the blind, deaf and dumb, drugged or poisoned, tottering from blows to the head, driven nearly out of their minds.

"All the rats have left the women's barracks," said Portman.

The women sang for all those who had lost someone, someone selected at daylight to be sent up the chimney and now no longer among the living; they sang to distract the bereaved from thoughts of the fires and of those who were alive only a few hours ago. The women who sang belonged to the Cleaning Outfit, which scrubbed even the trucks, scrubbing them clean of the dirt left behind by the condemned ones.

The singing filled the night with double voices. Double darkness. Double eyes. Double blood. Double snow, and far above the snow clouds, in a double star-filled sky. Double memory. Double hope and illusion. It filled it with all the things that man possesses only once in his life and loses.

"They make me nervous as a cat," said Portman.

You could not see the flames, you could only hear them. The women who had lost someone already—yesterday, the day before, last week or last month—sang for the mothers who had lost a daughter, for the daughters who had lost a mother, for the sisters without sisters, and for friends without friends and acquaintances who had lost someone they knew. At first the singing was low, then louder, and finally quite loud. They would sing for a short time and sometimes longer, although never too long, and their singing was joined by those who were afraid at first. Finally they were joined by those that were stricken, until in the end, everybody was singing.

"If you sing at night or in bed, that's bound to bring you bad luck," Portman said again. "If you sing at night, you'll be crying before dawn. If you're singing because you don't have a reason for doing it, someone will give you hell for it."

The whole month Portman had argued that even here there were good days and bad days. And that only children and old people could not survive their uselessness.

I waited, as did all the men in the camps, for the first tune—just as you wait for the first evening star, making believe that it has some special significance for you. I tried to imagine the faces or figures of the women from Norway, Belgium, and Holland, the women and girls from Rome, Warsaw, or Sofia, women and girls from Berlin, Paris, or the island of Corfu who had come here by boat and then by train, half dead with thirst. That which they were singing was, at least for the moment, beyond the reach of the hierarchy of the ruling and the humiliated, those who condemned them while they still had the chance to do the condemning. It reminded one of a fortress crumbling invisibly, even though its ramparts were strong and remained tall and unassailable.

The singing came from the darkness distorted, as if from a great distance. I felt something that no one could understand. It contained everything that I had ever waited for, everything I was afraid of and which filled me with mystery and fear, as well as with the wonder of life, because death had become simple, comprehensible, and ordinary. This is the world in which the killers were born together with us, but by killing would live without us; this was the world in which each one of us was the last in the world, before he disappeared and left behind a sliver of ash in the museum of an extinct race, remembered as someone who happened to appear for a couple of thousand years on the surface of this earth. It filled me with something resembling chloroform, which knocks you out like a fragment of a dream.

I waited to hear it interrupted by the rattle of the train on the ramp or a volley from a machine gun or a revolver. At the same time I hoped it would not stop. I wished that the women would sing, just as I wished to see the only thing that would make up for the destruction of justice: my image of two stars flying toward each other before they crash and crush the world that had culminated in this camp and in the killing of innocence in the name of an idea. It embraced something that I never could explain and which I probably would never be able to explain. Everything that man is and is not.

In those women's voices I heard all that is insignificant as well as all that is great, that which is pitiful and full of a silent glory, that which is comprehensible and incomprehensible, like every man and everything he has gone through and still must go through in the future. I understood that man in his smallness and misery is part of something greater, something that has had and will have many names, something that is unfathomable and great like the sea and the earth, the clouds and trillions of stars or galaxies, and at the same time lost like a grain of sand in the desert, or a fish or drop of water or salt in the ocean; that for which man wants to live, even in a place like this, permeated with death and killing, just as the sky is permeated with stars or a snowy night with snowflakes. I understood why man has the strength to die when it is his turn, so that someone else will not have to die in his place; and what he will share, when he has nothing left but his body heat and a spoon carved from an alder branch so that he can eat his soup and not lap it up like some dog, wolf, or rat.

I expected to hear the barking of dogs from the darkness of the night. I felt a different kind of fear and anxiety, different from what I experienced in the afternoon while I looked at the barbed wire, at the German uniforms, at the whip with the golden ring in the hand of the Rottenführer Schiese-Dietz. When I closed my eyes, I had the feeling that I was witnessing the birth of a new planet which was yet to be peopled, a feeling of going way back into time, into the very oldest times when the cooled-off planet earth had just become inhabited. I felt a new infinity, that infinity upon which man trespasses now and again with every breath, word, act or even the blinking of an eye. Something closer than closeness and more distant than distance, something so loud that it deafened me, and something so soft that it was like an incomprehensible whisper.

"Who cares about this," Portman growled. "I'd give them a better idea."

It probably seemed to him that he was watching how they would beat or shoot his mother, if he had ever known her. I don't know. Harry Cohen, too, let Portman's words float by as if Portman had not said anything the whole evening. This bothered Portman. It was a funeral rite, the singing that was born here and was not performed elsewhere, nor would be in the future. It probably both comforted and disturbed him that there would never be witnesses anywhere to this funereal singing that sounded like a martial song and like a suicide challenge, the invisible gauntlet thrown into the face of the enemy, because those who sang were in mortal danger. I don't know, I really don't know. For me it was something that I had lacked so I could perceive my life as less incomplete, and it was something that I do not understand to this day, somewhat like perceiving an echo that exists only in the memory, or a shadow that fell long ago, or a cry that memory has blurred.

"I don't want to hear them sing so I won't have to hear them cry," Portman added.

The women's voices were still mixing with the snowflakes, with the fire and the darkness. The singing came out of the wild night into which the women had brought it to subdue this night when people were being killed, like every night, every day, Friday, Saturday, and Sunday, on high holidays and on every working day, before the stars came out and when they were already fading in the sky. It came out of the night where words meant less than wind, snow, slivers or clumps of ash before they disintegrate, out of the night where innocent people were being killed in one part of the world, while in another part makeshift barracks were being slapped together for more and more prisoners, until all of Europe was German.

Not very far from us was a whorehouse to which prominent Jewish prisoners, henchmen and informers, and Jewish collaborators were occasionally admitted. We hated and despised them and at the same time feared them almost more than we feared the Germans. A little farther away there was another brothel for the soldiers, and yet a few steps further, mothers and wives of the soldiers and clerks of the Totenkopf SS garrison (entrusted by the Nazis with the cars of the prisons and prison camps) were reading fairy tales to their children about Hansel and Gretel and about the brave Siegfried. In one block, German doctors cut pieces of skin from healthy prisoners for grafting on frostbitten German soldiers from the Eastern front, or frozen airmen fished out of the English Channel. In another block two Jewish women pianists played a concert of Beethoven sonatas before being sent up the chimney. The prisoners and the jailers slept under the same stars.

The voices of the women came from the openness and closeness of the night, flowing together like a refuge created from nothing, like a shelter where you can hide for a moment without fleeing, where you can rest and gather strength or save the remainder of your strength. Their voices became a battleground upon which danger, for a few seconds, did not seem so dangerous. For just a moment, pain changed to painlessness and indifference to solidarity.

Over Auschwitz-Birkenau, below the low-lying snow clouds, in the thick smoke of the chimneys of the five crematoria, the singing of unknown women continued. Their singing came from the darkness, for a few seconds, almost a minute, two minutes or three, from the ever renewing sea of life and death, from the darkness and out of the wind, from the lips of women and from the depth or shallowness of the universe.

I was afraid that the women would stop. Then everything would be quiet. And then the only sound in the night would be that of ashes, snow, and wind.

"They're probably feeding the dogs in the kennels now," Portman mused.

Harry Cohen plucked hair from his nostrils and his ears, so that he would look all right in the morning lineup.

The singing of the women sounded like a river overflowing its banks. It colored the night the way the flames colored it or the red morning sky for those who are still alive to see it and for those who can only imagine it before they perish. It marked the night with a forgotten strength, forgotten tenderness, forgotten defiance, and forgotten understanding.

"How can anyone in Germany today think that a thousand years or ten thousand years from now this will be forgotten?" Harry Cohen asked.

"I can't stand the realization that all that remains of them is song and ashes," Portman said. He did not say that he divided people into those who'd already gone through it and those who were still waiting. He divided women into those whose families had perished long ago and those who had lost them to the trucks only this afternoon or at dusk.

"It's like catching sparrows in a cage," Portman added. "Everyone knows what to expect for that." His voice was full of anger and death. "I wish they'd shove it," he added.

Harry Cohen held a piece of bread and a bloody pork sausage under his ragged jacket. Was he about to eat it? He had to be hungry. But he did not eat. Was he waiting for the women to stop, just as I was, in the same way as before, when we waited for them to begin?

"They've lost their minds," Portman said. "They're more stubborn than I thought. They're more persistent than salt."

I could imagine the way the women looked. Some were swollen from hunger and irregularity, while others for the same reasons lost weight. Some sold themselves for a piece of bread, while others sold a piece of bread for a bowl of water so that they could wash. Sometimes I saw them humiliated because they had to strip naked before the SS soldiers or the Ukranian guards, or doubly humiliated because their heads had been shaved, destroying their femininity. They had already lost their capacity for bearing children. But now they were singing.

"What's the good of it?" Portman asked. "Why don't the smarter ones make them shut up?"

"With what? With ashes?" Harry Cohen asked.

"It makes my teeth hurt," Portman said. He was afraid that he would get another toothache and that without his teeth he would never be the same.

Did he huddle up so that he would not hear them? Did he pretend that the song no longer interested him? Was he interested only in his own breath? I no longer understood Portman and probably neither did Harry Cohen. The more we exposed our lives, the less we understood each other.

The women sang lullabies that they had brought from their homes, songs about love and joy, about the freshness of children. Their voices brought back a world which no longer existed.

"Yesterday Schiese-Dietz picked out the redheads," said Portman. "He probably knew why."

Portman feared who the rottenführer would pick out in the morning. Sometimes he picked out people who had prominent chins, or those who had small receding chins—sometimes people with white teeth and sometimes just the opposite. He'd picked out people with small heads and small brains, or with big heads in which he expected big brains even though the selected one would stare at him with the eyes of an idiot. Portman did not know when Schiese-Dietz would start selecting people with big ears or untrimmed fingernails, with thin or flat lips, with thick or sparse eyebrows, cross-eyed ones and people with long fingers.

But Portman sometimes dreamed about being selected for the Canada commando special unit, who cleared the arriving transports and had lots of food and drink, at least for a day, for themselves and their friends—bacon and bread and strawberry or plum jam, and thermoses with coffee, cocoa or hot tea, and vodka or schnapps or French cognac. He dreamed about this in spite of the fact that it also meant clearing the ramp and the railroad cars of dead infants and small choked children, carrying a bunch of them at once like bananas or shot hares or killed or choked hens. Portman dreamed around the clock of a full belly, but there was no chance of his making it into the Canada commando.

"It's my father's birthday today and the anniversary of his death," Harry Cohen said. "I'm as old today as he was when he died. He died in his bed. He was reading a book, closed his eyes and whispered that the end had come."

"Congratulations," replied Portman. "Do you think this has some special meaning here? That it's perhaps some kind of prophecy and you have a right not to let me sleep?"

Suddenly I realized that I was holding on to Harry Cohen's elbows and wrists and that Portman was pressed between us. Our lice crawled from one collar to another. I took their warmth and they took mine.

The unknown women had sparked an image of what could be because it had been once before. From time to time, the wailing wind interrupted the singing. Then the voices became clearer again, although the wailing wind did not die down. They floated through the network of electrified barbed wire, somewhere into infinity. I no longer waited for what Portman would say to mask his envy of the living and the dead. He was sometimes afraid of the dark so he had to talk to hide his even greater fear of the Germans. The singing roused something in him that he thought was dead. It was somewhere on the limits, the nakedness of everything that was still living. It was the heart of his existence, on the thin border of his moral and physical strengths, like the moments of selection, dependent upon decisions made by someone else, but also upon his own decision on how to accept it. Only he and his consciousness, no traitor to himself.

"I'll give them another minute," said Portman. Suddenly it sounded as if he did not have enough air in his lungs. Maybe he had tuberculosis already. "Count to sixty."

The women were singing a popular German song: *"In den Sternen steht es alles geschrieben, du sollst küssen, du sollst lieben . . ."* Probably those who went into the chimney were German or Austrian Jewish women. It was an old coffeehouse hit, but in this moment it carried some immediate, close, pure and direct sincerity and courage, some surprising truth about who is who, no matter where or when. There was in that song now everything that was still unselfish or honorable, even when it was weak and abased.

"Well, really, who cares? When it takes so long it's no good," Portman added. He was being sarcastic about the thought that someone here was singing about kissing and passion or the desire from which children are born.

I held on to my wish that the women would not stop. Did Portman want them to stop because he feared for them? Besides the fact that in the end he turned his anger upon himself?

"Do you want to cry for them?" Portman asked. "This is idiotic solidarity and does no one any good. It just makes the Germans madder. The women have paid for it a couple of times already, as far as I know. Wouldn't it be better to let the Germans sleep at night at least? Do they want to test whether it's true that the devil never sleeps at night? Do they think they're in America—where they can sing whenever and whatever they please?"

Portman turned his face to the planks of the bunk. "They'll knock their teeth out if not worse. I've seen a lot of toothless ones here. And then later I didn't see them anymore, precisely because they had lost their teeth."

I held on to the last bits of the melody, which was already becoming blurred against the night. My brain, along with hunger and the smell of human bodies in the barracks, was floating off into the numb wake-

fulness that precedes sleep. I suddenly realized that I needed to have
Ervin Portman beside me, even with his anger and superstitions and
fear, and I needed Harry Cohen, just as they both needed me. Even
when the people—both the living and the dead—get on each other's
nerves because they have nothing to offer each other and just vegetate,
even on the way to the showers. What makes a man forgive others is
not born of weakness or of strength, but from the fact that human life
is irreplaceable and that nothing else matters.

Portman was bothered by my lice and by Harry Cohen's fleas.
Portman picked them out from the ends of his short hair before it would
be cut again for blankets and army coats. He pinched them with his
nails and threw them down from the bunk in a curve resembling the
flight of crows. When someone below grumbled, as though he'd swallowed them, Portman stopped. I felt Portman's hot breath, just as Harry
Cohen felt mine.

"When I was a kid, my mother used to believe that if two people
started singing the same song it brought them luck," Harry Cohen said.

"I never sing or whistle when I play cards," Portman said. "That's
sure to make you lose. I don't rush headlong into hell if I can remain
at least a little while at hell's entrance. I prefer to look at smoke instead
of looking straight into the fire. That's one thing they've taught me:
that it's better to have your hand in the water than to have it in the
fire."

"Hell isn't down below, in the center of the earth, in the crevices of
mountains, rocks, and passes. It's up above, on the surface of the earth,
like scales on the body of a fish. It's in every man, under the stars,
under the snow, under the enormous firmament," Harry Cohen said.
"It's in every uniform, in every whip, bullet, or dog that is set against
people. I think that hell exists fivefold—in each of the five crematoria.
Or in the eight-meter pits where they burn people when it's not snowing
or raining."

"They're still singing. They're more persistent than salt," I said.
"They're braver than geese or wild swans. I wish I had their marrow
in my bones."

"A lot of good it would do you. You'd really end up in a fine mess then," Portman said. "Don't count on me."

The uniqueness and worthlessness of human life—like two sisters—floated through the night, over the camp and over all of the camps of Germany and the occupied territories. This is what in five, six years the German war had done. This is what made one doubt man and his existence, victory and defeat, good and evil. What caused the first to be last and the last to be first. The wind distorted the singing of the women. It drove the snow against the wall of the barracks and filled its enormous arms with ashes which it carried away farther or closer, spreading them on all sides—ashes that will remain on the face of the planet like a birthmark, even if every last Jewish man, Jewish woman, or Jewish child should perish.

The ashes silenced the echo of the first shot. It lasted only a few seconds. Definitely less than half a minute. The singing mixed with the shooting, then there was only shooting and its echo. It definitely was nothing unexpected; Portman was right about that. It sounded like the rottenführer's switch for camels. Last time, Harry Cohen remembered that a camel will never forget if somebody wrongs it. But, Harry Cohen added, they never forget the good that someone does for them, either. I was sure that he was now in his mind with that Aryan girl in Prague, Maruschka. Maybe she could read his mind, but she could never know what he knew.

In the air, among the snowflakes, a kind of echo remained from the shooting of the machine gun. It was all ordinary, just like the snowflakes. Like the smoke from the chimneys. Like mud.

"They could have figured it out," Portman said. "Unless they've become blind, like moles in the winter."

"Maybe they did figure it out," Harry Cohen replied. "But I don't believe it, just as I don't believe that moles go blind in the winter."

"I'll go to sing with them, once they get the idea of throwing rocks at the rottenführer and at the scharführer at the same time," Portman said. And then he added, "No one will give a damn."

Someone went to the bucket. Nothing had changed in the least in the daily routine of the barracks. From the sounds of the steps and movements you could tell who had diarrhea, who had dysentery or even typhus, who had tuberculosis, pneumonia, or only asthma—who would not make it till morning or midnight and who would manage to infect his bedfellows before he died.

I bid farewell to the singing of the women and looked forward to tomorrow's, just as I had looked forward to my grandmother's bedtime fairy tales. Where does a man find strength when all that he has is weakness?

"Schiese-Dietz believes that Jewish children are born hairy, like animals," Portman said. "He also selects the hairy girls first, even before those who are skin and bones."

I knew that I would be able to hear the women singing again, and yet it occurred to me that they would be singing when I wouldn't be there—nor Portman, nor Harry Cohen. I thought about life and death in Auschwitz-Birkenau. What is the purpose of human existence? Why is man plagued by feelings of futility and worthlessness? How do you find out how to do the right thing when it comes to it? It was again a moment of unanswerable questions. But there was some change in the air, even if there were no answers. How many people had they shot? What would the women appeal to tomorrow with their singing? I was lost in the echo of their chorus. I felt the snow, the ashes, and the silence around me. I felt the urge to go outside, for which the guard would immediately shoot me before I got to the barbed wire. I wanted to touch with my lips a sliver of ash or snowflake. I listened. There was no sound. The women had sung themselves to sleep. Others cried themselves to sleep. And still others had been shot into an eternal sleep.

"At last," said Portman.

It did not sound like relief or satisfaction, though sometimes Portman thought that women had nine lives, like cats. Perhaps he hoped that it was true. Everything that had to do with cats Portman believed to be ill-fated, an echo or foreboding of misfortune, even when it was born only in his head.

"Couldn't they have gone to sleep long ago?" Portman asked. "To-morrow they'll be dropping like flies, even those who were not hit." And then he continued, "There's no sense in wasting your time or your strength. It's a waste of every drop of blood when you spill it on your own and for nothing."

I tried to call back the echo of the women's voices, the image of birth, of something that for me was always connected with women, something which I knew little about and probably never understood. I felt the familiar shame, but for the first time, maybe knowing why.

"Do you have the shakes or what?" Portman addressed me. And finally, "They'll drive me nuts with their singing."

Portman curled up to sleep. I wished the remaining women would fall asleep and not be cold. Harry Cohen began to chew his bread and blood sausage. He was, maybe, concerned with the number of possi-bilities everything and everybody had, has, or should have, or doesn't have at all. He wished to be somewhere else, someone else, where people do not live a miserable life, where they don't have to ask every other second why they were born, about things for which there were no solutions.

Portman's fleas and lice were feasting on me. The smoke rose slowly toward the sky. Black snow was falling. I have never forgotten the black snow with ashes in Auschwitz-Birkenau, which that night I saw for the first time in my life before I fell asleep.

"Good night," Portman said in a conciliatory tone. He repeated to himself the tattooed number on his right forearm. He probably no longer envied the dead.

"Good night," Harry Cohen said. It was one of the possibilities.

"Good night," I managed sleepily.

We were swallowed by the silence into which Samson once disap-peared and in which every night and every man seems to be the last. Infinity engulfed us.

A Man the Size of
a Postage Stamp

❖

Don't react to a mad man if you don't want to be like him.

Answer a mad man's madness so he doesn't think how wise he is.
———Jewish Proverb

Nobody knows anything. Nobody is going to know anything.
Not even we know anything.
———Heinrich Himmler

The dead can't carry the dead.
———German Proverb

1

H ey, still the hair and whiskers?" said Feldwebel Karl Oberg, a leader of the garrison band.

He was as surprised as he had been on Thursday that nothing showed on the teacher's face. "What do you think is so smart about not shaving or cutting your hair? You still believe that he who lives to see next spring will survive for one whole year?"

Karl Oberg's coat had been tailor-made for him when he had been the military bandleader in the Warsaw garrison. Polish nobility patronized the same tailor. Feldwebel Oberg said he didn't expect the teacher to reply. He hadn't answered last Thursday, either. The teacher hadn't said a word the whole day there and back. The commandant had ordered him to bring the old man again. The feldwebel wondered what the commandant could want from the teacher.

They were halfway there. Alongside the old teacher, Feldwebel Oberg
felt like a strong young sapling in springtime next to an old tree. Thinking
about an old tree, he could imagine the labyrinth of roots, a hiding place
for poisonous snakes. The old man's back was bent. His eyes were dim.
The bandleader's eyes were blue. He was slender and well built, and there
wasn't a speck of soot on his well-shaven face. His black shoes were well
shined. He was careful to keep his shoes clean.

They passed the bakery and the storehouse and the office of the
accountant and the camp's army-supply depot. After that, the two were
joined by the bandleader's German shepherd.

"Come here, Suicide," said the feldwebel. "What are you doing loose
here? Isn't it dangerous to run free? There must be a bitch around
somewhere."

It was cold. The wind was still. The coldness lay across the land like
silence. It patched the marshes together.

"Still got all that hair and all those whiskers," said Feldwebel Oberg.
"Yet we can't import seaweed, mattress stuffing, or sponges from all over
the world anymore like we used to."

He exhaled and his breath came out like white steam. "Doesn't all this
ever remind you of the sea? Or perhaps a rock at the bottom of the sea?
Hey, wake up, Whiskers! We still got a few minutes to go."

Feldwebel Oberg had gone to the trouble of arranging one of the Jewish
melodies in the morning. He put its funeral-like rhythm into a march. He
would introduce it next Thursday evening at the casino.

You could hear trains coming and leaving on the ramps.

"Some people keep silent to make themselves feel bigger," the Feldwebel
said. "We're almost there, Whiskers."

Karl Oberg began to whistle "The Entry of the Gladiators." Something
occurred to him.

"You not only have all your hair and whiskers like you did last week,"
he said, "I understand you've still got your name, huh Whiskers? But you've
got a number too, and a tattoo on your left forearm, isn't it so? Still got
everything, hair and whiskers, the name, even your civilian clothes. You
ought to be more grateful."

He kept on whistling. He glanced briefly at the teacher's face.

They were almost there, and Henryk Bley tried to straighten up so he could keep pace with Feldwebel Oberg. Walking warmed him up a little, but it exhausted him as well. The dog kept circling and jumping, sniffing and snarling. Not even the rapid pace was enough to keep the teacher warm. He had once told the children in the camp orphanage to stand in clusters and hug each other to keep warm.

The German shepherd stopped in front of the commandant's house.

"Take it easy, Suicide." The feldwebel addressed the dog. "Don't you like *Menschentieren*?"

The German shepherd eyed Karl Oberg from the doorway. His nostrils quivered in anticipation.

"Faster, Whiskers. Try to catch Herr Commandant, if we haven't missed him already like last Thursday."

Karl Oberg let the teacher pass through the gates between the sentries and then followed him. The guard told the feldwebel that his escort should stay in the waiting room.

2

Herr Commandant Oscar Adler-Bienenstock was with his son at the park. He didn't have a wife, only a twelve-year-old son who had come here afterward. Herr Commandant had been wounded at the Eastern front. They both liked engines and music, which, as Schopenhauer said, mimics the world, the mystery of life, the great nothingness; the melody to which the world's text is set. But that was all they had in common.

Herr Commandant had taught his son reading and writing, physics and arithmetic. He taught him the mysteries of birds and animals, the importance of discipline, and the secrets of engines. In winter the marshes froze, and in the springtime they melted. It was hell for engines. But worst of all was keeping the machines going and repairing the engine's disorders.

People began to whisper that Herr Commandant's little son, a blue-eyed, fair-haired little angel who did not look like Herr Commandant but probably resembled his mother, wasn't quite right in the head. He had big bloodshot eyes that were wet and glassy, a skull that narrowed in the back, a high forehead, and big ears. Only his complexion was lovely, just like his shiny hair, like a girl's. His bottom lip was large and wet from the way he kept running his tongue over it; even if he wasn't eating or drinking he found something for his tongue to do.

The boy listened to his father's explanations. Had the father forgotten the time? It seemed that the boy liked to look at things backward. Trains coming and going—and vice versa. Sometimes the boy seemed scared and other times indifferent and still, or aggressive before submerging into his indifference again.

Islands of leafless forests stretched above them and into the countryside. The sound of engines carried far into the marshes.

Herr Commandant ordered the forests cut. He had the timber hauled off for the Reich. That way, not even the maimed forest could give shelter to the fugitives. Only miles from here there were forests untouched, silent and deep; in their midst, wrapped like a gossamer in needle leaves, was T.II., the brother camp.

"What happens to animals when they're with people?" asked the boy.

"Why?"

"Because of these children here."

"Oh, I see," Herr Commandant said.

But he wasn't sure. Was it that the boy saw the children in the camp, as he did the rest of the prisoners, as animals? Hopefully, the boy didn't know any more about the people they put behind the wires.

But the boy saw them, every day. He would grow with it as German children were growing among farms and gardens or factories and schools. They were coming and never leaving, but their numbers didn't increase.

Sometimes the boy thought it was strange. Were they entering some underground river, disappearing into an invisible sea?

Herr Commandant grabbed his shoulders and called him a man; but the boy didn't like his embrace. For a second, he looked through his father as though he were a stranger.

"Which side of the fence was my mother on?" the boy asked.

"Your mother?"

When it was too cold to watch the band practice outdoors, or to watch and listen to the engines, the child's attention was captured by the waves of greasy smoke that rolled in on the wind from the marshes or over the forests from the camps at T.II., and the dumping station. The boy watched as the wind pulled the smoke across the sky and created letters, numbers, or signs. Sometimes the clouds were thick, and black ash fell from them like rain. And sometimes the clouds resembled engines and trucks. The pond was half frozen.

"You're going to like the military maps," Herr Commandant said.

"Why?" asked the boy.

Military maps weren't what the boy liked. He was fond of new army trucks with red crosses painted on them. Three weeks ago he had seen soldiers taking out stiff human bodies. At first, Herr Commandant forbade the boy to watch, but it became routine, everpresent.

The pond resembled a sunset in the midst of the day, reflecting dry clouds split from a dark ocean. The boy looked up at the smoke writing its incomprehensible messages in the sky.

There was no river in the town or at the camp at the side of the marshes, so there were no bridges. Only once had the boy asked for the bridges he remembered from Germany. All that was left of the church was the bell tower. German pilots had aimed at it when the town was still Polish. After that, the young German cannoneers used it as a training target. A small handful of military families comprised the German garrison. It was the army that created the atmosphere in the town, even though it was represented by few people—the way a country was represented by a ship, a flag, or a reputation. The boy didn't like other German boys, and vice versa.

"In a map you can taste the time, like you can tell the taste from the smell of an apple," said the father. "There are many things you can taste and feel—time, tradition, courage. Maybe later, a woman like your mother."

Was it too complicated for the boy?

The boy seemed not to listen. There was an inscription on the garage that fascinated the boy: "We Germans came into the world in order to die." It reminded him of the truck with red crosses on its sides and on its roof. The ambulances had no windows, like birds without wings or heads. Something was missing, or rather, had been added—a sheet metal neck that led into the strong, eight-cylinder motor. And instead of legs, it had two big exhaust pipes, like the wings of a bird in flight, curving like fins; but why did they have no windows? The boy wondered. Why did the exhaust pipes curve inward instead of out? What happened to people from the moment they stepped into the ambulance until the cab was empty again? Man never asks, the father had said. The boy's thick, fair hair was combed back, like a mane, and his blue eyes shone.

It struck Herr Commandant that his son looked like an angel. Only angels do not know and ask why. There is no why for people in command. Why did this happen to me? That brought to mind some lines from Nietzsche about the dead god who had killed the conscience— who said that beauty is watching someone you have helped to create (in this case his boy) glide across the pond's level, performing the backstroke. It was necessary to scorn death, maybe to love death. The killing and the possibility of being killed. To understand life and death as one. How to teach that to his son? How to introduce him to the great killing, teach him to despise and defy life?

One's name—being a father—being a son means very little in the light of some things, Herr Commandant thought. The new kind of love is tough, not fragile like Christian love—or, forgive me, that of the Jewish swine who ended up on a Roman cross and good riddance to him—I've got a feeble-minded son—thanks to whom?—I must love him in a tough way, like a master without weakness. But the commandant was thinking about the Reich's laws and institutions like Brandenburg, Hartheim, or Eglfing-Haar hospitals or a mental hospital in Kaufbeuren, and what was called "the merciful act."

When he took the boy out of school to look after his education himself, his son confused the points of a compass, north, east, south, and west. He could never remember the four elements, fire, water, earth, and air. There was some fifth element between his temples. He had trouble with everything that included four, the ideal number of Pythagoras. He only comprehended the number three of Aristotle. He didn't know that swamps can belong to both elements, water and earth. He would concentrate on light, or on sounds, and always on voices. But he could never get them all together.

It seemed as if the boy's interest could not be aroused by talking about animals and what happens to animals in the company of people. Only about engines. Then he started to make wet circles with his small, full, red tongue.

"Why don't you listen when I speak to you?"

"I'm looking," the boy said.

"At what?"

"At the ambulances. They look like birds. Like fish. Like swans."

"They're good cars."

"They don't have windows."

"They're disinfection trucks," the father told him. "Yesterday, three of them broke down. They've got new engines already, or I hope so. I will show you four new ones."

"They've got exhaust pipes like elephant trunks," said the boy.

Maybe he should have been born a girl, Herr Commandant thought. What am I going to do with him? And through the father's mind flashed the thought how the boy would be better off.

The boy looked up at the sky, at the picture the smoke was drawing in the still air and at the rolls of huge, black, sooty, vaporlike balloons. The blue sky was endless.

"There will be a concert this evening," Herr Commandant said. "'The Entry of the Gladiators.' That's a nice march. *Einzug der Gladiatoren*. Will we go listen in the casino?"

The father looked on as the son played ducks and drakes with flat pebbles. He always took three stones at once. Then the boy threw the stones into the water and watched the circles. They never touched the icy margin.

"Why don't you say something?" asked the father.

The boy remembered the morning he visited his mother in her bedroom in Berlin. It was a clear day, and his mother had said that she would have nothing more to do with his father. His father hit her in the face with his fist. Her back and head struck the wall of the bedroom. She bled from her nose. His father became furious at the sight of her blood and he hit the boy's mother again and threw her onto the bed, tearing her dress and her underwear from her. "I can't stand you," said the mother. "Go away. You're disgusting." The boy was hidden in the wardrobe with his mother's dresses and shoes and flacons of perfume. Nobody knew the boy saw. His father didn't know he was there. The boy could only guess what it meant, why the mother refused to share the bed with the father, why the father had gotten so mad. He left her lying in her blood, her face toward the ceiling.

Sometimes the water brought it all back to him. Or the smoke. And sometimes the trucks. But near his father he always remembered it. When he was four or five years old, his father broke into a fit of anger at having an imbecile for a son and beat him with his fists about his head and face and nose and eyes, and that happened often. Only later, after his mother left, did he stop beating him.

"To understand animals is to understand people; and to understand people is to understand war," said Herr Commandant.

"Why do animals fight?" asked the boy.

"From an instinct for survival," answered Herr Commandant. "To live."

"Look there," said the boy.

"Where?" asked the father.

He looked up at the sky where the smoke was thinning out and into a stream from the castle at T.II. Puffs of it floated in the sky like a map that Herr Commandant could follow—the same way sailors at sea can read the stars, or the way a blind man can move with confidence along a familiar path. The smaller dots were towns and villages, and the tiniest circles were camps.

"Let's go, I have a meeting at the Commandatur and Führesheim. You wish to go with me?" He touched the boy's shoulder.

His eyes flickered with a distaste he couldn't put into words. He thought about fathers and children. Four elements. He looked back from the ambulances, away from his son and the inscription over the garage door and back to the sky.

3

Henryk Bley waited, as Feldwebel Karl Oberg told him to, in the commandant's waiting room. Ever since last Thursday, the teacher had racked his brain about why Herr Commandant summoned him, then sent him away without bothering to see him. He ruled out the possibility that the commandant had wanted to ask him to teach or advise him on his son. But he hadn't ruled out the possibility that he might be interested in knowing his views on his son. The teacher had years of experience in that field. Last week, Feldwebel Oberg had mentioned that at the castle at T.II.—they weren't just exterminating bedbugs and lice and rats with Cyclon B.

There was a loose-leaf calendar on the right side of the door leading into Herr Commandant's office. Easter Monday was printed in red. The teacher could hear Feldwebel Karl Oberg talking with an orderly at the other end of the hall. They both laughed. The noises of trains on the ramps were coming and fading again.

The orderly, Sturmman Fritzinger, on the way to the ambulances, had a good story for the bandleader in his native German about what the last Gypsy king had said: "Big in his own eyes, small in the eyes of others."

The office of Herr Commandant was in the left wing of a stone building whose windows overlooked a garden with huge poplar trees. From the corridor and the waiting room you could see the frozen trees wrapped in ice which melted at midday and froze again in the afternoon, forming droplets of ice like pearls. Stubby icicles hung from the drainspouts, reflecting the feeble afternoon sun. The corridor was decorated with framed portraits of German military leaders, right up to the most recent one, who had brought the Reich together. Some of the portraits had mourning bands across the right hand corner.

The teacher heard footsteps in the hall. Herr Commandant had lost one leg below the knee fighting on the Eastern front in Suwalki, Lithuania. That place was marked on his map in red.

Henryk Bley stared at the toes of his shoes. He tried to concentrate on Easter Monday, or on a distant picture of the city of Susa, in Persia, where he'd been once. The muddle of the village came closer and then faded away—fragments of an image. There was also a man in a regal robe, embroidered with pearls, gold, and rubies, who'd wanted to exterminate them some hundred and fifty generations ago but had decided not to at the urging of the queen, one of his wives—maybe a little whore in the king's harem—but certainly someone clever, brave, and most probaby just.

The teacher tried to imagine the woman who had kept the king from killing them. He was brought closer by comparing her to the eldest girl in his orphanage here, Noemi Astach.

But thinking about the black, deep, sad eyes of Noemi Astach reminded him again of Herr Commandant's boy. The teacher's stomach rumbled. At one time that would have embarrassed him. He paid no heed. It gave him a slight pain. What was worse? Hot or cold? Hunger or fear? The silence from behind the woods? Fear now or fear five minutes later? Which fear is the worst of all man's fears? Which fear takes away from him and which fear gives him strength? How long had he been here already?

The waiting room was clean and warm. The pellets of ice in the old man's beard were melting. Some of the drops looked like wet salt. Why doesn't man have the quality of salt? The teacher licked the drops from his lips. His stomach growled again. He dared to raise his eyes to read the sign again and glance at the calendar marked for Easter Monday; the teacher's eyes were hazy—like the haze when evening falls; or in the morning before it lifts. He didn't want to think of being hungry, of fear, of Easter Monday, or of the deep, black, sad eyes of Noemi Astach.

He remembered the breakfasts and the suppers in the orphanage before the war and the way the children were taught. How the cook explained to them how she couldn't hear when they all talked at once.

It was when they only spoke one at a time that their words, wishes, and explanations were understandable and could be listened to—sometimes even when they just whispered. The teacher thought about the fibers that bind the past with what no longer exists.

The rumble of his stomach echoed into his thoughts of how they had arranged the tables and chairs, deciding where each should sit, where he should keep his clothes hanger, bath and hand towels, or from which plate he would eat. He recalled how the children came into the dining room in groups: first, second, third. Or which children had to nap after lunch and which ones preferred to play.

The commandant's waiting room reminded him of the house from which he had just come—the way the day reminds of the night, the dryness of the damp, or the way being hungry reminds of being fed, and thirst conjures up an image of a glass of water.

The door of the commandant's office remained closed. After thirty minutes, Feldwebel Oberg reappeared in the waiting room. He had a dog at his heel and was holding its collar.

"Come on, Whiskers," said bandleader Karl Oberg. "Pull yourself together. It's too late for our turn. Maybe next time . . ."

4

Outside, Karl Oberg mounted a horse and reined it next to the wall on the sidewalk beside the teacher. The feldwebel felt good in cold weather.

"Well, Whiskers, we're back where we started."

They continued side by side, the feldwebel on horseback and the teacher on the ground. They took up the sidewalk. There was nobody around. They went by the warehouse. The feldwebel patted the horse's neck with his pigskin glove. The dog, trotting alongside, barked.

The horse turned his long magnificent neck here and there.

"After the Germans, nobody will return anywhere, not to Poland, not to Germany, Whiskers. And if, thousands of years from now, someone asks, 'What's the difference?' the answer will be 'Yes, this is the difference.' The moment of no return, Whiskers. No exceptions."

The hooves of the horse rumbled on the stones. One, two, three, four. One, two, three, four.

"You're already alive for a few extra Thursdays beyond average, Whiskers," said the feldwebel, from the loftiness of his horse. "Here we are, it's the middle of the week, and it's as though nothing has happened. Just when the band boys are at their best. And I've had to leave them when they're all warmed up."

Sometimes the horse nudged his nose against the teacher, pushing him closer to the walls of the buildings they passed.

Feldwebel Oberg pulled the reins, eased them out. The horse snorted. The dog bared its teeth at the marshes; maybe it sensed what a person or a horse couldn't. Or just a bitch; dogs can smell a bitch for miles.

"Hair and whiskers," mused Feldwebel Oberg. "As if you didn't know, Whiskers, that what's appropriate today can be a drawback tomorrow. You've outlived your old woman, your family—many families. You enjoy surprises you can't take credit for, don't you, Whiskers? Who knows what will happen by the time next Thursday rolls around? Come on, faster. You've got legs like a ballerina. And you don't say a word, Whiskers, as if you were trying to tell me something. By now you ought to have some idea of how far it goes, your being an exception. In winter, everybody's got thin skin. Yours must be like paper."

The horse stumbled because the feldwebel had pulled on the reins. Then he recovered and resumed his pace. Stones stuck out of the pavement.

Feldwebel Oberg patted the animal. His ruddy face looked sunburned. The feldwebel's black calfskin riding boots pressed against the horse's flanks. He eased up on the bit. "Whoaa . . . "

The teacher also stopped, without the feldwebel even telling him to.

They were in the middle of the camp in front of the home for Abandoned Children, Street and block Ch. 13. Farther from here was the canteen, blockführer house, and the hauptwache next to the casino.

Henryk Bley said nothing. He waited for the bandleader to dismiss him.

"Your hair and whiskers are like rocks at the bottom of the sea," Karl Oberg chuckled. "By the way, Whiskers, wouldn't you like to know what happened at T.II. with the lady of your heart? Children were with her. Does that make sense to you, Whiskers? You certainly know what I mean, Whiskers. And even when you shave and get your hair cut, it will still be like a stone at the bottom of the sea. So, go, go, go, Whiskers—*dalli, dalli, dalli . . .*"

5

"I'm here," said Henryk Bley when the door closed behind him. He listened to the echo of his words. He wanted to assure himself that he was speaking, breathing, still living. Was he?

Inside the house he could feel the moldiness, the smell of cold, stagnant air. The teacher waited. Where are the rest?

Man is a stranger in the world, but there are some places where he's more a stranger than others. And places that are good, at least a little better than others. That brought his thoughts to the postage stamps. He remembered his collection, which the Germans had taken as they'd taken everything. One of them had a silhouette of Flavius Josephus, the Jewish military leader and historian from the years 37 to 100 in the common era. During the Jewish war against the Romans, the largest war ever fought against Rome, Flavius led and gave up a rebellion in Galilee. He commanded the fortress of Jotapata and handed it over to the Romans. He claimed that in surrendering he had at least saved the lives of some of his people, even though he'd taken the honor and dignity of those who'd already fallen and of those who survived. The teacher sighed. He prepared himself for the first thing he'd say. It's a miracle we're all still alive, he thought. The teacher had only a few teeth left. Almost every day he was beaten. Only the first beating is memorable.

The cold came in through the windows the children had plugged with paper and rags. It's a good thing there's no wind, he thought. An icicle hung from the waterspout. He knew the children were in bed already, pressed close together to keep warm. This was something he didn't have to teach them to do. He thought about the silence that swallows up all voices together.

"I'm back," the teacher said.

He continued on his way toward the stairs that rose from the long corridor on the ground floor. The stairs led up to the attic. He had his bunk next to the hallway where fifteen-year-old Noemi Astach, the eldest girl in the house, slept. The rest of the children slept downstairs. As the teacher went upstairs, the treads and planks creaked, as did the wormy boards. He told them to stay in bed as long as possible, the longer the better, to beat the hunger and the cold.

The teacher stepped on the third stair and its squeak sounded as it had since last Thursday, echoes of two hundred children whose faces, voices, and names he couldn't remember. He was afraid these faces would get lost, because later, from afar, a person is not much more than a face, and when all that is left is a memory, the face is the first to get lost. Then one forgets the name and, finally, the memory of the memory.

In his mind's eye he could see the window the sun came through, against which the wind blew. He thought about what the children learned: German, English, Spanish, Hebrew, French. Syllables, substantive nouns, adjectives. Subtraction, addition. Division. The mysteries of Ludolf's number. Numbers and principles of Pythagoras or Archimedes. The beauty of Baruch Spinoza. He could hear the song all the way in his office when the windows were open in the spring, summer or fall. He recalled the lines he'd written for the children to read. Isn't it terribly cold here? Not as bad as outside, at least.

What did he really want them to know? What's good and bad? Right and wrong? Just and unjust? Why man lies, steals, and kills? Why he doesn't lie, steal, and kill? Why man is born? Why he dies? It seemed so simple. He wanted to make them forget today and yesterday and to look for tomorrow. But that was a lie. He thought of how he'd called them into his office for their medical examination. He breathed in the cold, musty air.

"I am here," he repeated.

6

Noemi Astach came in before he could draw the blanket in front of his bunk like a curtain.

"They took away a third child while you were gone," she said. "Natasha, Diana, and Aneta are gone."

"Aneta." The teacher's voice sagged.

"They said she needed medical treatment. And that you knew about it. They loaded Aneta into an ambulance."

"Without a window? When?"

"An hour after the feldwebel took you away."

"Who?"

"The driver and his helper. Herr Commandant's son was with them. He was sitting in the front cab."

"I don't know anything," Henryk Bley replied. It was as if with each word he were wiping away each thought, vision, and echo he'd brought here to his nook. The girl looked at him before lowering her eyes.

"Last Thursday when you left the ambulance came, too."

Noemi Astach wore a kerchief on her head like an old woman. Her reddish hair was closely shaved.

"It's cold in here," the teacher said.

"Where were you?"

"At Herr Commandant's headquarters."

"What did they want you for?"

Three girls gone, why? Noemi Astach was eight years old the day her parents had been stoned to death in their country town and people sent her to him. Now she had a piece of burlap wound around her neck, the same piece she wrapped her feet in during the night. It was an old coat sleeve and she wore an even older coat. Henryk Bley knew that she had nothing on underneath. She'd given her clothes and underwear to the younger children. She'd given her sweater to Aneta, the girl they'd taken away during the time he'd been gone. Before that, she gave her socks to Diana and traded her shoes for Natasha's.

He glanced at the walls. Flies, lice, and bedbugs were frozen against the stone. Some had been killed with pins. That morning the children had found a rat frozen in the cellar. The teacher took the blanket left hanging in front of his bunk and wrapped it around her shoulders.

"I don't want to think only about what they're doing," he said.

Patches of mold grew on the walls. They'd scraped them off the evening before, but they were there again in the morning. Blotches of dampness appeared, encircling the mold. The roof leaked only when the ice on it melted at high noon, not during the evening or at night.

"I knew they were going to take someone away when you weren't here," Noemi Astach said.

She looked at him. It was a double anger against herself, the teacher, and the rest. She had brown eyes.

His lips quivered, purplish with the cold and moist from the melting ice. Was he still preparing himself for what he was going to tell the children about Easter Monday? He looked at the moon. Framed inside the icy hole in the roof, its craters were visible. The teacher recalled in a half voice the names of the seas and mountains and valleys of the moon. It was all very distant. The icy tart that was the moon looked remote and thinking about it brought to his mind the image of Herr Commandant's boy—his blue eyes, the strange way his small but long tongue kept rolling around inside of his mouth like a windmill, and that curious, amazed, inexplicable expression of his. And it brought home the resemblance of Noemi Astach with her sad eyes to the German child. He knew his first impression was not mistaken when he had gone away and then come back. Easter Monday, he thought to himself. And again he was overcome by the premonition he'd feared. The moon sailed through the clouds. It looked like a round jellyfish in an icy sea. It was only after a while that he realized that Noemi Astach had left.

7

Henryk Bley was awakened by the cold. How long had he slept? He looked up through the hole in the roof. A few minutes? Or seconds?

It was a long time since he had had dreams at night. As unbelievable as they seemed to him, they frightened him before he could forget. In his first dream, there had been the blind girl and deaf boy he taught walking along the sunny beach—both of them healthy, healed of their muteness and blindness, but twenty years older, bathed in sunbeams and reflections of the blue water of the Mediterranean. Things had shifted into the future. The image even had fragrances—of cypress and warm, dry air, white, wet sand, and salt water. The once-blind girl had met her sister as if she hadn't stayed behind at T.II., and they walked together, side by side, along a sandy path, and their shadows were cast on yellow and white rocks. Along the bottom of the rocks a moss grew. But high on top, the rocks were bare and smooth. Beyond the rocks lay Haifa, the port, and the hills of Carmel. The highway next to the path curved toward the new town of Tel Aviv. Both young women were pushing baby carriages. The path and highway were bordered by magnolias and oleander bushes. Far ahead, the oranges in bright green trees stirred in the wind, and so did the lemon trees, half of whose fruit was still green, half just beginning to turn yellow. On the left the water was heaving, tireless, a sea with its white and silver waves and foam. Glistening fish leaped above the surface and then plunged back again in a game that's lasted unchanged, and will last until the sun goes out. The young women passed a garden restaurant where music was playing. The restaurant took up a long stretch of beach where palms grew.

In his second dream, Henryk Bley was chatting with Herr Commandant Oscar Adler-Bienenstock about his son, as if the Commandant had requested his advice. From his papers, Herr Commandant knew that Henryk Bley was a teacher and a physician, an educator and writer, or rather, he had been all that before he came here. In his papers were hints that the inclinations of the teacher weren't completely comparable to others, but at the same time there were enough records of dates with women to whom the teacher had been close in his years. Herr Commandant asked the teacher to sit down. Henryk Bley sat on the edge of his chair. It occurred to him that he'd leave later, and when he returned to his children, the house would be empty. Herr Commandant was staring at the globe. Germany was right there in its place, close as a hand in a glove.

"We're turning the world back to the way it used to be and forward to where it should be," Herr Commandant said.

On the small Polish mahogany table—the kind a little lamp or vase of flowers belongs on—there was an empty white bird cage. A full bookcase was against the wall.

The teacher noticed that there was no clock in the room.

"*A bove majore discit aratrore miror*—the bull learns to plow from the ox. *Absent naeres non erit*—the absent one will not inherit," said Herr Commandant.

He stretched as if he wanted to get up, but it was only the upper part of his body that moved. His crippled leg with the prosthesis and his other leg with the amputated toes remained immobile.

"In the breast of many a father, a mother's heart beats," said Herr Commandant.

Outside, the orderly Fritzinger opened the door of the stove and threw in a shovelful of coal. The wall shook and the door of the desk opened. The inside of the door was inlaid with bits of colored wood.

"Even if you wanted to shave and have a haircut, I'm afraid you're going to have to wait until Monday. Isn't it Easter Monday?"

His face grew sober. The door creaked. Herr Commandant's son came in.

"Three," he said.

"Four," Herr Commandant smiled. Then he said, "We can't move ahead by always looking back." Then he went on, "I'm sorry, old friend, but I'm the Commandant here; I'm not the Commandant there." He said no more.

Suddenly Henryk Bley didn't know whether he heard his own voice or Herr Commandant's. Everything, even the castle at T.II., was transformed into a small railroad station with a garden and a field and a forest at the end of the meadow. This was his third dream. The guards

opened the doors of the freight cars—forty men and twelve horses—
and ordered the children to get out. The children looked around, dazzled
by the sun.

"Yes, Herr Hauptman," the stationmaster said.

"Of course, Herr Kriminalrat."

"Where is orderly Fritzinger?"

An auxiliary engine pushed the rest of the train toward the gateway.
The air was clear. Everything was still. The blue sky was the color of
the sea, and flowers were blooming in the meadow. They went across
a long path in the grass and as far as the woods, but not quite to the
trees where the meadow turned into a plain. All went in silence as if
in the night. The blue sky was still full of sun. The children began to
sing. It was the song Henryk Bley had composed with them before they
went.

> *When you go into the unknown, far away,*
> *Take just the flag and hope*
> *So board, my little ones, the longest train . . .*

He could still hear the children's voices and see the meadow, the
forest just ahead, and the sunshine; where the forest began and ended.
The children kept going and singing. Suddenly the pine trees turned
into German soldiers, spread out on chairs, their legs apart, with machine
guns in their hands. The machine guns were aimed at the children, but
the soldiers didn't shoot. The children kept on opening their mouths,
but their singing couldn't be heard anymore. All became mute. You
couldn't even hear the machine guns. Led by him and Noemi Astach,
the children melted into the stillness of the forest at the edge of the
abyss; no matter where they turned, each of the trees became a German
soldier.

The teacher forgot all three dreams at once. He saw the chunks of
ice on the roof again. The moon was full. Stars glittered in the sky.

8

"On Monday we're going to move," the teacher said.

"It's Sunday already. Where to?" asked Noemi Astach.

"We don't need to worry about packing," he added. "That's good."

You could hear the whistles of two trains as they passed each other at the ramps. One was just arriving and the other was just leaving.

"Did you find out any details about my brother from the band-leader?" asked Noemi Astach.

"No. He talked about Leona."

"Are they going to kill us today?"

Noemi Astach's dark eyes deepened, like a well in which the first and last thing drowning was fear.

Henryk Bley knew who the girl reminded him of, although it wasn't just a likeness. He remembered his friend before she'd boarded the train to T.II. She was tall, firm-breasted, and narrow-shouldered, and her hair was black as coal and smelled of cinnamon when she washed it. She still had long hair when she got out of the freight car. He remembered her hands.

"Don't be afraid, and don't let the others fear," he said to Noemi Astach.

"It's easy to say."

The teacher was preparing for what he was going to tell the children—that they should look upward and not slouch when they walked or rode away, as if they were about to spot Allied planes in the sky, coming to punish Germany. He thought about both things at once, about how many times the Germans had postponed what should have and what was supposed to have happened in Warsaw or in T.II. The teacher was listening to the trains. By morning one was gone, the other already empty.

When they were downstairs, he looked at the children. "I want to tell you about Susa in ancient Persia. I was there once when I was still a young man."

The teacher saw relief in Noemi Astach's eyes and questions in the eyes of the other children, except the blind girl and the deaf boy. He glanced around the floor for a trace of the rat that had lost its life here—a bit of hide maybe, but he found nothing. The teacher thought about what the blind girl wouldn't see and the deaf boy wouldn't hear. "About good things," he added.

Through the tear in the window's paper cover, the clouds could be seen floating slowly. The first light of dawn was pushing back the night. The walls had long since begun to sag and the teacher wondered whether the house might not collapse. It had been a short night.

Smoke and the stench of fire came from the marshes beyond the town. The earth breathed with the approaching spring, with the smell of winter, of mold, darkness, and ice that was turning into slush. It mingled with the smell of mold on the rotting walls.

"There are some things that are good for us," he said.

The morning star was still visible like the evening star had been the night before. It was before five. The teacher caressed several of the children. Their skin was rough, dirty, and chapped. He tried to cling to the image of the rocks by the Dead Sea and Easter Monday in Susa. He heard a motor. He knew he had just a moment left before the ambulance with its red cross stopped in front of the house at Ch. 13.

The teacher calculated how much time he had before bandleader Karl Oberg would bang at the door or somebody else would come to tell them where they were going to be moved. He thought that he would tell the children of his pleasure at how quickly they'd awakened and gotten ready.

He talked fast about the bloodshed which had once been prevented against their people in Susa and how many fathers had stood before their children like he was standing with them now. Those fathers had probably thought at that moment about what they'd done right, what they refused to do differently, and about the mothers who had given them life and what it all meant. About how a brave woman was found (a distant cousin of one of them, or all of them), one of the wives of the Persian king at the time. He'd always envisioned her as slender, pale from fear or from the chill that ran along her spine. She couldn't help being afraid of what was coming, of what was so close already, of what she alone could handle—or couldn't. She'd heard the stories that were later confirmed to her by her uncle, a dignitary in the king's court, when they ate at the table with the king.

Henryk Bley spoke more quickly; he heard the noise of the ambulance and then the brakes, and the door opening and then banging shut again.

He tried to breathe life into his words with the image of the king's table in far-off Persia, spread with a white damask cloth, the crystal vases filled with flowers, and bowls the servants carried to the tables. Henryk Bley described the wine goblets on the royal table, the water, and the platters of the finest food. He realized that he was describing acorns, which the children had gathered last fall, and bran, which neither belonged nor would have appeared on any royal table. He described the glow of candles in hammered silver candlesticks that stood on the tables, and the light of more candles in golden chandeliers that hung from the stucco ceiling, thinking about the wax that must have dripped on the table when they burned low before their lights went out. And then he talked about the king's throne and cushions.

In the meantime, he couldn't help hearing what the children were hearing, the omnipresent footsteps of the feldwebel and of two other pairs of feet in high jackboots, the kind people wore in this part of the country during the winter and early spring. He heard a dog bark. The children turned their heads and looked at him, but he kept talking as though he couldn't hear what everybody else had.

He spoke of the king's wives—who sat on the king's left at the table and who resembled his friend, Leona—and their mothers, and Noemi Astach, looking the way the children remembered her from before.

Henryk Bley heard the bandleader's first thump on the door. Without talking about it, he went on imagining the desire and gentleness the woman beside him had aroused in the king long ago, and the events that set one against the other because somewhere someone took the first step that made the other steps inevitable and prepared the way for the massacre of everyone who'd been born of the same mothers as the queen.

Before he'd become the director of the orphanage in Warsaw, Henryk Bley had had a stone paperweight that had been found at the bottom of the Dead Sea. The sea was shallow. It had just as much strength as the thousands of years that crush stones. He could see the stones, softened as a sponge.

"We'll all stick together," the teacher said now. "This will be good." And as he nodded to Noemi Astach to go and open the door, bandleader Karl Oberg kicked it open with his polished boot.

"Good, good," the feldwebel said in German. "Of course. *Sehr gut.*"

The feldwebel grinned at the teacher. "Still all that hair and whiskers, Whiskers, as if nothing had ever happened?"

His face was ruddy from the cold. "The mud stinks here, Whiskers," said Feldwebel Oberg.

Beside the ambulance stood the driver and the commandant's son.

"Are you ready?" asked Karl Oberg. "You'll get warmed up in a little while."

There was a quickness in Oberg's voice, a kind of exuberance and a reconciliation with fate, either with what he was missing or because he had again to abandon his military music-makers. "Hair and whiskers—still like the rocks at the bottom of the sea. You won't listen to reason, old man." He turned to the commandant's son. "Have you ever heard of a *seeschwein*—a sea pig?" His eye was caught by the teacher's tuxedo trousers with the satin ribbon down the sides. "How many are you, Whiskers?" the feldwebel demanded.

"Where are we going?" asked Henryk Bley.

"Far and near, Whiskers. Don't worry about that. Just resettling. A little to the East as always."

The feldwebel knew that the teacher and the Commandant's son were hanging on to his every statement. "I don't want to overload the ambulance."

"Ten," said Henryk Bley. "Eleven with me."

"That's all right," said Feldwebel Oberg.

"Where are you taking us?" asked Henryk Bley.

For a fraction of a second, the teacher thought of those who were no longer living. At the moment he needed to concentrate on those who were.

9

The ambulance stood twenty paces from the entrance of a half-ruined house called the Institute for Abandoned Jewish Children, at the edge of the camp. The vehicle was angular, like German ambulances, manufactured during the Second World War by BMW and by Mercedes-Benz.

"Come on, get going, Suicide," the feldwebel said to the dog at his feet. With its tail between its legs, the dog growled and ran over to the ambulance. It sniffed as though it were on the scent of something that would lead him home. It didn't dare to jump inside.

The ambulance stood with its back to the house, facing the little garrison town which, in honor of the forty-second birthday of Herr Commandant Oscar Adler-Bienenstock, had been given a new name on the maps of Germany—Festung Adler-Bienenstock. Marshes stretched out on every side, under maimed trees of what had been forests. The driver watched what the bandleader was doing, always as if for the first time. The commandant's son stood beside the ambulance, his mouth wide open.

"Everybody is to get in and sit down as soon as I say so, Whiskers," started Feldwebel Oberg. "But only one at a time. You'll have two minutes from the time I give the word. Everything's got to click. But first, I've got to have your signature on this paper, stating that you're moving and leaving the house in order."

The feldwebel drew a folded piece of paper from his sleeve and spread it out in front of the teacher.

The driver opened the rear door of the ambulance.

"If you don't want to sign, I'll have to leave you here and the children will go ahead," the feldwebel continued. "Since your bed is made, you must lie in it."

Even before he caught Noemi Astach's eye, the teacher signed his name.

"Well, now we're quits, Whiskers. I can see you don't want to stay by yourself if there's a chance to go somewhere together," said the feldwebel.

The driver closed the door. The commandant's son had noticed there was no handle on the side of the door. Then he noticed there were scarred and scratched wooden benches on both sides of the van, a little window behind the driver's seat with bars on it, and a curtain of steel chain which could be opened and closed but only from the driver's side. The ambulance had no other windows. The floor, sides, and roof of the vehicle were steel plated like a police van. That was why it went so slowly and made such a lot of noise, like a troop transport. It showed signs of wear, as though it had gone several times around the world.

It looks a bit like an iceman's van, the boy thought to himself, or like one of those trucks that transports gold and money to banks. Like a watertight steel safe-deposit vault.

He was disappointed the children hadn't sung the song he'd expected. Even though, there'd been a gleam in his eyes since he was witnessing something so strange as the trip they were taking—going from somewhere to nowhere.

The bandleader's words echoed in his head. The commandant's son had finally understood what it meant to move from somewhere into nowhere, the trip whose destination was the swamps. Was that what his father meant when he said the worst is the best and the best is the worst, making sense of things that hadn't made sense before?

"All right, Sturmman Max Hans," Feldwebel Oberg said, sitting up in front as the commandant's son, the sturmman, and the dog got in the cab of the ambulance. "Let's go."

The driver switched on the starter and the vehicle moved off. The feldwebel looked content. He'd already rehearsed the afternoon concert for Herr Commandant. It would start off with "The Entry of the Gladiators." Then "Alte Kameraden," "Vöglein Singen," and "Bummelpetrus."

"Some people don't ever shape up," the feldwebel said at length. "How many times have I told that old man to shave and get himself a haircut?"

He turned to the commandant's son, who was sitting to his left. "By the time you're a few years older, you won't have to wait to know how things are. I can see you're not as scared this time."

The commandant's son was thinking about the words "disinfection" and "resettling" and about lice. About the posters in the garrison and in the camp: One louse means your death. *Eine Laus dein Tod.* What was it his father, Herr Commandant, had said? *Jedem das Seine.* To each his own. He thought about the animals in the jungle, where the elephants go to die, and about what he felt but had never understood.

Dim geographical zones—the whole world at once—floated through the boy's head the way nightfall swallows the last sources of light, changing sunset into darkness. He thought about what he'd overheard. Then he thought about the scorpions that hid in the sewer pipes, in the shower faucets, in garages, and in clothing when it wasn't changed often enough.

The boy thought about fleas. He always seemed to arrive at fleas even when he started with elephants. Then he thought about bees, which carry poison along with their sting. Then snakes, fish, and birds. Finally about lions, tigers, and crocodiles, which knew how to kill men. These thoughts also made him think of rats.

The commandant's son was thinking about the rats that seemed to spread faster than people. As his father had said, the spreading was dangerous because it robbed people of food. He thought about the fearlessness of his father. And finally, the strength of engines.

"What are you thinking about?" asked Feldwebel Oberg. "About the sweet land of forgetfulness?" Maybe they should at least castrate these people, like so many others, he thought to himself.

"What happens to animals when they're with people?" the boy asked.

"What do you think?" replied the feldwebel.

The boy didn't answer yet; he was thinking about what was going to happen before they reached the marshes. For a moment, he had the feeling that as they approached the marshes they were melting into them, as if the marshes could think, and as if, at that moment, he could guess what it was the marshes thought about at times like this. Bubbles rose to the surface from the dead bottom of the swamp, like swollen stars that burst in silence down below. There were three bubbles. Again three.

His eyes caught fire as if he had chills and fever at the same time. The next time his father started telling him about how and where the elephants die in secret places in the jungle and how Indian tigers get a taste for human flesh and blood, he would say, "No, it's the marshes. It's the engines. The trucks. Ambulances without windows. Exhaust pipes like elephant trunks. Like birds without wings. Or like fish with wings and birds with fins."

All of a sudden from somewhere, his father's eyes looked at him.

"Is it true that they call them in Polish *duschegubky*—soul-eaters?" the boy asked suddenly.

"Are you telling us or asking us?" the feldwebel wanted to know.

Where could the boy have known it from? One of the young German inventors, SS-Untersturmführer Becker, invented these ambulances, and came here to test them. They forced carbon monoxide into the van instead of outside. The head of SS-Einsatzgruppen, Otto Ohlendorf, had objected to the unloading because it was not a stimulating view for German soldiers to look at the *menschentiere* in their own blood and saliva and excrement. The SS-Untersturmführer rode around to the single units of the SS-Einsatzgruppen to teach the drivers how to handle his invention correctly: not pushing the accelerator to the floor right away, but gradually and patiently at the very beginning; putting the prisoners to sleep and then choking them, not the other way around. That will get rid—he claimed to the soldiers of the SS-Einsatzgruppen—of the view of distorted faces, of the people who had expelled what they were not able to digest when they were unloaded.

When the boy didn't answer, the feldwebel went on. "Are you coming to the concert? How about you, Max Hans?"

The feldwebel decided that there must be strange ideas getting themselves entangled at the moment inside the head of the commandant's slow-witted son. Should he test him on the four cardinal points of the compass and the elements?

"How much farther are we going to go?" the commandant's son asked. His glittering eyes were like marshes at sunset.

"It'll take twenty to twenty-five minutes before we get there," replied the feldwebel.

"Where?" the commandant's son wanted to know.

"There," answered Feldwebel Oberg.

"There—nowhere," the commandant's son echoed.

It was as though understanding had suddenly come to him from afar—of everything it meant and encompassed—and now was carrying him on implacably toward the same goal the children inside the ambulance already sensed.

The mystery of the marshes, he thought to himself. The mystery of the engines. The secret of animals who were killed because they were animals. He turned to the little barred window. It was more transparent than the points of the compass and the elements—water, air, earth, and fire—which canceled themselves out in his head. One, two, three, and one is four. He toyed with his tongue. It was better than trying to make a difference between the north and water.

They drove past the stables, warehouse, the dog kennels. They passed the command headquarters casino and turned off toward the marshes where the camp began. The vehicle left hardly any exhaust fumes behind.

"They haven't emerged from paradise yet," the feldwebel said to the driver, who didn't answer. "Sometimes it feels like an eternity from Thursday to Monday. Or sometimes the opposite, from Monday to Thursday." He chuckled. "Are you giving it the gas, Max Hans?"

"Full gas ahead," replied the driver, who was wearing an SS-Einsatzgruppen uniform and had a gas mask at his feet.

"Step on it, Max Hans," said the feldwebel after a while.

"It won't go any faster," replied the driver. "The gas pedal's right to the floor."

Karl Oberg grinned. The commandant's son looked at him. There was an innocent understanding between the two of them that excluded the Commandant Adler-Bienenstock. Everything was going the way it was supposed to.

"Good, no?" asked the feldwebel. "The world's a fine place. As long as you know how to get by. *Jedem das Seine. Eine Laus dein Tod.* We Germans were born to die." He calculated how far it was to the marshes. "Do you feel like a regular fellow?" asked the feldwebel. "I think so."

"You're a regular fellow," echoed the commandant's son, as if he'd just discovered what it meant to be mature, to be grown up, to be a *man*, and he gazed at the bandleader with his watery blue eyes. His eyes were like bluish stars, like an angel's bells. His mouth, in which his tongue revolved, was rosy.

The SS driver kept his eyes on the road and the vehicle he was driving. "Forty kilometers an hour here is probably like driving ninety on an empty autobahn," he declared.

"Can you give us a little heat, too?" asked the feldwebel.

"Why not?" the driver replied.

The lights in the ambulance and in the cab were watertight. After about ten minutes, Karl Oberg switched them on, turned around, and looked inside. A second later he switched them off.

"They seem to be coughing," remarked the commandant's son.

"They are coughing. It's cold," the feldwebel confirmed.

"Yeah," the driver declared.

"It'll soon be spring," said Karl Oberg.

"Yeah," agreed the driver.

"It's about time," admitted the feldwebel.

"It's dull here in the springtime," the driver said.

"That's the truth. Not much grows here. Too many wars have passed this way," the feldwebel said.

They listened for a while to the sound of the motor. Then the bandleader asked the boy if he liked the springtime.

"I wish I were with them now," said the boy.

"Where?"

"There," replied the commandant's son.

The boy began to sweat. Tears started rolling down his face, which was twisted as if he were laughing. But he wasn't. He was thinking about the sheet metal neck on the ambulance. About the strength of the engine. Although he didn't dare to turn around and look into the back of the van like Karl Oberg had done, he had it before his feverish blue eyes. There was the closeness in the eyes of Oscar Adler-Bienenstock's son and a distance, too—an emptiness. His ears were singing with the song he'd heard once about distances, strange flights, about souls that flutter in the wind like flags. About trains going somewhere.

The glassy light on the roof inside the ambulance gleamed in the dark like an icy full moon. Like a fish eye, like an empty eye socket. They were already in the marshes and the vehicle lurched along. Karl Oberg rapped his knuckles against the glass of the cab to the rhythm of "The Entry of the Gladiators."

10

The driver shifted the lever, changing the course of the engine's exhaust. When he did that, Henryk Bley's words and thoughts were snapped off as if a fragile thread had been torn. The children and the teacher pressed rags instead of handkerchiefs against their noses and mouths.

That was when the commandant's son heard the first noises in the back of the van. It was as if sacks of potatoes were falling on the floor, or as if those sacks had ripped open and the potatoes had rolled out, or as if the teacher and children inside were fighting. That was when it occurred to him that the exhaust pipes looked like the trunks of old, sick, dying elephants in some unknown jungle. Drops of sweat stood out on his childish, almost girlish forehead. His tongue remained quite still inside his mouth.

That was when the children and the teacher began to choke. The teacher already forgot his vision of the black-haired queen; there were no palms in the corner of the banquet hall anymore where the king and queen were dining, nor was the sky above the couch in the royal chambers, nor were the amorous murmurs of the king interrupted by the pleadings of his wife who, more than saving her own life, wanted to prevent mass murder. The queen's adversary, the minister, was not there either. He was drawing lots to find out what would be the best date for the massacre and he'd hit on the spring festival. Susa, which had been a populous city at that time in Persia, had become just a heap of mud and greasy stone in Henryk Bley's day. But then it was a place of gilded silks and brocade draperies with heavy fringe in the shape of pine cones or bells or flowers, a city of carpets woven with blue and crimson horses and dogs' heads and bodies of bronze leaves with veins like a candelabra. And the statues of men like Hercules, capable of strangling a lion with their hands. That was all gone. Henryk Bley, sensing all the emptiness and terror and relief that surrounded him, felt the weariness that stars must feel when they're dying. The sun had gone out. The volcanoes grew silent. He heard his coughs and the coughs of the others who were choking to death with him. He heard cries, including the cry of the deaf boy and the cry of the blind girl, all of which were lost in the turmoil of everybody else's screams. But it was only for a fraction of a second. He could feel Noemi Astach lurching against him, her head bumping his forehead as if she'd had some kind of seizure. He could feel her finger digging into him on one side and the blind girl clawing him on the other. But he couldn't speak anymore.

Like the rest of them, he began to cough and scream although he had told them not to scream, not to let themselves be broken at the last minute, gasping, choking, on their way to distant places far away. Finally he began to cough up blood and foam from his mouth and nose, like a person drowning. This was the end. He didn't want to think about himself. But now he did. It was the last moment of his consciousness. He felt how alone they were, how alone he was. Just one of many. It was only for a fragment of a thought, maybe just an echo of a thought he'd fortified himself with while waiting for this moment. His mouth closed when he bit one of the fingers on his left hand. Then his face became distorted. There was only darkness, which veiled and swallowed everything up.

The ambulance pulled up to the swamp. There, above the gateway, was the inscription made of pine branches and brushwood: "Next Year in Jerusalem."

11

The commandant's son listened for sounds from the back of the van. He couldn't hear anything. His tongue rotated like a windmill inside his mouth and he kept repeating to himself north, south, east, west, wagging around his saliva like a paintbrush. He felt something he couldn't understand.

"They're done for," said Feldwebel Karl Oberg. "*Vollgefressen.* Fully eaten up."

"I've got to dump them," the driver said.

"Don't lose too much time," the feldwebel said.

"Hope not."

"I don't want to hang around here too long," repeated the feldwebel.

"It might take five minutes. I've got to do it by myself," the driver said.

"Five minutes is all right."

"We don't waste time."

"I've got a concert this evening."

While the driver unloaded the bodies, the boy and Karl Oberg left the van and walked over to the deepest point in the swamp. They didn't speak. The sky was high. Already the moon was visible. There was silence all around. No wind. It was far from the barracks to the lager commandant bureau, his adjunct's office, telephone central and block-führer's house, far from the lager post office.

Finally, the bodies and heads disappeared like dead hens in the swamps. The driver splashed the blood and excrement from the bodies in the truck with a few pails of water.

"Ready, finished," the driver called.

"Yeah, one moment," the feldwebel called back.

The bandleader Oberg threw a stone into the water. As soon as it sank, circles appeared. The boy's eyes were foggy.

"Are you looking?" asked the feldwebel.

"At what?"

"At the circles."

"Yeah."

"Still?"

"Yes. Those are the largest."

"All the time?"

"Yes."

"Do you still see them?"

"Weakly."

"And now?"

"A little."

"Still?"

"No."

"So you see."

"I don't see anything."

"That's it."

"What?"

"Nothing."

"Nothing?" asked the boy.

"That's just what happened."

"What?"

"Nothing."

"How come?"

"That's the difference between right and wrong," the feldwebel said. "There's no difference in them when you don't see what you don't want to see. You see? It is just like when you throw a stone into the water. It doesn't stay. You throw a stone, it whirls up the circles on the surface, and then they spread out and disappear. And now imagine it's foggy.

Nebel. Do you know what *vernebling* is? Fog. Night. Like brother and sister."

"No," the boy replied.

"You'll see in a moment," the feldwebel promised.

But from the boy's expression it was obvious he knew what to expect.

"What is it now?" he asked.

The feldwebel still didn't explain the main thing to the boy, just as his father hadn't explained it to him before and wouldn't explain it later.

Feldwebel Oberg turned to the commandant's son. "Well, you've seen it. They're just *Menschentiere,* as your father rightly said. Nothing more than *Menschentiere. Schweinehunde.* Sow hounds. When you're studying the elements, don't forget about fire, water, earth, and air. The fifth element is us." He grinned. *Das Tausendjährige Reich.* The thousand year Reich. *Blut und Boden.* Blood and soul. The Nuremberg law for protection of German honor and blood. He pulled on his yellowish pigskin gloves, as if he didn't want to touch anything anymore. Sometimes ashes fell into the marshes. That made them look like pools of black water lillies.

"It's good, isn't it?" he asked.

The driver circled the van. Then he entered the cab and started the engine. The smoke coming from the exhaust pipe seemed to poison the air around them. The dog was trembling, looking at all three of them, and then at the commandant's son.

There was a light in the boy's eyes that almost set his forehead aglow. It was like the sun, like springtime and fire. Or just water? The marshes seemed brighter and even the little islands of ash, several layers of it, were flooded with daylight at the meridian. He was dripping with sweat, as if he were in a steam bath. The sound of the motor reminded him of the song he'd heard once and never afterward, and he had the feeling he could hear it now, even though he couldn't make out the words. He was happy to listen to the strong engine. They went back to the van.

"Would you like to ride in the rear?" asked the feldwebel before they boarded for their return trip.

"Yes," answered the boy.

"Go ahead. Get in."

"Thanks, *danke*," said the boy.

"*Arbeit macht frei*, and here is the number *drei*," said Karl Oberg as he smiled.

The commandant's son had the feeling he was looking at his father's face, eyes, words. Three, not four. Number *drei*. He looked in the ambulance and out, where there was a dumping station in the swamp. The dog jumped into the cabin.

"Everything for a good German family," said the feldwebel.

He closed the door of the van. Karl Oberg coughed. Then he turned to the driver.

"I've got a new march based on a Jewish funeral tune, like the idea I got last Thursday to turn a Gypsy wedding melody into a funeral march. It makes sense when you turn it all upside down. Don't you want to come to the casino and listen?"

"If I've finished my work at the garage," replied the driver. "Too much overtime work. Then I have to go to the dentist at his apartment. I think his phone extension is 34."

"Yeah, you're right. It is 34. Did you get a new motor?"

"Yes, but I doubt it's a brand-new one. It's probably been over-hauled," the driver answered.

The driver thought to himself that it wasn't nice to confuse the feebleminded boy with talk about the elements, since even the birds in the trees talked about how he couldn't keep the points of the compass straight in his head.

But the boy wasn't thinking about elements now. He was still thinking about how the exhaust pipes looked like elephant trunks. How strong, beautiful, and powerful the engines were. He thought that knowing why elephants wander off and why tigers hunt people instead of people hunting them was more important than knowing the points of the compass.

The three of them—two in front and one inside—drove back faster than they'd come. The truck felt lighter as it bounced and jiggled along the road to the marshes like a young horse. The red cross, painted three times in brilliant military colors, looked guileless, as though it were offering something. The motor rumbled, and black, sooty vapors sputtered out of the exhaust pipes that looked like a swan's neck or fish fins. They left thick, oily fumes behind, and because there was no wind, it took a while before they dissipated in the fresh air. But soon the smoke from the ambulance disappeared altogether and left the air behind it clean. The dog was quietly grooming itself.

They were on a huge plain in the middle of a spreading wasteland between the Baltic and Azov and Black Seas, reaching out in all directions like a frozen spiderweb, an occupied country, like an island to which no ships come sailing, lost in the leafless forests and lost in the world. Far away but still visible by eye, as a tiny line on the horizon, were green forests growing from time immemorial, so deep and high and thick that everything disappeared in silence, as though every living thing would stop.

It was a cold, still day at the end of winter and the beginning of spring. Easter Monday. The ash settled in between the empty husks of grain and snow which, at noontime, had turned to slush. Crows flew, cawing high above the untilled fields. They were huge birds, darkening the sun.

For the fourth day and fourth night, rolls of black smoke floated across the sky. There was still no wind.

NIGHT

1

The moon swung low and was swallowed by the river. A trail of sedge and gray ashes from the ghetto was washed ashore.

"Enough," rang out a strict voice.

A small crowd of men came to a standstill.

"Get on," the voice continued. "Anyone opening his mouth . . ."

On the white road made gray by the night, a truck waited. Four benches placed close together were in the back, under the canvas. The men climbed in. The policemen who had come with them stepped back into the darkness. The young SS officer who had taken them over looked from one to another with half-closed eyes.

"Let's go," he said in the direction of the driver. The engine turned over.

"Where are we going?" asked a voice, quiet and tired, like an old man's.

"Shut up!" bellowed the young SS officer.

Suddenly the truck left the road. It went around something like a fortress or a plowed field, and the sharp whine of the brakes cut into the night. The man with the tired, old-sounding voice was big and strong and belonged to a commando of carpenters and diggers. The child beside him was his son.

"Out!" bellowed the young SS officer.

From somewhere nearby came the acrid smell of burnt ground. The night was dark and no one could see anything. They walked, holding each other by the hand.

"Hold on to me, boy," said the tired, old-sounding voice.

2

The SS officer said, "Stop." He wore a green field uniform. Apart from the burnt ground, the spring night was full of the smell of rye fields and young meadows, and from the distance the wind brought the smell of potato fields in June, of flowers, and a certain chill. The young SS officer went ahead to report to his superiors.

They had been picked out of bed earlier, but none of the policemen told them what was going on, where they were going, or why—except that they had to be male. Then the young SS officer and a German driver took them over. They had already taken away one unit the day before, and nobody knew where they had gone or where they were now, because they had not yet returned. That unit had contained thirty-six men, and today's unit comprised another thirty-six.

"Sixteen and twenty men, Herr Brigadenführer."

"Good."

"What are your orders, Herr Brigadenführer?"

"Send them here."

"Yes, Herr Brigadenführer."

The young SS officer returned to the group from the ghetto. The acrid smell of burnt ground still lingered, along with the ugly taste of timber doused with petrol, and paraffin set on fire, and the taste of charred thatched roofs and walls which the wind kept carrying away and returning.

When he brought them, he reported: "Unit is ready, Herr Brigadenführer. Attention! Sixteen and twenty men, Herr Brigadenführer."

"Take a deep breath," said the general.

Then he waited and said, "There was a village here. Now it's gone. You're going to work. A bullet for the first one who opens his mouth."

A silence spread again over the hilly countryside. In the darkness the trees were invisible. The more distant hills and the remnants of the village were also invisible. Later, birds flew across the sky.

Their gaze penetrated the darkness a short distance ahead of them. There was a village here, but now it is gone. From somewhere close by, the cry of a crow rang out. From nearby came the bleating of goats.

"Show me that wall," said the general.

"Here, Herr Brigadenführer. A hundred and seventy-three men. At dawn we identified them with the help of the village records. Immediately afterward . . ."

"Enough, thank you," said the general.

"The wall, Herr Brigadenführer."

"Carry on," said the general. "*Weitermachen.*"

3

"There are goats here," said the tired, old-sounding voice. He leaned toward the boy and supported himself on the boy's shoulder.

"I saw sheep, geese, and ducks," the boy added.

"Don't cough," the tired, old-sounding voice added. "Don't draw attention to yourself."

The boy was irritated by the smell of the burnt earth. Smoke from the other end of the village, from where the fire was no longer visible, still penetrated everything.

"Quiet!" somebody in the general's entourage shouted toward them.

"These are Jews from the Terezin ghetto," a different voice said to the brigadenführer.

"Who ordered this?" asked the general.

"You, Herr Brigadenführer."

"Oh," said the general. "All right. Let's move."

"Yes, Herr Brigadenführer."

A tractor rattled somewhere nearby, rolled over a hillock, and disappeared into the darkness. The voices of the men from the general's entourage, who were no longer visible, could be heard again. Suddenly the wind brought the smell of quicklime.

When the general's entourage reappeared, the general said in the direction of the young SS officer who guarded them, "Let them know."

"Men," said the young SS officer. "You must dig a mass grave. You're going to bury the dead. A hundred and seventy-three bodies."

The general added, "By morning this will be flat earth."

Before the young SS officer took them to the marked pits, they heard somebody in the general's entourage say, "Pioneers will be deployed here, Herr Standartenführer—one commissioned officer, one noncommissioned officer, and thirty-five men. This squad won't be able to manage it, Herr Standartenführer. It's necessary to deploy two strong squads, equipped with the best implements, for a fortnight."

"Nonsense," said the general.

Where the pits were to be dug, the smell of freshly turned earth was added to that of the burnt ground.

"Get on with it," sounded from the group of men in leather coats.

"Get on with it," shouted the general in the direction of the young SS officer.

"Get on with it," shouted the young SS officer, as the pistol in his hand gleamed darkly.

"What are they going to do to us?" the boy whispered.

"Don't be afraid," the tired, old-sounding voice whispered back. "We are here together. All together."

"Here," said the young SS officer. "Get working."

Then they heard, "We have deployed three squads of Reichsarbeitdienst, which will also be used as a clean-up unit in order to secure further valuables—such as farming machines and metals suitable for scrap—Herr Standartenführer."

The first man lifted his pick. Its head flashed through the darkness. They started to dig and toss out earth. They could only think that they were digging, throwing out, and treading on the remnants of a village that had lost its living souls during the night—a village which had succumbed to fire and was now to lose its dead. They heard fragments of what the unit officers reported to the general. They could not connect the work they were doing with the idea of the village.

Because of the darkness, it was impossible to guess how big the village had been. Only shadows and darkness covered the plain and the hillock, the remnants of the houses, as if it were a derelict fortress.

They could hear the sound of the picks, the birds of the night, the soft blades cutting softly into the spring soil, which was ready for summer. They could hear the gentle clink of spades striking against flint, a buried horseshoe, or a discarded cooking pot. They could smell the scent of the earth piling up beside the pits, hear the touch of metal on soil, the breath of the men digging, and the sounds of the night.

"Three meters deep," said the young SS officer.

"That'll be enough," said the general. And to somebody in the crowd of men in leather coats, "Let them be useful again for a while."

Somebody laughed.

4

The men who were digging were almost up to their shoulders in the ground. They kept throwing out earth as birds flew overhead, along with insects, in a gentle spring breeze. With the advancing night, the wind brought a chill that was made greater by the fresh earth. They dug and cast out earth for those who had still been alive the day before, for those who had owned houses and the land on which the houses had stood. They listened to the wind, the birds, the trees, the horses, the goats and the sheep, and now and again to a cockerel whose call failed to separate night from day.

They were forbidden to speak, even though the young SS officer had disappeared into the darkness. Soon they were in the ground, the earth looming over their heads. Sometimes, a star would appear among the spring clouds, disappearing when the clouds thickened again. At one moment in the middle of the night, a falling star came tumbling down and the sky resembled a pit being dug out of the earth. The men were no longer visible; only the mounds of earth which they threw out were. From time to time, the general of the security police, or the men in the leather coats, or the young SS officer would appear near the hole in the ground.

"Don't cry, son," whispered the tired, old-sounding voice. "Don't look there."

"Quiet," said the general.

"Quiet, men, or else . . . " said the young SS officer.

"Ten blows with a stick for interrupting work," said the general.

"I could think of a stricter punishment," said the standartenführer.

"Yes, Herr Standartenführer," said the young SS officer.

"Put it away," said the general, looking at the mound of bodies.

The general and the men in leather coats were leaving.

"It's my son, sir," said the tired, old-sounding voice.

"Who asked you?" said the young SS officer.

"He has never seen a dead man," said the tired, old-sounding voice.

The smoke crept into their noses and throats. Every now and then the wind would spin around in circles. The clouds dropped. It looked as though it was going to start raining.

The men at the top began handing down the first bodies, where they were lined up along the charred wall like logs, to the men at the bottom of the pit. Some of the bodies were half-dressed, others only barefoot, others in their underwear.

"Perhaps some of them are still alive," whispered the boy.

"No," said the tired, old-sounding voice.

"More earth, faster," said the young SS officer.

"Come on," the tired old voice prompted the boy.

The boy looked toward the charred wall that the village men had been facing, hands up, before they were shot. He continued throwing earth onto the corpses while looking at his spade, the earth, the wall that the dead had been touching with their hands before they fell. The wall had been blackened by flames. The first signs of morning appeared in the distance, but it was not morning yet—just a brilliant ribbon, the first touches of light, the final touches of darkness. The eyes of the boy, accustomed to the darkness, started to distinguish the ground plan of the village, which until that moment had been one with everything else. He did not want to look at the dead. He did not want to look at the earth that was falling on the fingers, noses, and eyes of the dead. Here stood a house, here a shed, here a barn. This is where a fence stood, a lane ran by, here the tractor had driven through earlier. This could have been the school, this the savings bank. Before them, behind them, beside them, under them, above them was a village that no longer existed. He threw the earth very quickly, in order to see the first bodies covered and from then on to see only the earth. The echo of the young SS officer's words that they should throw more earth, faster, faster, reverberated in his ears. The handle of his spade was warm from his hands, moist with his sweat. The dirt rained down. The dead had no shoes. They were burying them barefoot. He kept looking at their feet. Sometimes a shower of dirt threw up an arm, moved a finger, a head. Their feet were already covered.

"Enough," said the young SS officer. "You've five minutes for a meal. You can go eat."

5

The young SS officer took them to a tarpaulin on which stood bottles of water, bread, and a round of cheese.

"Eat up, Jew-boys. There's a feast for you," he added. Then he went to one side and squatted down near a mound of earth.

"Son," said the tired, old-sounding voice. "Stay close beside me."

"Ten blows with a stick," whispered the boy.

Here they were, those thirty-six people who had left the day before and had not yet returned, the village which was and is no more, the smoke that rose to the sky all through the night and which was carried away and brought back again by the wind—those one hundred and seventy-three men shot and dead, another life, strange or familiar, distant, which had come and gone.

They could see one another as much as they had been able to before they had been moved onto the truck the previous night—before they had been brought here.

The echo of words, fragments of reports that they overheard. Forty eiderdowns, seventy-four cushions, three baby carriages. Eighteen radio sets. Ninety-six pairs of men's shoes, eighty-three pairs of women's shoes. The food they were now eating. Grain, oats.

There were stars in the sky, clouds.

"You don't need to," said the man with the tired, old voice to the boy.

"Nobody?" asked the boy.

"People will pray for them later, perhaps, somewhere abroad where there aren't any Germans," said the tired, old-sounding voice. "And perhaps even somebody, somewhere in Germany."

"Nonsense," said the younger of two brothers nearby. "They wouldn't have given us anything to eat."

"I can't," said the boy.

"Where are we?" hissed the elder of the two brothers. "Does anybody know anything?"

"It's a mining area," said the younger brother.

"Do you have to talk?" asked a man with glasses. "Isn't it enough just to look?"

"And for you?"

"I hope you don't feel like the Maccabees," said the man with glasses, swallowing a piece of bread and cheese. "Perhaps for that matter we have only our bodies and muscles." And then he asked, "You're not going to eat?"

"It's burnt out as though they had the plague," said the elder of the two brothers. "This was not the act of pioneers. I'm sure you know who I have in mind, though."

"Did they drive us for an hour, or was it two?" somebody asked. "I've lost all sense of time. I only know that it was night and now it is morning."

Steps, noise, snatches of voices could be heard. The answers were contained in the questions. After they had eaten and finished the work, will they also . . . ? The young SS officer returned. They fell silent.

"Finished?" he asked, looking at the tarpaulin. Most of them had not even touched the round of cheese or the water or the bread.

"You can take it with you," the young SS officer said. "Put a little life into it. Get a move on. The unit before you wasn't even given a scrap. The general wasn't here. You're lucky. You've escaped the stick. You've done a good job." And then he quietly added: "If any of you find anything—a ring, money, or something like that—hand it in." He started whistling "Heimat deine Sterne." He rubbed his hands as if they were frozen.

"Into pairs," he ordered them in the end, until they were all paired off again, a digger and a man with a shovel.

6

"Faster," bellowed the general.

He stared at his watch. The sky was still dark, but only above them and further toward the west. In the east, day was already breaking. He tried to guess how long it would be before it was actually daybreak. The young SS officer swallowed dryly. It was chilly. Dew glistened in the grass.

"A littler more dirt here, where I'm pointing. Cover it up properly."

It seemed to him that the man with the tired, old-sounding voice embraced the last dead body on the pretext of moving a stone. Could he be putting it under his head? Why did he throw so little dirt on him? What did he see in the dead man? Was he perhaps the mayor? A priest? An assassin?

"*Scheisse*," said the young SS officer. "Have you lost your head? Do you want ten blows with a stick? A bullet? What are you doing with him? Cover him up. This minute. Make him eat dirt."

The glow of daybreak swept over the pale face of the dead man, who could not have been much more than sixteen, eighteen at most.

The man with the tired, old-sounding voice did as he was told by the young SS officer, but he looked away from the boy, who tossed dirt down to him from above, farther to the west, where it was still night, as if he could not hear or see and could not perceive things through the reflection of the night.

"Cover him up properly," repeated the young SS officer. "I won't tell you twice. Throw a few shovelfuls on top of him." He started toying with the leather tongue of his gun holster.

"Throw all the quicklime in there, nothing left over," he added. "Do you hear me?"

The man with the tired, old-sounding voice watched his son pour out a sack of quicklime, then stepped back and climbed up. They all emptied sacks of quicklime.

"That's it," said the tired old voice.

The young SS officer spat. Then he went to report to the commander of the security police, who stood erect, as though he were also making a report as well as listening to one. By the light that was now spreading over the land, the commander could see that the earth and lime had filled the pit, the communal grave, up to the brim. A tear in the clouds spilled light softly onto the scarred earth. Beyond the tear, day had arrived. Once more, they could imagine that this had been a village. They could imagine the days, the months, the centuries through which it had flourished. The place where the church had stood. The path that had been trodden by foundrymen, miners, their wives, mothers, sisters, children. The fields plowed by the men now in the pit, their necks, heads, and chests pierced by gunshot wounds. The women who had been taken away the day before and who had given bread and milk to the children they would see no more. Their relatives and friends who would learn about this from the next announcements following the news from the German Supreme Command.

The general looked around the plain, the mound; his eyes returned to the remains of the village.

"Excellently done, gentlemen, I think," he said and put his hands into the pockets of his overcoat.

He looked around over his shoulder, toward the men in leather coats. These men had nothing to do here now. Their cars drove up at 4:30. They got in.

The general stayed behind. He cast an eye over the village ground plan once more, noting what no longer existed. The clouds drew apart and the moon sailed out once again. The general watched the wisps of smoke, which no longer had the strength to float high but were torn by the wind and kept near the ground in curls, as though the burnt earth and the freshly-dug pit was a body of water.

But there was no longer anything here, apart from the wisps of smoke that merged with the morning mist. The bleating of the sheep and goats could be heard again, like the cry of the departing night, of the arriving day.

"Back to the truck," ordered the young SS officer.

Beside their truck and behind the mound, which up until this time had been invisible, there was now another truck, the two like brother and sister. On the other side, the general's black limousine waited. The right mudguard sported a flag of the commander of the SS security police.

The man with the tired, old-sounding voice now looked like an old man who had aged overnight, in a morning, in a single journey. He motioned for the boy to climb up.

"Get down," said the young SS officer. "I haven't given the order to line up yet."

The white bodies of the goats and the white wool of the sheep emerged from the misty morning.

"Load them on," said the young SS officer. "Half of them onto each truck. Sixteen men and sixteen sheep. The goats that won't fit onto the vehicles will be taken away by a different unit. Make space for the animals. I don't want them to suffocate."

"No," the general interrupted him. "Take the animals separately."

"It's a hundred and forty-four goats, Herr Standartenführer," said the SS officer.

"OK, put the goats onto one truck and the unit and the sheep and a few goats, perhaps, onto your truck," added the general.

The SS officer did as the general ordered and signed a piece of paper, which he handed over to one of the military policemen.

"Let's go," said the general.

"Let's go," said the standartenführer.

"As you command, Herr Standartenführer," said the young SS officer. And to the men he said: "To your places. Quick. Faster."

7

They rode along with the animals, through the misty morning in which the stars no longer shone. For half an hour nobody spoke, even though the young SS officer sat in front, in the driver's cabin. Nobody drew the canvas aside, not even a crack, so they could see which way they were going. There was the chemical reek of blast furnaces, the breath of the coal shafts and of the plain, swept by a raw wind, a wind carrying the odor of the brown-coal surface mines and even still the smell of burnt ground—then the noises of towns, small or perhaps large, of crossroads, of railway crossing barriers and of the road, cut in half by the railway line. They traveled a road that followed the railway line and ran through a mountainous region, and perhaps through a pass, before reaching the lowlands again. The man with the tired old voice was silent, as they all were, not knowing at that moment, as they did before and later, whether they would reach their destination. The truck was loud with the clipped bleating of the sheep, the braying of the goats. The sheeps' eyes were dull, without interest or fear. The space was made warmer by the breath of the animals. They pressed themselves into the front half of the vehicle. Even in the twilight, under the canvas, the animals, thick with wool, gleamed white. Now and then, light could be seen as it bore down on the canvas from above, before the invisible sky became once more overcast with clouds.

The landscape through which they passed was silent. The truck drove through the sound of its own engine. It was still early morning.

They could only surmise which way they were going from the maps they held in their memories.

"It's behind us," said the tired old voice to the boy.

"Right," said the boy.

"Perhaps. Let's hope so," said the elder of the two brothers.

It was first and foremost the village that was no longer, the people who were and now are dead. The village that had disappeared from the face of the earth, as a river running dry, a fire dying out, a breath merging with mist. The men, shoes removed, shot, some of them undressed, trousers gone, left in their underwear, without papers, faces to the wall—nameless, jobless, futureless. The village that had disappeared like a mountain swept away by an earthquake, as night fades into morning, day into evening. An extinct volcano, a burnt-out star, a village. A village become a mass grave, filled with earth, night, day, quicklime. A pit that will become overgrown with grass, trees, and weeds.

When the canvas loosened from the long journey and the bottom straps were fluttering in the air, the men saw a river. The driver followed a road nearby. An early morning moon, as white as quicklime and blood red, floated on the water. The water was turgid—banks of mud and occasional stones.

The man with the tired, old-sounding voice put his arm around the boy's shoulder. He could feel how cold the boy was. He was cold, too. It was a chilly morning.

After an hour, the truck stopped.

"Get out," said the SS officer on the embankment.

The young SS officer looked back, probably waiting for the other truck, which they had lost on the road.

The men got out. The tired, old-sounding voice suddenly said, "I want to stay with my son."

"Why?" asked the young SS officer. "Do you want ten blows with a stick?"

"I want to stay with him no matter what happens," the man repeated.

"Help the animals, carefully. Unload them," said the SS officer.

"What is going to happen now?" the man asked the young SS officer. And to the boy he said, "Stay with me."

The man with the tired, old-sounding voice looked at the river and held the boy. He looked at the river, but his gaze was turned inward. He saw a village, one hundred and seventy-three men shot dead, one hundred and ninety-eight women imprisoned, ninety-eight children abducted, a pit filled with earth and quicklime. At the same time, he saw the river, himself, and the remaining men. Those other thirty-six who had left the day before and had not returned. The men by the wall before they had been shot, with the priest, who like the rest no longer had shoes on. Who was he, the man who had been forced to remove even his underwear? The houses doused with petrol and paraffin and set alight—the first house at seven in the morning, so that by ten o'clock all would be on fire. A blaze, kindled according to the instructions of the German military police officer, so that there would be no need for firemen to control it.

The man with the tired, old-sounding voice breathed in mist with the wind, which his son also inhaled, and watched the river flow, the moon recede.

"Take the animals down," said the SS officer. "Carefully. Whoever harms those goats and sheeps..."

Just like his father with the tired, old-sounding voice and the others, the boy did not mutter a word.

"Keep your traps shut back there," said the SS officer, describing an arc with his right arm in the direction of the river. "Otherwise..." And he drew two tightly closed fingers across his throat.

8

The banked walls of the military town were illuminated by the late spring morning. There were no longer any soldiers in the fortress, only fortifications and ditches, in the south, in the north, the west, and the east. The fortress now served as a town donated by the Führer to the Jews, and as a warehouse and off-loading point. The moon hung over the town, blood red with circles of dirty gray around the sharply defined crescent. Everywhere, above and below, clung mists.

They passed a Jewish guard beyond the no-man's-land, surrounded by old battlements and new police boxes.

"*Heil,*" the young SS officer hoarsely greeted a senior constable. To the men, he said, "Take the animals to the gardening area. You will make a sheep pen." To the police, he said, "These men can sleep all day."

"Yes, sir," answered the senior constable, nodding to a policeman on the other side of the fence and to the Jewish guardsman, who had a wooden truncheon and a cap bearing a yellow ribbon.

The animals trickled through the gate, their hooves gently clattering on the stone pavement.

"Son," said the tired, old-sounding voice. "Give me your hand. We are back safe and sound. We are alive."

The man with the glasses said, "I don't feel like pretending we were the Maccabees. They've the right to say that the first bird to stick his head up will be shot."

"It's just as well that it was at night—you couldn't see anything," said the tired, old-sounding voice.

"Right," replied the boy.

"Back there," said the tired, old-sounding voice. "Everything there, what happened there. Poor people."

"I didn't see anything. I didn't look," said the boy.

"Good," said the tired, old-sounding voice.

"Nothing, nothing, nothing," said the boy.

The man with the tired, old-sounding voice looked at the entrance to the barracks, from which they had been picked up at the beginning of the night before, at the paraffin lamp with its painted blue shade which allowed its light to fall only close by, in line with the blackout regulations. Suddenly he remembered the smell. He sniffed around several times and felt that the barracks didn't smell as it used to. His nose was full of burnt ground.

The boy remembered the emphasis which his father placed on his last word.

"Good," the boy repeated. Then he leaned against a ram, and with his palm, covered in calluses—some of which had broken and were marked with loose skin and blood—he grasped the coarse curls of wool on the animal's back and on its neck, touching the leather collar at the animal's throat. The ram looked at him with dim dull eyes.

The elder from the barracks, together with the elders from their ward, came out to meet them.

"At last," said the elder from the barracks. "Are you all back?" At the same moment he recognized on the man and the boy the smell of burnt earth. It was the kind of smell that couldn't be washed or scratched off, as if it were a tattoo.

"All of us," answered the tired, old-sounding voice.

"Sheep?" asked the elder from the barracks.

"Sheep, goats. Perhaps even horses, cows, and pigs," answered the tired, old-sounding voice.

"They demolished houses and undressed and removed the shoes from the dead. They pulled their socks off."

"Yes," said the tired, old-sounding voice, stroking the boy's head as though he wanted to cover his ears.

"Did they beat you?"

"No."

"Have you eaten?"

"What's he got there?" asked the man with the tired, old-sounding voice. "What are you holding on to?"

"Nothing. A collar," answered the boy.

In fact, it was nothing more than a leather strap from which someone had torn off the bell.

They looked for an owner's name, but didn't find anything, even later when they inspected the leather by the light of day, except the name of the blacksmith who had been and was no more, or the name of the harnessmaker who was no more. There was indifference in the dull eyes of the animals.

"You can go and get some sleep," said the tired, old-sounding voice to the boy.

It seemed to the boy that daybreak would not come for a long time. The moon turned the color of the sheep's hair and blood and eyes, and of the dirt of something that was impossible to name. The moon drifted above the river again. Slowly, the sun began to shine.

FIRST BEFORE THE GATES

1

I t was rumored that Captain Johann Wolfram von und zu Wulkow, with his silvery hair and polite, reserved manner, was a German count who spoke fluent French, English, and Latin, and wore a magnificent uniform. His signature glittered on the public notices glued to the passages in the houses and the walls. During the last week of April, he built his headquarters on the highest hill in the center of Prague, near the monastery and the steel lookout-tower above the Moldau River, overlooking the city from all sides of the Compass Rose. Nobody had seen him in the streets, down in the quarter. It was said that he was ready to leave the city as a warrior, without looking back. Though he never made speeches like his predecessor, he was said to speak to the people in his mind, never for more than a minute. And it was rumored that the Captain had a teenaged illegitimate son somewhere in Germany. But everybody knew that Captain Wulkow's new military camp lay by the cemetery wall. At the thought of the cemetery, the old woman, Maria Kubarska, about whom the story later came out, said at the end of the night to herself, "It won't be long and I'll by lying there, too, like so many others. In a few days I'll be seventy-two. I've lived long enough." She had other thoughts, too. There was a feeling in her that the boy didn't understand her, that he didn't understand himself and what was going on.

"Child," she whispered, "you are like a sieve and your head like a leaking pot."

The words "rite of passage" passed over her lips, followed by the word "Nazis." Small things of great significance and great things disappearing into nowhere. She often repeated words from an old prayer book that she found in a trash can where Emanuel Bloch was deported to the East, together with his mother. It was said that the old woman was ninety-eight years old and was not permitted to sit in the streetcar but had to stand on the platform of the second car, the place for dogs and freight.

Each time the night streetcar, number seven or twelve, drove through Carmelite Street past the Church of the Triumphant Virgin Mary, where Maria Kubarska prayed on Sundays, the glass-paned door of the house rattled. She thought about why, at the end of the six-year-old war, the life of one person was so valueless, as if nobody cared whether you lived or died. And why so many people were going about their business as usual in spite of the fact that day after day so many people were being killed in camps, on the gallows, and in places of execution.

"Why aren't you asleep?" asked the boy drowsily. "Why don't you pray during the day? If I don't get enough sleep, I'll feel like a fly by morning."

"There's a new big shot among the Nazis here, Johann Wolfram von und zu Wulkow, a count."

"I saw people tearing down all the posters with his German name," said the boy.

She felt contempt in his voice and it came, first, because she kept him up at night, and second, because he didn't see the sense in something she'd picked up from a trash can almost three years ago, and kept like a treasure. He didn't like it when she repeated the Jewish prayers like an echo of an echo, from far beyond. The old woman returned to the rumors she heard on the block about Captain Wulkow from the fresh military unit which had pitched his tent only a couple of streets west of their house on the top of the hill. What kind of man was he? A notorious killer who had come directly from Russia or Poland, where survivors still told tales about him? Or from France or Italy, where they had already chased away unwelcome Germans? The grocer insisted that he was a German of noble origin who talked without shouting, read poetry, and listened to music, and seemed not unaware or unconcerned about the end of the war, which was quickly approaching, but wanted it his way. Somebody heard that he was stationed in Paris during the summer of 1943.

The darkness of the new moon had deprived Maria Kubarska of sleep for six years, just as on this night. She had gotten used to her insomnia. She didn't need so much sleep now. She couldn't blame it on the boy, whose bright red hair shone in the dark, nor could she blame it on Germany, old age, or even the grocery store owner's noisy rooster. (It had finally been slaughtered and eaten for Easter, so the old woman couldn't hear it crowing.) She didn't even blame her insomnia on the grocer's five years of cooperation with the Germans. Only sometimes did she fear nightmares in which death was a woman in black rags, resembling her, coming to the foot of the bed to announce that it was time to stop lounging and to come.

"Why are my nights so heavy—my thoughts an endless maze?" she wondered.

"It's night still. Sleep," said the boy.

"I can't," she said. "I wish. You should sleep. Sleep, please."

Was it the dead who talked to her—her husband and her daughter and Mr. Emanuel Bloch and his mother? Deprived of sleep, she thought about her man, who had been executed on June 23, 1942, not far from here on the shooting range of Kobylisy, near the water tower and the old Jewish cemetery. She kept quiet. She thought about the reasons the boy would wet the bed, often three times in one week. The feeble person is of no use to anyone. Children need protection. Did he have bad dreams? Was he sick? I have to be strong, she thought.

Maria Kubarska thought about Mr. Emanuel Bloch and his ninety-eight-year-old mother. They were part of her thoughts when she was scrubbing the floor, the restrooms, and the cloakrooms at the railroad station, and when sweeping the hall around the bumpers of the railroad cars—triple blocks of cement ending in a dull pyramid which stopped the train. In her mind she saw Mr. Emanuel Bloch drink water from the faucet in the hall or go to the common restroom with his hands folded as in prayer. Was it true that Mr. Emanuel Bloch and his mother prayed facing east? Was he dead like his mother, like her husband and her daughter? Who ate at his table now? Who sat in his chair, slept in his bed?

Sometimes it occurred to her that she linked the living and the dead through the language of Mr. Emanuel Bloch's prayer book. *Who is he who possesses wisdom? It is he who learns from every man, it's said. From all who can teach me I learn. Who is he who possesses strength? It's he who overcomes his own desire, as it is said.*

"God," said the boy in a half-whisper. "You must be crazy from all that. Are you trying to be Jewish or what?"

"Don't blaspheme. Did you forget to buy bread? I can go to the monks for sheep's milk before daybreak...Here, take a bite, suck my blood," added the old woman. "Today we have to go to the doctor. I've got a summons to show up with you—a subpoena." She prayed from the book of an old, and by now, dead Jewish man to prove to herself that the Nazis couldn't destroy her mind—but maybe the body. *It is said, sometimes a man goes to his mate, and sometimes his consort comes to him. A man is easily appeased, but not a woman.*

2

Otto Kubarsky, Maria Kubarska's grandson, waited only two minutes to make sure the old woman was asleep. At every night's end she was exhausted from waiting for something to happen, so at dawn she closed her eyes as if dead and slept. Should he burn the book or throw it away— back into the trash can where she'd found it? For a split second he thought about how she became silly, while blaming it on him. Did she really believe that the prayers of a dead man could save her life? He had to forget about the old woman and her accusations that, in his mind, changed into the fear of weakness.

He thought about bats—how they're equipped to fly on a starless night and avoid invisible cobwebs; and about chipmunks, small as distant stars, leaping from tree to tree somewhere in Bolivia; and about butterflies so weak the wind can carry them off, yet able to fly over an ocean. Sometimes he wanted to be one of the birds he'd read about, to fly thousands of miles alone, to fly across the world twice, from north to south and from south to north, only to return next season right to his nest, to the same tree or roof or cliff he'd started from.

He thought about Nazi tanks, like the Königstiger, King Tiger, the Panther—the best tank of the war, or the Hummel, Bumblebee. He also thought about soldiers, the *Panzergrenediers*, always part of the Nazi army in Prague, essence of the Blitzkrieg, which had now lasted for six years.

In two or three minutes he faced the hill with the stairs to the cable cars and the steep slope close to the Hunger Wall on the way to the Premonstrate's monastery. There was no moon and the skies were black and starless. He trembled with cold, fighting the moist wind and fear as well as the muddy path, coming closer to the monastery's rear wall with its narrow wooden door.

From his place now he saw the tents of the military camp; the guard didn't see him and the dogs couldn't smell him. In the distance near the cemetery was the tent, a flag with a swastika flapping in the wind. Otto Kubarsky, too, had heard the commander was a count, von und zu Wulkow, and that he had a whole cable car to himself going up and down the hill, always alone except for his adjutants. He recognized the big guns, looking from the top of the hill down on the city in all directions. For another split second, he imagined the old woman could see him. Her Jewish prayers would come in handy. He stood and watched how they unloaded artillery and ammunition from cable cars.

Five minutes later, carrying a pot of milk, he passed the long shadow of the big tank guns. He went back the same way, his feet wet and trembling from the cold, looking forward to being in his bed again.

3

"Oh my God, boy, you'll be my death," the woman whispered.

She stroked the boy with her hand. Her palm was hard like a scrubbing brush, soaked so many times in hot or icy water and full of oil, dirt, and grease. So now he's become a thief as well? What next? *To whom does God give wisdom? To one who is modest? To the brave and honest who don't steal and lie? A woman prefers a poor young man to a wealthy old man.*

"It's cloudy," she said without looking outside. His shoes next to the bed were wet and covered with mud and grass. "Where have you been? You must be sick in your head. Isn't there a German military camp out there?"

Outside, the loudspeaker announced five A.M.; then came the military march. The old woman lifted her arm and her head. The headquarters of the high command announced that tank traps, which forced some troops into a tactical retreat, and then to reassemble as in the Ardennes, had caused temporary difficulties. Beethoven's march was played. There was static and squealing in the loudspeaker.

"Are you working today?" the boy asked.

"You talked about bleeding in your sleep. A doctor ought to look at you. Ready?" said the old woman. "Let's go."

She had a harsh voice. Maybe it was the way his eyes were spaced that made him seem so far away. They were set wide apart, close to the sides of his face, so that the pupils always seemed to be unfocused, as though the world could run together. His eyebrows too were set high above his eyes, making the skin beneath lengthen and cast shadows at the corners. They were like the eyes of her daughter, Marta, with their hooded faraway look. But they were also selfish eyes, though she couldn't say in what way, except that he proved a thief, stealing at night, and he didn't see the danger of the German camp. And to steal so close to a cemetery—wasn't that blasphemy? Life is a sorrow, yes. Were his the eyes of a child and a man at the same time? He was small for his years and had thin shoulders, long tapered fingers, and a narrow face that gave him a girlish look. He was one of the smallest boys in his class.

"Put on a sweater or you'll catch cold," the old woman added. "This is the birth of Jack Frost. It's blowing in from everywhere. It came early this year." Then she said, "I won't let them kill you as they killed your Grandpa, or Mr. Bloch and his mother. What did you dream? Tell me."

The boy didn't answer. It was better thinking about birds and butterflies that could overcome great distances in spite of their weak wings, or about the chipmunks of Bolivia.

She almost threw the coat over his head. It had been her daughter's and she had altered it for the boy. She watched as he fastened the buttons with his fingers. Then the old woman started drinking the rest of the milk.

The dark May daybreak lingered above the courtyard. She could see from her bed the contour of the garage with its caved-in roof, the ash cans, and rotten wooden cages left by the former landlord, who had raised budgies and finches. Sometimes on sleepless nights she imagined the grocer being forced to exchange his apartment with them as a punishment. Many people became rich during the war, but the poor became poorer.

Her bones creaked. Her coat had wide lapels and sewn-on rabbit skin. "Comb your hair. Your head looks like a rooster tail. And tie your shoelaces."

4

The German doctor was tall and bony, with black hair plaited into braids pasted close to her head. She had the cheeselike complexion of a person who hasn't slept. Her lips were close, thin, and mannish. Her white coat was buttoned under her arm. Maria Kubarska had never seen such a coat. Inside the office was a couch covered with white, waxed linen and a table full of papers. The doctor stood at the desk with her legs apart.

"Am I supposed to examine you," the doctor asked the old woman, "or the boy?"

"Him," the old woman answered.

"Such a handsome young man," the doctor said. "What's wrong with you?"

"He wet himself twice during the night," said the old woman.

"Nothing so bad," the doctor said slowly. "I've seen such cases. The mother smothers the boy and won't let him be a man. What kind of proceedings are you in, criminal or civil?"

"We're not in any proceedings," the old woman said.

"Many people are sick today," said the doctor, who looked at Otto Kubarsky and then asked, "What do you dream about?"

The old woman's face reddened. So did the boy's, which the doctor noticed without moving her lips. The old woman looked at the doctor's nostrils. Could the doctor incriminate them merely for his dreams? The doctor looked the same way the secret police officer with the hunter's hat and the driver who showed them the way to the door had.

"I dream about fire," the boy said, trying to relieve the old woman. "One time a viaduct was burning, a transport was moving on it, they called for help. I had a fire engine and hurried to put it out."

"What else?" the doctor wanted to know. She had been interested in aberrations of behavior, in the structure of certain chambers of the brain, its parts, its composition; she'd been promised the brains of criminals, including German deserters, from the Gestapo office. They were giving them away after execution. The expression on the doctor's face was suddenly animated. Interest grew in her eyes.

"It's always some fire," added the boy.

The old woman grabbed the boy by his hand.

"It was only a dream, doctor. It has nothing to do with politics. We're alone. All our people are dead," Maria Kubarska said.

"Of natural causes?" the doctor wanted to know. "Give him less to drink in the evening. I don't know if I can place him in the German institution, especially now. There are no more free places in Castle Hartheim. Maybe next time."

The old woman's brow was wet with perspiration. Her chin shook, chilled by the cold. Her thin wrinkled skin was covered with little black hairs.

Once they'd left the doctor's office, she said, "They're making a fool of you."

"I won't drink," said the boy. "That's all. Why did you drag me here?"

He thought of the birds, flying over thousands of miles. The old woman's feet hurt and the veins in her leg were swollen. The speaker in front of their home on Carmelite Street was noisy. *Das Obercommando der Wehrmacht gibt bekannt.* Behind the hillside the glossy material of the tents reflected in the sun.

"Johann Wolfram von und zu Wulkow," Maria Kubarska said in the midst of the announcement. "Yes, no more than Chanan, John, or Ivan. The lamentations of Jeremiah . . . She will never see you. Only how she stared at you. You're not an animal, I will cure you. Just wait and see." And she quoted the papers from the trash can of the old man, *man is paired with the woman he deserves.* And, *a man should not think evil thoughts in the day as they might lead him to uncleanliness by night,* and then, *for a man whose wife dies in his lifetime, the world is deepened.* But how is it vice versa?

"What did you say?" she asked.

"Nothing," the boy answered.

The boy thought again about birds and butterflies and about boys who poured sugar, if they had it, into the gasoline tanks of German automobiles and sand and dust into the oil cylinders of wheels on the railroad freight wagons where the old woman worked. He knew the old woman would start her prayers again.

5

In the evening, Captain of the Wehrmacht Johann Wolfram von und zu Wulkow noticed a boy in a black flannel coat standing by the fire.

He put away his personal field mirror, saying to himself, *"Avoir des Cheveux d'argent."* Silver hair. *"Silberne Hare."*

The captain went to inspect the condition of the troops and to decide whether the fire was breaking safety regulations. He liked the new moon and the dark sky; the stars, hidden by clouds, seldom shone. The wind wafted through the city like a vanishing song. It was Rainer Maria Rilke's city, the place he described as a "miserable town of suborned existences." *"Reiten, reiten, reiten, durch den Tag, durch der Nacht, durch den Tag. Reiten, reiten, reiten. Und der Mut ist so müde geworden und die Sehnsucht so gross . . .* (Riding, riding, riding, through the day, through the night, through the day. Riding, riding, riding. And courage has grown so weary, and longing so great.)"

The captain smiled to himself. He held the monocle to his eye. In the distance there was the sound of a streetcar clanging, the roar of a military motorcycle, and the whistling of a long freight train. He was surprised that he remembered a railroad station, the faces of people who had been sitting in a compartment of a train when he'd gotten on, how much the ticket cost, and how the telegraph poles flashed by.

He watched the slender body of the boy. He thought about what the military camp of the victors meant to a child of a close enemy tribe. Captain Wulkow thought then of history, of what makes it greater than man.

To sit in an open city like Prague wasn't the worst of fates, he thought as he watched the boy by the fire. It was almost time for taps. The soldiers had returned from the local beer halls, "Under the Lookout Tower" and "At the Local Gimlet." You can't change human nature. He saw his soldiers as men of force, as the oldest, most ancient yet contemporary men, prepared at any second of the day or night. But the war was going to be over soon, and he was going to leave and not turn his head back, maybe never.

In the glare of the fire, Captain Wulkow noticed three wrinkles on the top of the boy's forehead. From the nearby monastery, the chapel bell sounded for late evening services, and from the other side of the hill the bells from the Church of the Triumphant Virgin Mary called back. The men gathered around the corporals, who were roasting a ram on a spit. The meat was partly a gift and partly booty from the Premonstrate's sheep fold. Only the strongest and most ruthless will survive this time, this place, this world, the captain thought, not the most civilized. The monks thought it was good to buy the favor of the soldiers with a flank of mutton. The walls under the observatory in the middle of the gardens, a broken plow forgotten since last fall, and the tall and bushy pear trees—all reminded Captain von und zu Wulkow that the ram from the monastery's flock was something slavishly pagan. On the inside he smiled again.

In German nothing sounded as it did in the Slavic language. He could take the words "rock," "rifle," "fire," and each was always just what it said. He tried it in French, Latin, and English. Tell me what language you speak and I'll tell you who you are, the captain thought, and he resolved to enter this observation in his diary. It was a long war, a lost war. Most probably it was not his last. It was not over yet, of course, but it would be. No turning back. There was something very old in his mind; he couldn't say exactly what, but it was older than the first water, heavier than the stars and the air, and more unattainable than the darkness.

The captain watched the fire, the roasting ram, the soldiers half German, half French, both corporals and the boy. It reminded him of a woman he had been in love with in Germany as a cadet in a military school. She was the wife of the commanding officer, professor of strategy and tactic, a leading expert of the army. The commander was proud to have a son with features resembling his lovely wife. The captain sighed. The boy reminded him of that German-French woman. It was the past, a bridge where a man shouldn't turn his head backward. But he did, in secret, for himself.

He stayed in the shadows where he knew they wouldn't see him until he chose to make his presence known.

Earlier the captain had read through the evening military mail and the posted orders. Then, before sunset, he looked at the city camp and studied its architecture with the aid of a map. He was fascinated by the gardens. This city, he knew, had been built by the German architects Parler, Brokoff, and Braun. The beautiful churches linked the inhabitants to Germany, whereas the neighboring Poles—while they still had a country—turned to Rome. The presence of the churches brought peace to the captain's soul, a hazy idea of Slavic tribes, even though during his entire stay at Prague he had never crossed their threshold. His mind was full of foreign landscapes, strange faces, and distant languages.

Captain Johann Wolfram von und zu Wulkow felt the invisible solidarity and the intangible presence of thousands—hundreds of thousands—and millions of German men in arms: flyers in the air, men in submarines in the dark waters deep under the sea wherever they were, from Gibraltar to the Caribbean Sea and from the Atlantic to the Pacific Ocean. He felt their spiritual, almost physical, presence here in Prague at the top of the highest hill, under the low-lying wet heaven, in the only world where there was never enough space and air for all, for the victims and the defeated.

The boy stood by the fire. The sentry had brought him there when he muttered that he had gone to the cow shed at the monastery for a pot of milk. They had scared him by saying that traitors would be hanged on one of the pear trees that grew in the park or on the hillside leading up to the camp. The boy was impressed and scared at the same time. He barely succeeded in hiding his nervousness in the presence of the soldiers. The black and blue mark beneath his left eye had been put there by the sentry's rifle butt as he urged him toward the camp at a faster pace.

Corporal Rudolf Kalkman said to the boy, "Everything that lives must die, but there are two catches: not everything that dies will be born again, whether an animal, man or flower; and each person makes that decision at different times."

The second corporal agreed. His name was Maurach, and he felt right at home in the Eastern European regions. He collected articles about the lives of Aryan Slavs fit for Germanization—he noted their conditions, signs, and inclinations. It's unbelievable how much depends on ears, noses, and chins, on the color of eyes and hair, and on the mouth. What was the curse of the weak who made brothers of his servants? There were only too many exceptions.

The corporal showed the boy a bayonet covered with blood. (The boy had offered earlier to bring an animal from the monastery, which he did.) Corporal Kalkman smiled, grinning in his coal black eyes.

"Good evening," Captain von und zu Wulkow greeted. "Is the animal perfect? You can tell the men to stand at ease, Corporal."

The second corporal, Maurach, began to play the harmonica, *Heimat deine Sterne.* The fire roared as the ram roasted, crackling as it came apart at the joints. The captain, his eye behind his monocle, peered into the fire. He watched the movement of the animal's skin touched with gold. Corporal Kalkman had been a butcher in civilian life. Now he refreshed his skills; he hadn't forgotten anything. In a stable, goats protect horses from diseases and bring luck and money to the farmer. A goat's horn under the pillow cures insomnia. But sheepskin also has its mysteries in daylight, and in moonlight, and in different seasons.

There was hesitation in the flames, and in connection with the sheep it created strange music in the captain's ears.

"The meat is superb, Captain," Corporal Kalkman answered. "It was a black sheep. That doesn't mean calamity when you cut its throat fast, Herr Captain."

His eyes were bloodshot. He'd been standing very close to the fire and hadn't slept for several days before the camp had moved to the hillside. He watched the drops of fat running down the skin of the animal and into the fire. Tufts of black hair protruded from the corporal's nostrils. He was careful never to show weakness to anyone. He kept away from Hungarian and Romanian soldiers in order to avoid any suggestion that he looked Jewish, or, as he once said, Mediterranean. He didn't like Italian, Romanian, or Hungarian soldiers. He envied Corporal Maurach's blond hair and light brows as well as his thin beard, light as straw, and his blue eyes. He was glad Captain Wulkow was not blond and blue-eyed. Captain Wulkow was a silvery brunette, with green-gray, almost colorless eyes.

"Come with me to my tent, I'll see that you're well treated," the captain told the boy.

The captain thought about how his mother believed that seeing a sheep at night meant a storm or a death, and that only a ram drives away the evil spirits of man.

They walked next to each other in the soft grass under the dark pear trees. The first star appeared on the north side. Captain von und zu Wulkow felt a tension in the boy he thought he could explain.

In the tent he had the boy pronounce certain Czech words. He enjoyed the musical quality of the language. As soon as the German and Atlantic armies jointly defeated the Russians, the language of the Czech tribe would die out as would the language of the Jews—like the mysterious language of the Aztecs or of the lost continent of Atlantis which had died thousands of years ago.

So weit die braune Heide geht . . . The captain opened the portable record player he took along with him wherever their expedition went— from Moscow to Kiev, from Kiev to Paris, from Paris to Warsaw, from Warsaw to Prague. He wound the spring. The melody was Beethoven's Sonata in G major, opus 30. A bat passed through the air behind the tent; then an owl hooted. The captain smiled. By taking only one step backward, he felt as though he flowed back to the times of the twelve Teutonic tribes. The tent and the large travel trunk were covered with small carpets of Turkish and Persian design.

What was it? What was the boy awakening in him? He thought of his secret, half French-half German woman and the son of the commanding officer and teacher of strategy and tactics in the military school thirteen years ago. The captain looked in his field mirror. He thought about the boy's frailty and the slash marks on his face. He thought about the many German boys who had fallen, and about secrets of fathers and sons, unknown fathers and secret sons.

He picked up the telephone. It would be necessary to announce that today, May 4, 1945, at 8:16 P.M. winter time, the criminal elements in town abused a German soldier. Punishment must be handed out.

Captain Wulkow took the boy by the shoulders and led him back to the fire. The fire swished and crackled. With the back of his hand he touched the frail, white face, the chin and the nape of the slender neck. He urged the boy to walk faster and slapped him a few times on the shoulders with his gloved hand.

6

At that moment, the German doctor wrote an inquiry to the Gestapo's Prague office, asking them to provide her with more brains of local criminals. It was similar to a request she'd made yesterday when the skirmishes and attacks against German soldiers began on the streets. The Gestapo advised her also to ask the commanders of local units. Only a few German university laboratories were busy with similar research. She hypothesized that there were connections between head trauma in childhood and aggressive attitudes toward German occupation and forces in general—particularly with aberrations in behavior.

Comparing the addresses of the two Kubarskis, she wrote a second letter to Count von und zu Wulkow. She took pains to explain her purpose and the future importance of her brain research. It would be ideal to be able to conduct the experiments on some people before and after execution. She had already studied the brains of ten hanged criminals and of twelve others shot or frozen in the laboratories of a certain castle. She had no doubt that her research could contribute to science and the scientific prestige of the Third Reich. There was no better place than Prague, the center of Europe.

She thought about the front line, about where Schörner's army, with one million fresh German men, was now and what obstacle presented itself to this city, its inhabitants, their future being closed in by the American army. She thought of the pride of this city, of how some of the people demonstrated pure madness. Did they think they could defeat Germany? No one should underestimate German capacity and resolve or Nazi ability to act with ruthlessness. Nobody is permitted to touch Germany. It was a pleasure to know that her commander had a fun-

damentally different approach than the mad dogs in Prague expected.
She sent her letter by her personal messenger under her seal to the
quarters of the Count von und zu Wulkow.

7

The wind brought the fragrance of the blue and white lilacs and the
pear trees to the fire, which mixed with the night and the scent of the
roasted animal. Below, the town seemed submerged in darkness. Planes
occasionally hummed overhead. Down on the street, a streetcar or
motorcycle droned in the dark.

"Are you cold?" the captain asked the boy. "Get closer to the fire."

Corporal Kalkman gave the order to stand at attention and then at
ease. He handed the captain a metal plate with a helping of meat. He
knew the captain would refuse it, but would let the boy be served.

The captain thought about the boy, about what he would do with
him. The town below reminded him of a sacrificial ground that German
knights in armor once rode to with clanging weapons and spirited horses.
It was Friday, the fourth of May, a new moon. The moon seemed to
be hidden behind a dark curtain through which it would break, a tiny
crescent, perhaps tonight or tomorrow morning. The captain thought
about their Teutonic past. That age didn't seem so far off. Nor did it
seem difficult for him to look forward a thousand years. At one time,
the Teutonic tribes ruled Europe with an iron hand. They were strong
and healthy. Had they let themselves become dominated by the Greeks
and the Romans or by the dubious wisdom of the Jews? On the hillsides
overlooking the city, he felt close to all of that. He absorbed it with
every breath, with every step he took in the grass under the cool spring
sky. In the dark, he had the taste of something that even the German
language had no words for. He thought about how the dead and the
living penetrated from the depths of the past to the present, to this
place, to the fire under the sprawling pear tree, into the wood and the
aroma of the roast. Here they were, his Teutonic ancestors: lethal as
wolves, keen as hawks, proud as eagles. He breathed deeply in and out.

Again, in his thoughts he was with the wife of the commanding officer in the military school.

The captain turned away from the fire and looked out into the darkness over the city where black towers jabbed the sky. Smiling slightly, he thought about how all that was German flowed up at this moment, and he felt how one thing was connected to another. History didn't just follow. It is the result of individuality and resolve and conduct in unstable times. History made Captain Wulkow tell the soldiers to bring a small barrel of rum for those who were not on duty.

The captain stood next to the boy and looked into the fire. The boy's eyes also belonged to the fire, as though the fire itself was in them. But on his back he felt the wind shiver with hunger. The wind rustled in the treetops. The grass flattened, then stood again. The captain was observing how the boy caught the warmth of the flames with his forehead and chest and the palms of his hands. Does he think about me, wondered the captain? Does he think about light, sound, and voices? About childhood associations, in reverse, about the visions of his unknown future? Someone handed him a small slice of military bread. He ate slowly. The bread tasted like the pressed and baked sawdust bakers mixed with flour. From the other side of the fire, Corporal Maurach threw him a linen towel so he could wipe his hands and mouth.

It occurred to the captain that there was no other army in the world as companionable as the German army, descendants of the Teutons, knights of the Middle Ages, the Crusaders: born of song, blood, and the land, of honor, light, and voices, as hard as tungsten steel, lithe as a leaping panther, mighty as an ocean. That was the army keeping Europe *maustod*, dead as a mouse. The army which made the enemy *mundtod*, deadly silent.

In the evening, the town reminded the captain of a poem written by invisible hands, one that has lost its meaning. He left for his tent.

"We will put out the fire, you can pee with us into the flames," said Corporal Kalkman, and he smiled.

When he was leaving for his tent, the voices of the corporals and the soldiers merged in the captain's ears with the humming wind in the pear trees. He didn't turn.

8

"You're not going there anymore," said Maria Kubarska. "Only over my dead body. I won't let them shoot you like a dog."

"Living like dogs is OK?"

"Don't you understand?" she asked. "It's just not worth the risk." The old woman fell silent again.

The new moon edged toward its end. The dark blue curtain of the sky, purple and velvet on opposite ends, sailed through the clouds above the courtyard. Maria Kubarska lay next to the boy and wondered: What will happen? Am I prepared for it? The spring always asks how the winter was, or the past six winters.

"They'll kill you as they did your grandfather. They'd love to kill everyone." And then she said, "I wish you were my bird again."

The house and the courtyard were dark and quiet. Friday was falling into the past and soon Saturday would arrive.

She lay on the bed and looked across the room at the geranium. She had placed a geranium in the window that faced the courtyard. She wondered if it would start raining.

She thought of all those who'd been killed because they'd listened to Radio London or Radio Moscow, about all the maimed who'd gone to Gemany and worked in the Ruhr, Essen, or Westfall and were forbidden to talk to the German population, just allowed to work for them. They'd never returned, like Mr. Emanuel Bloch and his mother. They were condemned to *Todschweigen*. Killed into silence, as the Germans said.

"What are you doing?" the old woman asked. "Have you lost your tongue?"

"I'm asleep," the boy lied. "What did Grandpa actually do to them?"

"He didn't dispatch the trains at the freight station," Maria Kubarska answered. "Because of him something was delayed. And then the SS Gauleiter Reinhard Heydrich, general of the German secret police and the first deputy of Hitler, his darling, was assassinated in May 1942 like a stray dog. They killed him and Mr. Emanuel Bloch and his mother.

They dispatched three Jewish transports, thousands of people on each, and destroyed one entire mining village. Now we're going to pay for it. I can feel it in my veins. In these bad veins of mine, and in my chest. No, you're not going anywhere. There are others here. Grownups. They've waited for six years."

"There's too much on your mind," the boy answered.

"It's quiet; I don't hear any shooting anywhere."

"If it starts raining, I'll go right away," the boy said. "I'll be back in the morning. Where's my coat?"

"I sewed it and reinforced it with my own hands. It would break my heart if something were to happen to you. My veins would open, even where old wounds have healed. My breath is loud, just like Marta's. Turn toward the wall. You're the last of the Kubarskys. Marta wanted it that way, for your name to be Otto just like your grandpa and your father. Look out. I smell the stench of trash cans all the way here. I don't want to live here anymore, not even one more day. In the morning we'll go out together."

"Do your veins hurt?"

"They're open," the old woman nodded.

The night became darker. "Everything will be different," she whispered. "When it's possible to defeat Adolf Hitler, any vision—no matter how distant—is close enough. You have to be reasonable, my little boy. They're worse than you imagine."

She waited for the dawn when the birds would come—the sparrows and the swallows, in great crowds on their paths between the land and the skies—hunting and nesting, flying day after day, year after year. She envied the birds. She didn't know exactly why. Maybe it was their freedom, or maybe it was something more—and at the same time less.

The night seemed to her the darkest in six years. The Germans were here, astute and strong, though in other ways already weak. From one side the Russians were coming; on the other side the Americans were waiting for their prey. What would they be like? Maybe it was the last night of the war. She thought of everything that made the nights heavy and dark, as if they had no end. As if someone had killed all the roosters that separated daytime from evening and night from morning.

9

On Saturday, the fifth of May, when the field artillery pieces on the Petrin hillside and around the lookout tower were no longer covered with waterproof linen caps, a small, boyish figure brought two sheep from the Premonstrate's fold, tied to a rope. No one on the hillside suspected him. The monk who saw him didn't say a word about the boy taking the sheep. The sheep bleated and the boy pulled the animals behind him and wiped the sweat off his forehead.

On each side, three men in raincoats stood by each of the guns, prepared to shoot. The safety catches on their personal weapons were uncocked. Johann Wolfram von und zu Wulkow's unit was prepared. It was cold.

"Stop. Where are you going? Not a single step forward or you'll be full of lead," the voice of Corporal Kalkman cried out from behind the boy.

"I'm bringing you some sheep. You said you'd get hungry and you wanted another roast. I couldn't come during the day, there was shooting. I had to wait."

"Move on or you're going to trip over your own carcass," the corporal mumbled.

Corporal Kalkman passed him and looked into his face, at his darkly circled eyes. The corporal pressed the point of the bayonet into the back of the black flannel coat that had once belonged to the boy's mother. The boy felt the sharpness of the point, and the corporal guessed by the slight degree of resistance that he'd touched the boy's back near the heart. The shadows were pitch black. Once in a while the wind blew the remaining drops of afternoon rain off the leaves and branches of the nearby pear trees.

He ordered the boy to wait by Captain Wulkow's tent. With his heels and toes together, slightly bent forward, he announced to the captain that the boy was here again and that he'd dragged in two sheep. They were on their way to the field kitchen near the supply wagon.

The captain sat looking over a map near an oil lamp. He was in uniform with high riding boots, and across his arms lay a coat with silver epaulets. He was uneasy about the large number of streets and connecting roads by which the rebels could attack or—after the attack— retreat. There was the winding Swedish Street; and to the north, Belcredi Avenue as well as a clump of streets around the Institute for the Blind; and from the east, Italian Street. This led to the market and to Carthusian Streets, a channel of roads with many windows and doors. He'd come to an agreement with the High Command of General Reitman's staff that he would assume alert status. But someone had cut the telephone wires and disconnected the electricity five minutes before. And now Corporal Kalkman had interrupted him.

Captain Wulkow's silvery hair flashed in the darkness. "Did you frisk him to see if he had any weapons?"

The captain put on his coat and buttoned it up. He heard the bleating animals and it occurred to him that someone could zero in on a unit by following their noises. He didn't say a word. He saw the boy under one of the pear trees. Voices were coming from the direction of the guns. From the monastery, the evening bells rang.

"Once, Corporal, you told the men that your father wanted to beat you over the head with a chair. A man like you only attains age in life, nothing else. You remind me of a lumberjack who cuts down a tree for his friends to make a casket for him. You're still only a butcher, Kalkman. Destroy the animals on the double."

"I'll destroy them on the double, sir."

The captain thought: To obey is as beautiful as to give orders, but on a lower mental plane. For people like Kalkman, only one rule applies: to bend and be bent. Man is his muscle and not his sorrow; life is an orgy, not higher principles. Only the present time—no eternity. Simple matters, no concern for the cosmic; no harmony, only chaos. Light, sound, and voices, but what kind? From where?

Corporal Kalkman killed each sheep with a single blow. He rammed the bayonet through their hearts. They gave a single bleat, then fell, washed by blood in their white wool.

"You don't understand a thing," Captain von und zu Wulkow said, and in his mind added, *avoir des mains de boucher. Hände wie ein Fleischer.* He saw the corporal's hands covered with blood. Captain Wulkow departed from the corporal and went uphill along the line of pear trees to his staff, hidden in the dark. He took no notice of the boy.

In three circles, sentries made their way noiselessly around the camp. They stepped quietly in the grass between trees, as if they were separating from their shadows and merging with them again. The rain began, small cold drops.

On the other bank of the Moldau River, a fire not even the rain could dampen was burning. Several German squadrons were flying east to west.

The lights of the flames didn't disappear until they were high in the sky.

They boy looked at the holster of Kalkman's pistol, put aside just like the coat on the open bed of the Mercedes truck. Only for a moment did he place his hand on the pistol. At that instant, he felt Captain Johann Wolfram von und zu Wulkow's gloved hand. The other hand that gripped him belonged to Corporal Kalkman.

"You know just a few types of meat, Corporal," the captain said. He let go of the boy's arm. The boy's shoulder shivered for a moment. To the captain, the boy's bones seemed frail under the thin flannel woman's coat. He remembered how once, right before the war, he'd run over a fawn during manuevers in the forest in Berlin. How strangely everything changes. Light, sounds, the mood. He coughed. Then he said: "Tie him to the cannon barrel of your tank, Corporal."

"*Zum Befehl*, Herr Captain," said the corporal.

"The most dangerous animal is a wounded one, Corporal. The worst war is a lost war."

"*Zum Befehl*, Herr Captain."

"Fire three rounds, Corporal."

"*Zum Befehl*, Herr Captain. Tie him to the tank barrel and fire three rounds."

The bell had stopped tolling. An old woman was coming from the bottom of the ruined walls, passing the cemetery wall. She crossed the peak of the hill. The guard's searchlight shone its bright light directly upon her. She reminded the captain of an owl and the corporal of a bat. She reminded the boy of an old bird who had wings but couldn't take off, a creature who could only move about with difficulty. She was seventy-two years old, to the day and the hour. In the searchlight, her wrinkled face flashed, her eyes squinted. Her mouth was open. Her lips were chapped. For another second, veins showed in her face and on her temples.

"In the morning, at ten, you'll be driving through the city streets in the center of the Wenceslaw Square, so shoot sharp," said Count von und zu Wulkow.

Maria Kubarska was coming in the black dress she had worn to her husband's funeral on June 12, 1942, with her head tied in a scarf and her hands clenched in fists, with the dark brown spots on her neck and aching feet. The old woman was fading in the night, tripping, as low branches hit her in the face, hands, and chest. She kept moving in order not to lose a second. Flashes of light blinded her, but she pressed on, determined not to lose a single step. Her arms were glued to her body; she didn't even use her right hand to protect her from the branches.

In the next flash of light the captain could see why. She carried the black prayer book tightly under her arm, protecting herself only with her left hand. The branches snapped against her wrinkled body.

A split vision of a man and his ancient fate many years ago passed through her mind. She walked slowly and with difficulty, as if her head weighed as much as the earth, the stars, and the universe. Her shoes were flat and worn. Her ankles, wrapped in muslin rags, were round and swollen over the tops of her shoes. She walked with slow determination, aiming directly, making way. So broadly do men carry their will against time and mountains.

The old woman moved her lips; she squinted her eyes and fought on, as if she wouldn't let herself be stopped by the night, the dark wild bushes, or the blinding light.

Everyone has his fool, and I have two at once, the captain thought again. *Wie Man sich bettet, so liegt Man.* As you make your bed, so shall you lie in it. The boy moved, as if he wanted to run and meet the old woman, but the corporal held him.

The woman caught sight of the three shapes near the pear tree, and she headed straight toward them. She felt her feet getting heavier all the time, but she went on over the wet, seaweedlike grass toward the pear trees.

The captain thought for an instant how bountiful their fruit must be. What year did the trees produce sweet and rich pears, full of succulent juices? What years not? Why can nature be virile at one time and barren the next? He imagined blossoms falling during the heat of summer; and then the fall reckoning what only the virgin knows. He thought how similar nature is to human beings, yet how people cannot narrow the border.

The old woman tripped in ditches and over hillocks, overturning pieces of turf and rocks. She was humming through bitten lips. *Let me not fall into the hands of man.* She whispered to herself and then almost aloud.

She thought about Emanuel Bloch, who liked to refer to some of his ancestors, most of them murdered. *Any man, alive or dead, will never be born again; some people are only born to do one good thing during their life—and maybe only to act out a notion.* She marched slowly and persistently forward, step after step, far up the hills, her eyes as dark and cold and hard as ice.

The old woman finally saw a man in a corporal's uniform gripping the boy's shoulder. When she came closer, she heard the crowing of a rooster cut into the night along with the breath of the boy and the voice of a man in a captain's coat, who said, "Do you have enough rope, Corporal? The old woman as well."

Clock Like a Windmill

*The town hall burned first in a fire started by the French in 1689 and again
in the ghetto conflagration of 1754. The two clocks were repaired in 1855.
The one in the tower has Arabic numerals; the second, in the gable under
the tower in the northern side facing the Altneuschul—the Old-New
Synagogue—across the narrow street, has Hebrew letters. The hands of the
Hebrew clock turn backward like leaves in a Hebrew book. According to
the Jewish calendar, it is 5,705 years since the creation of the world.*

Everyone in the cellar was captivated by the woman sitting on the
chopping block beside the door, although all she'd said since her arrival
was "Hello" and "Excuse me." She had been the last to arrive.

"The numbers . . . on the clock," she said now. No one answered her
and she added that the clock face showed everything backward.

"It's Hebrew," the caretaker said. "There are no numbers. Only letters,
and it goes backward."

"Yes," said the woman. "Yes."

There were two clock faces on the tower, the upper one normal, the
other with letters and hands that moved counterclockwise. The clocks had
been a part of the town hall for a few hundred years. The woman on the
chopping block was thinking about these clocks.

The caretaker had just announced that he was going upstairs to lock
up in order to keep anyone unwanted from coming to hide. He peered out
and up at both clocks before he locked the doors. They still kept time well.
They didn't need winding today. Mondays were always set aside for winding.

The doors were covered with thick sheet metal, and each had two
small windows at about the level of a man's head. Suddenly a barrage of
bullets hit the door near the caretaker's feet. The wooden paneling around

the door splintered, but the sheet metal which deflected the bullets saved him.

The woman on the chopping block jumped like a startled quail when the bullets exploded against the door. She was wearing a wrinkled beige suit, which made her look as if she were on her way to a meeting which for some reason had never taken place. Her forehead was finely lined, like an old woman's; the ripples looked like those on the surface of a pond. When the caretaker brought her down to the cellar to join the others, he noticed that she couldn't have been much older than his wife. The woman had told the caretaker that she was Jewish and had no place to live.

He looked out the window in the door. He saw a group of German soldiers leading two Czech policemen with raised hands toward the SS headquarters, located in the Law School building on the river bank. He felt relieved that neither of the clocks was ringing. There were no bells. It helped to make the place more inconspicuous.

The caretaker returned to the cellar. He sat between his wife and the woman on the chopping block; a stout woman sat opposite him, facing the children and the teenagers. He asked the two teenagers where they'd come from.

"Kelley Street, if that means anything to you," the older one growled. He made a wry face and turned away from the caretaker. Both of the boys were wearing jackets with rabbit fur on the outside. They could be concealing knives or weapons under those jackets—or at least it looked that way.

The woman in the crumpled suit on the chopping block seemed oblivious to what was going on around her. She was thinking about the clock that moved backward, perhaps because she had never seen anything like that. She thought she could feel the tension created by the two clocks, so near each other but in perpetual opposition.

In the twilight her skin looked pale, with unnatural spots of bright rouge on her cheekbones near the corners of her eyes. She looked like someone obsessed, or a person with a high fever. The woman sat on the chopping block as if she were dreaming. She made no spoken reply to questions; she would simply nod or shake her head. The caretaker didn't tell the others what she had confided to him upstairs.

"It's pretty boring here," said the younger teenager.

"Sit down here, if you don't mind," said the caretaker's wife. "It's only for a while."

It would be good for all of them to get ready for a long stay, the caretaker was thinking. He glanced around the room, saying lightly, "We haven't had so many people here since last Easter."

The German machine gun upstairs rattled again. The caretaker didn't mention the policemen he'd seen being taken away.

The chopping block had been cut from the trunk of an old, flattened oak. Near it lay an ax with a dull, jagged blade, covered with rust that looked strangely like blood.

"Thank heaven we cleaned up in here just a week ago," said the caretaker's wife.

"Thank you. You're very kind," the newcomer said shyly. "Please don't bother about me."

And then she whispered as if she were talking in a dream.

"Is anyone hurt?" the caretaker asked. He knew no one was; he only wanted to create an atmosphere of security and concern in the cellar. He pretended not to hear any of the sounds that penetrated from Maisel Street above.

The caretaker's wife seemed at home here; several times she had wanted to tell everybody her name was Olga, but the words didn't come. She gazed at the woman sitting on the chopping block as if she were trying to assess who she was and where she'd come from. Why was she so surprised that the lower clock turned backward?

"Here we're all as safe as if we were inside a great big granite boulder," she announced. "It's a good thing that none of our employees showed up. We wouldn't have had room for everybody. But, maybe. Yes," she contradicted herself.

"That's for sure," the caretaker joined in. He listened to the shooting down the street. "This cellar's a regular fortress. In a few hours we'll be able to go upstairs, just to make sure everything is OK. In the meantime, I suggest that you don't go near a window if you don't have to; it doesn't make sense to provoke them unnecessarily. After a while, I'll be able to go and take a look from the tower." He looked at the woman on the chopping block. "That's where the clocks are. You can see Paris Avenue and the Legion Bridge from there just as clear as can be."

"You don't think they'll go through every house?" the stout woman asked, heaving a sigh as if she really didn't doubt it. Her question emerged like a song from her heavy fleshy throat.

Both teenagers, looking like hunters or hoboes in their fur jackets, moved away from the window and retreated all the way back to the far corner.

"Consider yourselves guests, if you don't mind my putting it that way," the caretaker's wife said with a smile.

The children liked the way their mother spoke. They'd never seen her quite this way. She seemed pretty and resolute. Nevertheless, she was burdened with something she didn't wish to express. From time to time she turned away from the burning gaze of the newcomer's eyes. It occurred to her that it had been a long time since she'd last seen the sun. She sighed. As a child, she had imagined the sun to be an old man. In the garden of some mansion, she'd once seen a stone fountain engraved with an old man's face with the points of a sunburst radiating from it. The old man's face had been wide, cheerful, and beardless, with a carefully wrought smile.

Again, her eyes met those of the woman sitting silent on the chopping block. Life must be miserable for her, she thought.

"The Germans must thrust forward, break out, keep this street free for their sorties," the caretaker said. "When they get pushed back, they'll want to have free access to the bridge. It is pretty obvious that the bridge is of utmost importance to them—after all, the water's still cold." And then over the renewed stutter of the machine guns, he added, "Our people are doing all right. I'll hang out the flags when I get the chance."

"As luck would have it, I used up my wood sooner than the usual time this year," the caretaker's wife said. "Well, it was good for something. Every year we get a load or two of wood scraps from them."

"Who'd have guessed they'd wind up on our street?" the caretaker said. "They're always unpredictable. But what isn't, these days?"

The eyes of the newcomer remained indifferent to everything; nothing seemed to interest her.

The caretaker's children listened eagerly to everything said by the group. The caretaker's wife watched the teenagers in the corner. They seemed to be conspiring about something. They sounded raw and crass, but in spite of that, they had her sympathy.

"I noticed how many lilac bushes there are behind the walls of the cemetery across the street." In a conspiratorially low voice, the caretaker's wife added that she was fond of the smell of lilac, probably because it always reminded her of the forgotten sins of youth.

The stout woman laughed weakly. "My God, you're not going to talk about age, are you? How old can you be? Thirty? You can't even be that, Mrs. . . . ?"

"Belleles."

The caretaker coughed understandingly. "They wrote yesterday in the *Telegraf* that since the city is considered a military hospital zone, either today or tomorrow we should get food coupons for the next three months for sugar, bread, jam, and flour. They must have really had it."

"They can have my ration," the stout woman declared in her melodious singsong voice. The fleshy white folds of her throat trembled as she spoke.

"Hitler, yes, of course," said the caretaker, as if he were ashamed to pronounce the name of a man who, thank God, had been dead for five days. Was he really dead? Wasn't he still alive, in a certain sense, even after his death?

"Next time, I'd like to order wood from our old supplier," the caretaker's wife remarked, trying to keep the mood light. "I hope he comes back. The grocers and the carpenters will have their heyday yet. Some get frightfully rich off the war. And soon, after the war, they'll be getting richer. I wish they were getting rich already."

As the caretaker's wife spoke, the woman on the chopping block removed her gloves, one finger at a time. The leather stuck to her skin, making a disconcerting crackling sound as she slowly peeled them off.

"We couldn't have found anything better than this," the stout woman said. "We should meet again when it's all over and I'll bring my son." Then she turned to the woman on the chopping block. "No one should be so dumb as to take on this many women. But there's no need to worry."

"You should come at Easter—after the war—it's fun here," the caretaker said.

The initial tension had eased and he felt a wave of satisfaction. Everyone was more relaxed, notwithstanding the shooting which moved from the street closer to the river; only the woman on the chopping block still acted tense. The terse "yes" and "I wouldn't know" replies she offered to the stout woman and to the caretaker's wife seemed detached, offered so she wouldn't be considered rude. Her face looked sad and grave, as though she were being pulled in two, tearing in the middle.

The older teenager pulled the fur collar of his coat around his neck as if he were cold. "Is the policeman walking or isn't he?" he grunted to the younger one.

"There's no point in drawing attention to our house," the caretaker said, demonstrating that the situation was well within his grasp and he was able to keep track of what everyone in the cellar was doing.

There was a silence. The teenagers exchanged looks. The caretaker's children became restless and his wife scolded them; yet as she spoke, a vague expression of concern crossed the face of the woman on the chopping block.

By now, everyone knew that the six-year-old boy with the brown curls was named Toni; his seven-year-old brother was Oldrich; and the four-year-old was Olga. Little Olga wore long, almost new white stockings.

The caretaker glanced over toward the two teenagers who were whispering again.

"The paint always comes off the walls," the caretaker's wife said. "The rain leaks down here, and the cellar never gets a chance to dry out."

"We'd have to heat the place to dry it and that would be too difficult," the caretaker replied. "Where's the cat?"

Just before the newcomer entered, the stout lady had said that she was the mother of a pilot in the RAF. Shortly before her announcement, the two teenagers had appeared; the little one with the squeaky voice sounded as if he were too weak to speak louder, or just didn't want to expend the energy. The taller one's voice was changing. His Adam's apple looked almost like a man's but he still had the body of a boy. He watched little Olga constantly, as if reminded of someone.

The woman who came in last now whispered, "What kind of people are they? . . . What moves them? . . . I still don't know . . . maybe I'll never know . . ."

The caretaker lit a candle to break the tension that followed her words. The gray eyes of the woman on the chopping block stared into the small flame at the tip of the candle, absorbing it.

The older teenager yawned loudly and stretched. He exhaled, a long hissing sound, and then addressed his smaller companion, not paying attention to the shooting at the riverside. "So, have you made yourself comfortable here, you old Methuselah?"

His tone implied that no one in the cellar had said anything relevant, as if the others had been choking on the silence. He squinted into the dim, bluish glow of the candle.

"We're not getting back to Kelley Street anytime soon this way," he added.

"Mr. Belleles doesn't seem to mind having us here—so don't panic." The other one took pleasure in bundling up his fur collar as he spoke. "What's wrong with this place, anyway?"

A glint of light shone from the dim little window that was at street level facing Maisel Street. The waning day flowed in through the dusty glass, which was covered by a torn, rusted wire netting. The street could no longer be seen, even when the caretaker had put his eyes close to the netting to look out. It was hard to discern the facade of the house across the street with the balcony that hung away from the wall like a torn pocket. Half of the flagpole had burned down, and the other half

was wrapped in a red banner. Before the caretaker had descended the
stairs, it had become quite dark.

"I think they're still walking," the taller teenager murmured to the
little one.

"They're walking, all right," the little one agreed, unceremoniously
relieving himself.

The caretaker looked at his wife in silent consultation. She stood
and went upstairs, passing through the hallway that opened at a right
angle to the staircase. She returned three-quarters of an hour later with
a kettle of soup, half a dozen plates, and her heavy, festive silver spoons.
She gave the first serving to the woman sitting on the chopping block.
The thought came to her that those eyes above the vivid artificial blush
across the woman's cheeks seemed like two smoldering hearths; maybe
she wore rouge to disguise her fears. She seemed to age right before
their eyes.

"Eat hearty," she said to the woman.

She didn't even ask the woman's name. She'd probably made a
mistake when she hadn't clearly introduced herself at once when the
woman had first come; then at least she would know her name. But no
one else had bothered to do so either. She wasn't going to now.

"It will warm you up," she said. "A cellar is a cellar . . . it's cold down
here, after all . . . and warm food under any circumstances . . . it's the
foundation of everything."

"No one will dream of searching this cellar," the caretaker reassured
everyone again.

"What do you mean by that?" asked the stout woman.

"This is a town hall; nobody will need it anymore. The people
whose names are registered here left a long time ago and no one has
heard of them since. I trust you understand what I'm trying to say?"

"Are they still walking?" the taller teenager asked, his voice cracking.
He kept buttoning and unbuttoning his rabbit jacket.

"They're walking all right," the little one answered as weakly as
before. "So what?"

"They'll be walking till kingdom come," the taller teenager grunted roughly. He caressed the rabbit fur on his jacket.

The caretaker coughed in the direction of the teenagers.

"Eat carefully," he cautioned the woman on the chopping block. "It would be a pity to ruin your dress. Before you go, I'll lend you our iron. We have an electric iron and also a charcoal-heated iron I inherited from my mother."

Suddenly the caretaker's wife saw that the woman on the chopping block was exactly the person who'd been revealed to her through those smoldering eyes. She felt as though she'd known the newcomer much longer. She continued to serve the others.

"It's a bit chilly here because we're so close to the river." She told them she'd made the soup mostly to warm them.

The taller teenager turned abruptly to the little one. "They're not walking anymore, but don't get any ideas. They haven't been through here for at least an hour."

Without asking anyone's leave, the boys went upstairs to look through the peepholes in the entrance door to see whether the street was safe or if there were any German patrols on the prowl. They found a better lookout in the lower clockwork cabin in the tower. The turning gears smelled of oil.

Then they returned. The people in the cellar watched them crawl back into their distant corner like timid little pups.

"The landlord from across the street was opposed to hanging out the red flag," the caretaker's wife said after a pause. "The Germans shot the concierge and someone threw a grenade onto the balcony. It exploded and the entire balcony fell. Now the flag hangs down from the steel beams like a rag; so you can see it would be senseless to do anything like that now. She was too premature."

The stout woman listened carefully. She remarked, "That's bad. Maybe the woman had children at home."

"It's better not to talk about it," the caretaker said quickly. He turned to his wife. "I had no intention of doing anything now."

The teenagers could sense what part of the statement was meant for them.

The caretaker's wife caressed the children while she sat there musing. When children are too quiet, it's like an illness. She caressed them again. They seemed like small wolf cubs.

"So, you were a tailor?" the stout woman asked the caretaker, finally breaking the silence that had fallen over the cellar.

"Wouldn't that be something—you ironing our clothes?"

Nobody said anything.

The caretaker's wife glanced at her bigger son. He avoided her look and she again remembered the time when she imagined the son as an old man. She was sorry that it had been her husband's idea and not her own to bring down soup for everyone, even if he only conveyed it through his eyes. He always thought of things a little faster.

"Time is dragging on so terribly," the stout woman said. "Let's hope our patience is rewarded in the end. Here we are—stuck like nuts on a bolt—and up above, on the street, things must be coming to an end. This German horse isn't going to run very far." Her soft face puffed up when she smiled; her neck quivered.

Later in the evening, the caretaker took a second candle out of the box and replaced the one that had melted down to nothing more than a little stub.

"What are we going to do?" the woman on the chopping block asked suddenly. "What time is it?" She was trying to imagine the clock turning backward. Her voice sounded choked.

"We'll stay here—what else? What would you want to do? What could you do outside?" the caretaker asked. "You can hear the patrol walking right above us. And they're shooting all the time. The Germans won't surrender, and our side won't retreat. This is a revolution. It's either going to destroy us or them."

Upon hearing her husband's words, the caretaker's wife stopped feeling ashamed.

"A few bullets . . . you call this a revolution?" the older teenager said. His voice cracked and it sounded hollow and gruff, like it came from the shadow of the thick, damp walls themselves, condemned to darkness. He reached over and picked up the ax from the floor. "Whoever wants to can take this ax and go upstairs and try man-to-man revolution."

"They're still walking," said the little one, as if trying to temper the other's outburst. Walking soldiers meant passing danger. Their march kept time, and when the walking stopped, lives as well as time stopped.

It crossed the minds of both the caretaker and his wife that the two teenagers considered all of the inhabitants of the cellar—the caretaker included—cowards, even though the two of them were also hiding. The taller one constantly looked at little Olga. Then he'd spit or mumble in his low, cracking voice. Something was irking him. There was something dangerous in a voice like that, the caretaker thought. He'd never liked such voices. They were rough; you never knew what to expect of a person with such a voice. For a fleeting moment the caretaker felt he should get rid of the teenagers, kick them out of the cellar. Then he felt ashamed of the feeling.

"The doors are solid, there's no doubt about that," the taller teenager said to the little one, "a mass of metal plate nailed as tight as a coffin."

"Did you see the inscription?" the caretaker asked, intending his remark for everyone.

The taller teenager recalled the black metal sheet on the door of the building with the plate which read, in both Czech and German, "Prague Council of Jewish Elders."

"Jews," the little one said. "So what?"

"That's why, you idiot," the taller one answered.

"Who's an idiot?"

The children's eyes were riveted on the taller teenager. He looked secretive in his fur jacket. The rabbit fur was sewn inside out. The caretaker was sure the older teenager's sneer was meant for him.

"For all our bad luck, we've struck it pretty good," said the taller teenager to his friend. "I guess whatever isn't bad luck has got to be good luck, you old prophet."

The caretaker became annoyed. "It doesn't make any difference what you call it. The important thing is that without weapons—and we'd better not count on that rusty ax—it's better not to stick your head out. We wouldn't be helping anybody."

"They're walking," squeaked the little one.

Artillery fire could be heard outside.

The caretaker's wife turned and whispered to her husband that the woman in the beige suit was probably sick.

The caretaker wondered what it was going to be like when everyone tried to save his own skin. He coughed dryly, as if he had something important to say. But he didn't speak. The woman on the chopping block turned to him.

"I thought it might be safe to leave, now that it's dark outside."

"Possibly," the caretaker answered slowly. "But we'd be taking a risk since we have no idea what's going on upstairs. You can hear it yourself. Wait until I go up to the tower. From the tower gallery I'll be able to see everything."

They could still hear the chatter of the guns clearly; they'd just become used to the sound and were no longer aware of it as before.

"We can't eat up all your supplies," the woman on the chopping block said. Then she held her head cocked, listening. The German cannon was shooting at the Old Town Hall. "There are five of you including your children; we're strangers and I . . . "

She was interrupted by a loud crash. Apparently, a house nearby was tumbling down.

They could all picture the dust, the smoke, the roof fallen to the pavement. And then they listened, as if expecting ambulances and fire engines to pull up with their sirens shrieking. But everything was quiet, except for the rumbling.

"Don't mention it," the caretaker suddenly said to the woman on the chopping block. "The war is about to end, no matter how we end up down here. Those who will survive will have to learn how to live differently and to manage their affairs in a new way."

He spoke fast to make them forget the crashing sound. All of a sudden, he got the idea that he should tell them what he'd heard at the Black Hound Tavern on Soul Street—that bread could have been free in the East, if the Germans hadn't burned and devastated all the land from Nemen to the Volga. He felt they were ready to listen to him: He was gathering up all that was best in him, beyond himself, themselves, beyond Germany. But he only stammered, "Too much to explain at once. But it will be different for our children. I'm sure of that . . . "

The caretaker's wife wondered what he meant by all that; she was waiting for the crashing sound of the wreckage to stop. Suddenly she remembered that her husband once took his ration of bread to the Black Horse Tavern, claiming he'd get some unroasted coffee for it. She never got the coffee and he never mentioned the bread.

"Don't they have even a little bit of feeling—enough at least to show their better face before the end?" she asked.

"The sky's falling," the taller teenager broke in contemptuously.

He was caressing his fur jacket with obvious pleasure. It clearly wasn't made by a tailor.

The crashing stopped and it became silent again. Everyone wondered where it had happened, which house it had been. It could have been on Paris Avenue or on Soul Street. Or it could have happened in the small Market Square where the hardware store was. In the silence, all the imagined distances flowed together.

After a pause, the silence was again broken by the stout woman. She wore a camel hair coat and turned up its stuart collar to keep warm. "Oh God, oh God," she repeated over again. "To be caught so unaware."

The caretaker expected her to start talking about her son in England again. Her son was in some famous squadron with the word "Mandalay" in its name. She did begin to speak about him, and she told them that when her son came back as an officer, marching down National Avenue, she'd be there on the mothers' stand waving. They listened, but nobody had any idea what "Mandalay" meant.

She added a question unrelated to what she was saying before. "And how many of them fall into the sea? La Manche is there, you know.

How many were downed over Germany? What kind of people are we? Do we really deserve this?" And then, suddenly, "I have a bright apartment. All the windows are on the sunny side."

The woman on the chopping block looked up fearfully and then dropped her glance again, extinguished by the gray stone floor, the coldness of the cellar, and the shadows that covered everything in darkness.

"It's quiet now," the caretaker's wife said. "I'll go up and make some more soup. I'll thicken it a little; I've got enough. If you have any trouble going to sleep it's just the thing."

The caretaker turned to the woman on the chopping block. "You can't leave yet. You'll manage through the night, and in the morning we'll all go our separate ways."

He immediately realized that this might be interpreted as meaning he was turning them out.

"But only if it's quite safe. I won't let you out otherwise. Not now, not even in the morning. Not even in a week."

He didn't mention anything about going up to the tower to see what was happening and which house had been hit. Then he turned to his wife.

"Yes, go, you're right. If you have enough flour and margarine, thicken it up. Like when Oldrich came home from the hospital."

The two teenagers suddenly started conversing.

"They're walking. You can't stop it," the older one said. Walking soldiers could also mean approaching danger.

"Why stop it?" the little one replied. "Let them walk."

The taller teenager with the gruff voice looked about until his eyes rested upon the caretaker.

"Are there rats here?" he asked. "When I fall asleep, I prefer to be without rats."

The caretaker could always recognize the taller teenager in the darkness by his idiosyncratic voice. The caretaker answered, angry at the teenager for bringing up the rats.

"We used to have traps here, but recently the mice moved toward the river."

"The rats probably didn't have anything to eat here," wheezed the younger teenager. His head was completely shaven, but the hair was beginning to grow back in a semicircle that looked like a lawn sprayed with india ink. A gray stripe ran down the middle of his head.

"Where I'm from, it's the other way around," the taller one said, correcting the younger one. "So much the better."

"For crying out loud, how much longer are you two going to talk about this?" the stout woman with the son in the RAF protested.

The teenagers in their fur jackets paid no attention to her. In the meantime, the caretaker's wife had gone upstairs. The caretaker arranged the jute bags for the children and added canvas bags to the blankets so everyone could stay warm. "Well, here you are, like little Rockefellers. You couldn't sleep more comfortably."

He was wondering where the teenagers had come from. The story about the hospital on Kelley Street seemed strange. He listened to their muffled conversation, to the breaking voice, and to the voice that squeaked like a mouse. He felt that they were poking fun at one another. Yet somewhere in the noise of their words he could feel something else. They talked loudly, almost without a sense of the present danger, and the caretaker didn't want to ask them any unnecessary questions. Here today—and tomorrow, maybe at the end of the world. The second candle was burning out. Just as the caretaker was planning to light a third, his wife returned with the soup. He felt the presence of the city around him in the cold babbling of the river and in the wind and pervading darkness.

"They're walking," the taller teenager said.

"Well, is that something new?" squeaked the little one.

The caretaker was about to tell the female guests to lie down beside the children, if they didn't mind the bags; but the stout woman said, as though talking to herself, "My son is twenty-four. Maybe he's taking off just now on some mission, or maybe he's landing. And he doesn't have an inkling . . . "

The caretaker's wife returned with silver tablespoons for everyone. It was pea soup, thickened with white sauce she'd been saving for Olga. She had to wake the children. Throughout the war she'd been saving things, depriving herself for Olga's sake. She felt that if something happened to Olga, she'd hang herself. She'd improved the soup by dropping golden brown croutons into each plate. Again she served the woman on the chopping block first.

"Here," she said, "when I found the bread I was so happy I burst into tears. It's just nerves."

"Thank you," the woman responded in a low whisper. There was so much gratitude in her eyes that the caretaker's wife was embarrassed.

The caretaker again covered the wire netting on the window with a piece of rag. He removed the shade from the candle and they could see relatively well once again.

The woman on the chopping block squinted from the light. Her light complexion seemed more pallid than before and the blush on her cheekbones darker; her face had aged considerably, as if years had passed since it got dark and she began to eat. She placed her gloves on the floor and held the soup plate between her small red hands. In front of her she imagined the lower clock. She saw it as a windmill turning against the wind. The propellers of the windmill turned in a direction opposite that of man—not from life to death, but backward.

"It would be better backward," she whispered.

"This could be silver," the taller teenager said knowledgeably, holding his spoon in the light.

"It was a wedding present," the caretaker's wife told him. "It's all clean; you don't have to be afraid."

"I could tell by the weight." His Adam's apple suddenly jerked up and down. With a grin he said, "There's nothing I'm afraid of, Mrs. Belleles."

"Why don't you tell them that you had silverware at home, too?" the smaller teenager said with a smirk.

"It's easy to tell by the weight and taste."

"God," the stout woman sighed. "It really isn't just. We don't deserve to have to listen to this bickering."

"Please eat," the caretaker encouraged, trying to put an end to the conversation.

He wanted to say that this was wedding silver, reserved for special occasions. They had two dozen pieces, but after the war they'd never again be able to gather that many friends and relatives together, even if they counted both his family and his wife's.

Everyone thanked him and complimented him on the food, even the woman with smoldering eyes on the chopping block. She had eyes like a smoldering hearth, he thought. But in her thoughts were the turning clocks, both the lower and upper one, and she saw the way they opposed each other like beginning and end, or life and death. The stout woman with the son in England was nervously clutching a clipping from an underground newspaper. It was five years old. The article contained excerpts from a speech made by the British Prime Minister at a time when it seemed the Germans would conquer England just as they'd overrun Poland, France, and Holland. "Pea soup . . . that may lead to air pollution," the taller teenager remarked with a grin. "Well," he said to everyone, "at least it will be warm here."

The little one was grinning. "I'm always the one who gets the blame," he squeaked.

"Are there any more blankets upstairs?" the caretaker asked his wife.

"Only jute bags, most likely," she replied.

A volley of shots upstairs cut off her words. The shooting was on Maisel Street, not on Paris Avenue. It was followed immediately by another volley or two. It wasn't the revolutionary's machine gun from the corner house. The caretaker would have recognized that. He knew it wasn't a German cannon, either. The sound came from above, muffled by something. It sounded as though there was only a wall or a house between the person who shot and those who were listening.

"Oh, my God," the stout woman screamed, "it's the Germans."

"Put out that torch," said the taller teenager. "We don't want to get in the middle of any fireworks right away. So the gravedigger's after us," he added. "Mr. Belleles might as well prepare our shrouds since he's so good at tailoring."

The taller one laughed gruffly at his own remarks while the little one peeped, "Where was it?"

His friend's voice was cracking again. "It sounds close by." His sharp Adam's apple bobbed up and down.

The caretaker immediately put out the light. They could smell the smoke as the wick dipped into the yellow pool of melted wax. The cellar was riddled with the sound of crackling and sizzling. The acrid smoke filled their nostrils.

"I don't think it was the Germans," the caretaker said.

As he said this the cellar rumbled. They'd all become very familiar with the sound, the sound that had come before the roar of the house crashing down on Paris Avenue or somewhere close by. But they didn't know exactly where the house was because the caretaker lacked the courage to go up to the tower. Now everything trembled. The caretaker was glad it was dark in the cellar so no one could see him raise his arms suddenly, as if in surrender. He stuffed his fingers in his ears, which were buzzing.

"It didn't go our way," he said, listening to his own voice. "It's over for us."

"You might as well take measurements for my shroud," the taller teenager said. "If we luck out, I can always have it dyed another color."

Little Olga burst into tears. Her sobs came in spasms, as if she knew she wasn't supposed to cry aloud.

Her mother tried to stretch her arms around all three children—little Olga, blue-eyed Toni, her oldest, Oldrich—as if she could protect them in some way. She was no longer thinking of the things that could shame her. She felt something was coming—some sort of shame after all. She kept pressing the children to her. The caretaker was listening intently. He waited for the sound of the crashing wall. But it didn't come.

"It must have passed over us," he said after a while.

"I won't let anything spoil that silver spoon for me," the taller teenager mumbled. "'Cause if you can hear it and it ain't entered your flesh yet, then it must have gone over you."

The caretaker was suddenly grateful for the coarse tone of the teenager's words.

"Well, enjoy your food, you old Garden of Gethsemane," the taller one taunted the smaller one.

The children thought this very funny. The taller teenager grinned contentedly, glad he could quiet the little girl's tears.

"As I was telling you, my twelfth apostle, no matter how scared I am, I won't let anyone take this warm pea soup from me. Over my dead body."

"It's all over," the caretaker announced.

"What'll we do with the plates when we're finished?" the taller teenager asked calmly.

"Should I tell you?" the little one squeaked.

Then, in the darkness of the cellar, the group listened to the sound of their own breathing and to the warmth of human bodies around them. The caretaker wondered whether someone had managed to enter the town hall attic through the roof on Paris Avenue or on Red Street or maybe even Josefovska Street and, if someone did, had he set up his shooting gallery in the window above the clock running backward? There he could take aim at the German cannoneers across the street. He was suddenly sure you could take the best aim at the German cannon from precisely that window. It was no more than two hundred yards, straight across, over the crowns of the silver spruce in the nearby park and over the broken black statue of an angel. The caretaker imagined the yellow side wall of the town hall as it looked from Red Street and pictured the clock tower with the Hebrew characters instead of figures—everything reversed on the face. He imagined the window and the second clock above the balcony with brass ornaments that looked golden against the black of the old Hebrew clock. Again he imagined the fallen marble statue—the black angel—with its broken limbs and heavy pedestal. He could go upstairs to tell the sniper that there were women and children here; he imagined all of Paris Avenue and the adjoining streets, the sidewalks lined with the bodies of wounded men. You couldn't walk the street for fear of stumbling over the bodies.

Little Olga was still crying softly. He could tell where the others were by the sounds they made when they shifted places. He could hear the brushing of skin. The caretaker heard his heart beat. He was ashamed that it beat so loudly. He really should go upstairs, he told himself, before the cannon's single direct hit razed the town hall. Again he recalled the black marble angel in the park. The angel's head and the left side of its chest were missing.

He remained sitting, his head in his hands, pressing his temples. The upstairs clock made a sound like a whip thrashing his head. Olga was now only sniffling, "Mommy, mommy . . ."

"We should have left while it was still light," the stout woman said when all was quiet.

The caretaker was glad he'd suppressed his earlier desire to go upstairs. It was better that he remained sitting and hadn't been hasty. But he couldn't rid his mind of the image of the sniper inside the lower clock, firing, drawing attention to the tower. He imagined the next volley from the German cannon would bury them in the cellar, which had only one entrance; bury them under thick walls over five hundred years old, enormous foundations below, and a mountain of masonry above. Inside all of this were three children, three women, two teenagers, and himself—nine pairs of human eyes trying not to betray their knowledge of what lay beyond the walls around them. He tried to take his thoughts elsewhere. He'd been a tailor and had made suits and coats for people in this quarter. Then he'd improved his situation by becoming a caretaker. Maybe this thing about the sniper in the lower or upper clock was just an idea fixed in his mind.

The silence was broken by the voice of little Toni, who was whispering in the dark, "Kitty, Kitty . . . Fina . . . where have you been for so long? Come, Fina, warm us up." And finally, after a long pause, "Well, at last we're all here . . . the whole family's together."

The cat stayed with the children only for a moment. They could hear her meow and they heard the rustle of her paws as she slipped by them and disappeared.

"Cats are too tough for me," the taller teenager said in his gruff voice to his smaller partner. "Kids, does someone want my rabbit vest?"

"Take mine, too," the smaller one peeped, but no one answered.

The caretaker had to say something before he choked. He didn't want to lie, not even to himself. He was waiting for the sniper's shot above him and for the rumble that would follow. He heard the crashing in his temples. And then he imagined he'd hidden a flag under the mechanisms of the tower clocks.

"I want to go up for the remaining jute bags," the caretaker said at last.

"No," his wife replied quickly. "Don't go anywhere. At least not yet."

The caretaker felt her hot fingers as she clutched his.

"No," she repeated. "Not now." And then there was all the shame in her voice she'd wanted to hide, but she didn't release her clutch.

"Should I light the candle?" the caretaker asked.

Suddenly he knew the deep voice of the one with the sharp Adam's apple wasn't dangerous. He wanted to look into the eyes of the stout woman who clung so comically to the glorious feats of her son, the pilot with the squadron named "Mandalay;" and he wanted to look at the woman with the eyes like a smoldering hearth. He never thought it would happen like this.

He imagined himself still alive at the time when everything would be covered with rubble, when the cannon would have avenged the sniper's shots in the upper portion of the lower clock. He knew he didn't want to survive at the ugly price of failure, of making the unknown sniper lose his aim. He knew he couldn't control his thoughts, and he was ashamed of them; he couldn't prevent them and they persisted.

To his wife he said, "Don't be afraid; I won't go yet. Don't worry."

It grew silent, and the stillness of the guns above offered a fleeting feeling of security.

"If anybody touches that candle or those matches, I won't hesitate to give him a smack with the ax that's by the block," the taller teenager said calmly. He wrapped himself in his fur and looked like a hunter.

The little one squeaked, "As far as I'm concerned, I'd prefer to sit in the dark for a while, even with the rats."

The woman who came last whispered, "Isn't it all backward? Didn't they know what they were doing was wrong? They deceived him . . . they lied to him . . . to the end . . . could they have believed their own lies? Can they so easily swallow their murders?"

She looked at the children, then turned to the caretaker, keeping her eyes on the two teenage boys.

The voice of the taller teenager again cranked out in confidence. "With an ax. What do you say to that, you Mount of Zion?"

The children didn't understand this and didn't laugh.

"Let's see what happens if we close our eyes and try to sleep," the smaller teenager squeaked. "It can't do any harm. Anyone against that idea?"

Again, no one answered, but everyone was silent for what seemed like a long time.

The breathing of the children and the snoring of the teenagers intermingled. At times the caretaker thought the woman with the smoldering eyes was crying, although she hadn't made a sound. He could only make assumptions in the darkness. The taller teenager mumbled something. He tossed and turned from side to side, emitting a sound like a low howl. The little one calmed him.

"Nothing's happening, so let me sleep."

The caretaker tried to answer the puzzle that tormented him: the sound of a pistol upstairs, strangely close—where had it come from? He was expecting two sounds: first the pistol, then the avenging cannon. At the same time, he listened to his children's breathing. He placed his fingers in his ears to stop the sounds from entering his head; he still had to think. There was time to run upstairs, to get into the space with the lower clock, the hands which moved counterclockwise. His eyes felt as though they were popping out of the darkness. Finally, he closed them again.

"Aren't you going to sleep?" asked his wife, Olga.

"No. I don't have to. I'll sleep later."

She said quietly, "I'm going to try to close my eyes for a bit."

He felt this was both the beginning and the end. They were caught in between, pulled by the opposing forces. The last night of the war? For them, for the city, for the world? In this dark cellar? And so his thoughts continued to drift, moving forward and then coming back.

Early in the morning, they heard pounding on the door. The outer doors of the town hall were old; the wide gate and the small doorway for the servants and pedestrians creaked because the dry wood had rotted. The sheets of metal that covered the door and the quiet of the hall at daybreak made the noise seem much louder.

"They're coming for us," the woman on the chopping block managed to say with effort.

"Wait," the caretaker said quietly. "Maybe somebody else wants to hide here."

At the moment he said it, he meant that the person who was in the window behind the tower clock had perhaps climbed down and couldn't go anywhere else.

"I knew it," said the stout woman.

"Don't turn on the lights," the caretaker's wife pleaded.

The night continued on toward morning like a border that had to be crossed. The caretaker waited for the dry sound of the pistol to come from the gallery of the tower. All his thoughts were mixed with the vision of the broken black marble angel and the man in the clock.

"Get up, you old battle-ax," the taller teenager ordered the little one. "Move back into the darkness."

"All right," the little one peeped.

The two teenagers moved their jute bags to the edge of the chimney where the shadows were still deep.

"He's using the butt of his gun," the taller teenager said, demonstrating the motion with his hands. "I'll bet anything it's the butt of a gun."

"They'll knock the doors in," the caretaker said. "It will be better if I go and open up for them."

"They'll think we're all Jews," the stout woman blurted out. Behind the chimney, the teenagers silently noted how the stout woman was shouting that they weren't Jews, while the caretaker's wife repeated one word over and over: "Children, children . . ."

The taller teenager spat. The spittle landed on the jute bag.

"You pig," the little one exclaimed.

"You know I don't like it when officers are mentioned." The taller teenager muttered. "As long as I live, I never want to hear that word."

That was all he said and only the little one understood, but he didn't make a sound. The taller one was lost in his thoughts. In his mind he could see the officer in the old camp pick up his sister, taking her into his arms as if to fondle her. She was so little she could still take only a few steps. Then he had lifted her above his head and held her fast by the hands and feet as if he wanted to whirl her around. But he hadn't. The taller one couldn't forget how he had lost his sister, what the officer had done to her with only one pull.

The taller teenager was now stroking the rabbit fur diligently. "Don't be a fool, little one," he said to Olga. "You don't want to cry now, wait until it's daylight. I'd like to be standing by the wall with your cat, that Finis, Fina, whatever you call it. I'd like to wrap her around my neck like a muffler. And then I'd teach her how to dance on her tail to make you happy."

Little Olga listened to him, crinkling her nose and pouting. She took in the taller teenager's stares. Upstairs, the pounding grew stronger. "You're a real nursemaid, you know?" the smaller teenager squeaked. "Why don't you try comforting me a little?"

"Sure, you're the one who needs it," the taller one muttered. Now his voice wasn't cracking.

Suddenly the little one changed his expression. He peered into the corner of the cellar closet nearest to him. In a crevice that widened from the edge to the inside of the wall was a rat, staring into the darkened room with its bright eyes.

Both of them began to laugh, but only for an instant; the rat backed up and disappeared into its crevice. The little one felt lucky. His eyes held the assurance that where rats weren't afraid, neither he nor his companions had anything to fear.

"I know we're all right," the little one answered, as if he could see the wheel of fate begin to spin in the right direction.

The sound of the caretaker's footsteps as he walked upstairs mixed with the pounding on the door. Finally they heard the clinking of the lock and the doors opening. The hobnailed boots of soldiers clanked on the stone floor, which was made of big tiles in the shape of six-cornered stars. They could hear it all as clearly as if they were upstairs alongside the caretaker. The sound was quickly drowned out by another volley of gunfire which stiffened them with fear.

The woman with the eyes like a smoldering hearth covered her mouth with her hands, as though she'd been struck. She grabbed the hand of the caretaker's wife and breathed heavily.

"I should have been the one to go," the wife whispered. "I should have gone alone."

She looked across at the two teenagers.

"Germans," the stout woman pronounced.

"Germans," the caretaker's wife echoed.

"We shouldn't have let them wait so long...God...my poor son..." the stout woman said.

A heavy step, followed by the echo of another, was heard descending from the dawn. And then—in the glare of a lantern covered by protective wire netting resembling a dog's muzzle—the group discerned the figure of a soldier in a German battle jacket.

The soldier stopped by the dusty lattice doors, looked around, and said, "Pack of swine." This was his introduction. "Is anyone else here?" he added.

This wasn't said in the same threatening tone he'd used before, but he wasn't waiting for an answer. He took a long, sharp, skeptical look at everything the arc of his lantern revealed: little redheaded Olga and her two brothers lying on the jute bags, the two women holding hands, the kettle with the remains of the pea soup, the mess of the scattered plates, the heavy silver spoons. The light revealed a deep scar on his forehead. It looked like two scars that had run together, dividing his skull and his forehead.

The stout woman was shaking. The more she thought of her son, the more she shook.

"You . . . shaking like that," the soldier said gruffly. "Cut it out! We're human like you."

The scar on the soldier's forehead was furrowed by several wrinkles, as though he were in deep thought. He stared at the gleam of the German silver spoons and at the same time at the woman whose son was in England and who couldn't stop shaking, even after he told her to stop.

The soldier sighed. "Well, are we the ones who started the war? I'm not playing this game of my own free will."

His stare moved from one to the other, as if he were expecting a reply.

Hidden by the shadows, the teenagers watched him. The taller one still had the idea fixed in his head that if they got out of this one they would be home safe. He saw the man standing with legs spread in handsome leather boots. He kept staring at the soldier's epaulets, for the twelfth time reassuring himself that this was just a simple soldier, not an officer. At the same time, he stared a little at Olga; he couldn't help thinking that she was a redhead like his sister had been. He was clenching the little teenager's shoulder.

The smaller one studied the soldier's forehead. He was trying to decide what made the soldier tick and what could be expected of him. Words were only words, and so he was on his guard, watching the soldier's face, his every move. The soldier's helmet was set low on his forehead, covering as much of the scar as possible. He was well armed. He even had a grenade under his left thumb in the hand with the lantern. He had a double belt of grenades strung like beads across his chest and back; in his right hand, he held a tommy gun at the ready, and on his hip were revolvers in open cases. All he had to do was move and he clattered like an ammunition warehouse. It was obvious that he weighed less than the arms he was carrying. His green eyes glimmered like a cat's.

The taller teenager knew that with just one of the soldier's weapons he could gain more confidence. He crouched involuntarily, ready to spring. He bit his lower lip until it began to bleed. Hidden behind the soldier stood his three companions.

"How many times do I have to ask you who's here?" the first soldier roared. His scar immediately swelled and turned purple and red. He turned to the woman who was sitting on the chopping block, closest to the entrance. "Get up!" he bellowed.

The fourth soldier was armed with a bayonet instead of a tommy gun. He stepped forward and prodded the woman, aiming the blade at her back and pushing her toward the wall.

"It looks as though they've been feeding their faces here all the while," he said in German with a Saxon accent as he kicked the kettle and the block. Both rolled away noisily behind the woman.

"Everybody against the wall," shouted the third armed man as he, too, stepped forward. He was holding a grenade under his thumb like the first man.

"We're not Jews," the stout woman started. Her fleshy throat vibrated like a mass of white jelly, pushed and prodded by an invisible hand.

"Against the wall, I said," the third soldier repeated. "No exceptions. Against the wall."

The caretaker's wife grabbed little Olga and quickly dragged her across the floor toward the wall until her knees became bloodied.

"I'm not going to say it three times, you can bet. Down. *Dalli, Dalli* . . ."

The teenagers hadn't moved, although the order had been given twice.

"Officers," the stout woman's insistent voice cried out. The taller teenager bit his lip hard at the sound of this word. "It must be a mistake . . . we're not Jews, even if we are here."

"Face the wall," the third soldier said. His voice was a young man's. He couldn't have been more than eighteen, perhaps twenty. But he sounded coarse—much different from the days when he'd sung in the choir of the little town of Wolfen, not far from the city of Halle.

The stout woman whose son was in the RAF didn't have the chance to tell the soldiers that it would be a terrible mistake if they shot them now because they weren't Jews—or at least she wasn't one.

"Can't you hurry it up?" the second soldier asked.

"Down," was the immediate order from the first soldier, the one with the cleft and swollen scar.

"Down you scum," the third one suddenly roared, aiming his gun, as he discovered the teenagers by the chimney.

"And you think we don't mean you?" the first one said to the teenagers, swinging his lantern around. "Everybody against the wall. I'm not going to say it three times, the third time we shoot."

"You obey or you've had it," the third one said in an amazingly clear and sonorous voice.

"Hands up above your heads," the other soldier with a gun insisted.

The taller teenager continued biting his lower lip. The tips of his fingers almost touched the ceiling and he knew he wouldn't be able to get hold of any weapons, although he knew where some were.

The shorter teenager's hands reached only slightly above the taller one's shoulders with his arms extended, although they were now bent at the elbows. The teenagers quickly moved close to one another, not wanting to separate. The taller one rested his palms against the wall, and his companion also found a way to rest. The wall was pleasantly cool, and the little one was in the seventh day of fever. It had been with him for a week, yet he paid little attention to it, indifferent but at the same time confident that the fever wouldn't kill him. But now, he would have liked to overcome it.

The cellar became very quiet again. The first soldier coughed in a friendly sort of way, as if he were sitting in a German pub drinking beer. He kept looking at the silver spoons. Then he wiped his lips with the back of his hand. It was an effort for him to raise the hand with the tommy gun so he could perform this function.

Suddenly there was a rustle in the empty corner. The first soldier immediately loosed a volley of shots in that direction. The third soldier started shooting in that direction as well, while the second stood aside for them. When the first one let the lantern shine in that direction, they saw the cat, Fina, mashed to a pulp on the wall, just a big, black, bloody spot.

"A cat," the soldier with the beautiful voice said, sounding somewhat relieved.

And the first soldier, the one whose purple swollen scar divided his forehead from the rest of his face, said, "Tough luck."

The smell of the shots filled the cellar. The caretaker's wife, stepping from one foot to the other, stepped on one of the spoons. It made a clinking noise. "Where's my husband? What did you do to him?"

"Shut up," said the third one quietly. "Shut your dirty trap now."

"Mommy, mommy . . ." Little Olga was squeaking as though she were in pain.

"They're children . . ." the caretaker's wife said in a lowered voice.

The soldier with the scar repeated, "Shut your mouth, woman. Or you'll be sorry. No one is to speak unless I ask you a question."

His gaze wandered to the spot where the remains of the cat lay, then to the spoons.

"Keep standing," the third said in disgust. "And keep your mouths shut. We're the ones giving the orders here, and we hope you know it."

"Who else is here? What's in the back?" the first soldier asked lazily, as if it were some sort of great effort to speak. "Is there some kind of hole back there?"

"Oh, officers . . ." the stout woman started. The taller teenager squirmed in pain.

The soldiers paid no attention to her and were not flattered that she'd mistaken their ranks. They started whispering among themselves. Then the one with the scar said louder to the second one, "Search the house and the main staircase—take Heinz with you. There is nothing more back here. This dump is as old as Babylon. I can take care of things here myself."

"But if need be..." the second one answered.

They knew that the young one with the voice fit for a choir was named Heinz.

They heard the soldiers run through the house. All the doors in the town hall had been opened. They heard different kinds of steps returning noisily downstairs. Suddenly there was an explosion. The soldier with the beautiful voice, Heinz, had thrown a grenade into the wooden outhouse in the courtyard. He threw another grenade onto the staircase, shattering the white statuettes and the golden, bronze, and brass candelabras on the walls—and all this was mixed with the laughter and voices of the two men as they approached the cellar. The soldier with the scar was constantly whistling the theme from *Alte Kamaraden*. Since he was quite alone, he didn't scold anyone any more. His eyes were searching for more silver spoons; he spotted six of them lying on the used plates. Whenever he moved, his weapons clattered.

"Well," he said when the other two rejoined him. "If anyone's got anything, raise your hands—you won't be hurt." He was addressing his prisoners. "You two," he said to the teenagers, "put your hands down. Well, is anyone going to raise his hand?" He turned to the man with the bayonet and said lazily, "Search them."

The second soldier searched all of them rapidly with his free hand. He took just a little longer with the women, as if they could have weapons concealed in the inner side of their thighs, between their legs, or around their hips. When he touched the breasts of the woman with the smoldering gray eyes, he did it as if he were picking an apple or pear off a branch, and he held his hand there much longer than was necessary.

"Who are you?" asked the soldier.

"No one who could interest you," she replied in German. Her smoldering gray eyes stared at the soldier. The soldier spat.

"What kind of nonsense is this?"

"Do you want to be the first to get a bullet in the head, woman?" the third solider asked. "This ax is a weapon, too, and we're not used to playing around, you know. Give me your name and date and place

of birth. And hurry before I stick this bayonet in your grease." He ran
his finger slowly down the blade of the bayonet carried by his partner.

The stout woman kept repeating "Mandalay," as if it were some
sort of mantra or charm.

"Agnes Kant, typist, born in Prague on April 20, 1910," the woman
with the smoldering eyes replied.

The third soldier looked at her in surprise. "Kant. I've heard that
name somewhere."

He made the end of his gun whistle by bringing the barrel close to
his lips and exhaling abruptly.

"School in East Prussia—*Ding an sich*—does that mean anything to
you? 'The starry sky above me, the moral law within me?'"

Finally, he said with a sigh, "The same birthday as our Führer."

"Tell them we're not Jews," the stout woman again insisted.

"What is this place, anyway, that you can be sitting here and having
a party like this?" the first soldier asked.

"Stuffing their bellies," the second one roared.

"These are my children and we've been living here for eleven years,"
the caretaker's wife said, embracing all three children. "When will my
husband be back?"

"It was a Jewish town hall," the woman with the smoldering eyes
said.

"Did you know there was a shooting above?" the first soldier asked.

"Of course they did," the soldier with the bayonet answered for the
prisoners. "Unless they've lost their hearing or their brains."

"There was no shooting here," the woman with the ashen gray eyes
said quietly. "If you shoot, you'll be the first."

"How dare she . . ." the second soldier with the bayonet asked.

"Yeah, a Jewish town hall," the third soldier said in his beautiful
singsong voice. Then he added very matter-of-factly, "Every floor has
at least a dozen typewriters. What for? What else could they want to
write? Names? They can write them on the walls." And he hissed
confidentially to the second one, "Hurry it up, we haven't got this much

time." His voice was childishly clear. "There can be a few more names—do you get me?" He laughed almost guilelessly.

The second soldier couldn't stand the stare of the woman with the eyes like a smoldering hearth. He moved the gun into his left hand and hit the woman's face with his right. He muttered hoarsely, "Look at the wall..." The eyes that stared back at him were dead. "And you, too! All of you! Stare at the wall..."

The third soldier added more calmly, "Light the candle."

And the first one, whose forehead was scarred and who constantly watched the scattered silver spoons, added, "Heinz, light the candle for them."

"Wait, I'll do it myself," said the second. He held the gun's barrel under his arm, its butt rested on the floor; he struck the match twice; to the other two he said something in his Saxon German. It sounded like, "Don't fool around with them too long. There was an ax here."

He finally managed to light the wick. The woman with the eyes like a smoldering hearth didn't turn; she kept staring at the soldiers, as if she were looking for something in their eyes that she couldn't find. Finally, she searched the face of the younger soldier with the beautiful voice who might not have been twenty.

The cellar was now burning with the bright yellow light. The first soldier started to collect the silver spoons and was stuffing them into his pocket where, apparently, he also had grenades, which he removed and held by their chain in the hand in which he held the tommy gun. He held the last grenade in his left hand. The woman saw that it looked like an iron pear in a wooden holder, as if the grenade wasn't a weapon at all, rather a treat to be put into the oven to bake. The first soldier's helmet slid back to his nape and his cleft scar became more noticeable. The other two whispered to each other and moved back. The woman constantly stared at the youngest one; no one could tell why. There was no reasoning with her.

When all three soldiers reached the far end of the hall where it broke off into right angles, and where the fourth soldier stood waiting, they walked backward a few steps like crayfish. Then the first one with the awful scar on his forehead threw his grenade. There was an immediate explosion, similar to the preceding ones, but this time close at hand. The waves of fire and noise and the sharp blast of air prostrated the people in the cellar in front of the wall. The walls in the bend of the hall cracked and fell. The woman with the gray eyes staggered and fell over the back of the stout woman. More grenades exploded—probably because the first one with the kindly voice needed to free his hands and pockets. There were more waves of fire and blasts of air, followed by sounds of breaking and shattering bricks. The hall reverberated with the echo, magnifying the sound. The candle went out. The window right under the ceiling shattered and the light fell in. A red flag shot full of holes was flying from a burned mast on the distended balcony across the street.

"Children!" the caretaker's wife cried.

"What are you shouting like that for?" the taller teenager asked, and his Adam's apple went up and down. "Is anyone here still alive? It looked for a while as if we were all ready for the undertaker."

Upstairs, the doors slammed shut and someone was closing them from the inside with a bar. The caretaker's wife raised her head as if sniffing. "My husband is alive. Children."

"We're buried here," the stout woman said.

The taller teenager turned to the little one. "Rest your dumb head on my shoulder, you thrice-crucified Son of God. Let me feel if they haven't made a sieve of you. Boy, is your head hot! It feels like it's been boiling in a kettle all this time. Thank God these boys weren't from the Waffen or Allgemeine SS or die Herren Waffe. They would have taken everything, even our underwear. This one was satisfied with spoons."

The woman whose eyes looked like a smoldering hearth finally straightened up and remained standing.

"Oh, God," said the stout woman who had a son in England. "How well you told them. They thought we were all Jews. There's an ax here and it could have been suspicious to them. They thought we were Jews and had no weapons. If they hadn't thought that, we wouldn't be here. The Jews can't hurt them, even if there is a revolution." And then she added: "How can anyone refer to these people as 'boys'? What was it the young one said—about the names on the walls?"

"It's too bad about the cat," squeaked the smaller teenager.

"Oh, what are you saying?" the stout woman said. "My God, we should be rejoicing."

The taller teenager spat loudly and the stout woman sighed. "Why must people be like that?"

The skinny teenager stroked the top of his friend's head. The care-taker was just entering. They could hear him climb over the scattered bricks in the rubble where the hallway had caved in. His wife fell on his neck and felt him all over, as if she believed she saw a specter instead of her husband, as if she had to convince herself. She cried softly.

"Are you all OK here?" asked the caretaker, brushing himself off. He was covered with dust like a bricklayer. He went on, "I had to stand upstairs all the time because the fourth one wouldn't leave me. He poked me in the ribs with the barrel of his gun. He told me right from the start that if they found a single Jew in this house they would make a windmill out of the double clocks on the side of the town hall. I had to give them the keys. They cut all the telephone wires, as if they were still connected. They were suspicious of a wooden box with clips from some Portuguese sardines and of a rubber stamp bearing the name of the Central Agency for the Jews . . . I showed them that the stamp was on almost everything in the former reception hall."

"Why are people so evil?" the stout woman who had a son in England asked slowly.

"You don't have to look very far for an answer," the caretaker said. His words seemed to give some relief.

The taller teenager looked at the caretaker and asked, "You're a Jew, too, aren't you?"

The caretaker looked at him with surprise. "Why?"

And the teenager said, "Well, I asked if you weren't Jewish too— just curious. But your wife isn't Jewish and the children are mixed?"

The caretaker said only, "Let me catch my breath." Then he under-stood and smiled.

"It's only because of her," the teenager said. He tossed his head toward the stout woman. "Every Gypsy tells fortunes according to his own stars . . . some are full of courage and goodness when it's over . . ."

The taller one turned to the woman with the smoldering eyes. She straightened the chopping block and sat down. Her suit was crumpled.

"Why were you staring so long at that German? There must be something wrong."

"Nothing's wrong," she said defensively. She was quiet then, but at last the woman said softly, "My husband is a soldier like those three that threw the grenades and took the spoons."

The taller teenager stood up and opened his eyes wide. His Adam's apple went up and down several times. "And you?" he asked.

"My son renounced his father," said the woman. "If he had said his father was a soldier, he wouldn't have ended up where he did." And she added, "My son never said a word. He never owned up to his father. His name was Heinz. He had blue eyes and blond hair. Like golden fleece. He went to the gas chamber. He was there where you were."

"How do you know where we were?" the taller teenager asked. His Adam's apple moved even when he fell silent. "Just because we came from Kelley Street?" He was choking on his saliva.

The woman sighed and closed her eyelids, blinking several times. They were almost transparent, as if she hadn't eaten in a long time. She wept. The stout woman kept repeating to herself that a word couldn't be a talisman, even if it was "Mandalay" and it stood for a country or a city or some famous squadron whose number she'd forgotten. She had only been half listening. All she could think about was what she'd said before, "Why are people so evil?"

"I had a little sister and she went, too," the teenager said before the caretaker could put in a word. "She was just learning to walk. She could just take her first few steps. She waddled like a duck, but she could keep her balance." He wanted to say it as gruffly as possible. "She didn't make it; I would have been glad if she had."

It struck him as strange that he'd tell these things to her, that he'd tell these things to someone from the other side. "Don't think about it all the time. It turns a person into a walking cemetery." His insides turned upside down; he didn't even ask her if her husband was an officer.

The caretaker stroked his children's heads. Suddenly the machine gun from the house on the corner rattled unexpectedly, firing on Paris Avenue. Once again it was followed by the old sound, so very close that the caretaker turned pale. They could hear it more easily than the previous day because the grenades had shattered the windows. The machine gun became silent for a moment. Even now, he said nothing.

All the caretaker said was, "The house is locked. I won't open it again. I won't open it unless it is our men."

"Well, you could have started sewing our shrouds," the older teenager said.

He removed his fur jacket and placed it around little Olga.

Everything began all over again, but now it was different for the taller teenager, who watched the woman on the chopping block and who never took his eyes from hers. The caretaker just watched a cobweb under the corner of the ceiling. A hundred times he told himself he'd taken it down and a hundred times he'd left it there. He knew what would happen if the machine gun in the corner house continued to rattle. He looked at his children, at his wife Olga, at the two teenagers, at the stout woman, at the woman on the chopping block. His thoughts were interrupted by a blast from the German cannon which came to avenge the machine gun in the corner house. The charge from the cannon knocked down the weather vane on the town hall, which was thin and shaped like a star. The blast also hit the mast with its seven-armed candelabrum, and the mast fell crashing down. It sounded like the roof was caving in. Just at this moment, the caretaker's wife was joyfully saying to herself, although she lacked the courage to say it out loud, that the sun was rising and it looked like a cheerful, beardless old man. She was saying to herself that the war would be over, that they were still young enough, even though they had these big sensible children, and they could have been buried alive down here but they weren't, that everything was beginning over again. And she felt she understood what peace would be like.

Both of them were thinking that there would be a new beginning, yet it was actually quite otherwise. The second charge from the cannon hit lower, as the barrels of the German cannons were lowered. The path of the shell shattered even the pedestal of the stone angel in the park between Red Street and the house on the corner with the dead machine gun. Fist-sized pieces of schrapnel knocked down the mast.

The woman with the eyes like a smoldering hearth grabbed the two teenagers by their dirty and bony wrists and held them fast, sobbing. The caretaker's wife held her children, but her stare circled around the other woman's eyes; each an ember that glowed like a hot sun, warping the air around it into a half smile, then a frown.

At that moment, the German cannon was aimed precisely at the tower which housed the clock that turned backward.

RED OLEANDERS

Things remain only what they are.
———From an old song

Only man looks like a fortress that surrenders when it has stood its ground.
———A saying

Only in human eyes can loyalty seem faithless and love look like betrayal.
———From an old song

ONE

1

In Acre, between Nahariyya and Haifa, next to the cannery and close to the police station, they built an insane asylum. In one of the cells lived a man who had escaped from Auschwitz-Birkenau in the summer of 1944. He brought with him all sorts of documents and plans that detailed the fate of the Family Camp in B-II where six thousand people from Bohemia died in the ovens in a single night—most of them children and their parents. Among those killed were his wife, his brother, and the smaller of his two sons. He made it to Lake Constance on the Bodensee and sent his testimony to America.

The old man never spoke or wrote to anyone, nor did he receive any letters or visitors. He lost all power of speech, but not because the Germans ripped out his tongue in the experimental barracks of the prison infirmary as they had done to his other son who had survived the war. The last thing that the sick man said was that after his escape from Auschwitz-Birkenau the Germans still managed to kill over a million people there, and that some people tend to forgive and forget in order to get on with their lives.

It was reported that he watched the sea constantly, as if waiting for someone's return. He had a biblical name no one remembered and became a legend in the area for his silence.

Before the sick man died, he watched from the window of his cell how they loaded old freighters with wheat, engines, and coal. It was known that in the winter of 1945 and the spring and summer of 1946 the old man had, with the assistance of the Hagana, organized transports into the Promised Land for displaced persons waiting in the camps in West Germany. His eyes always held unanswered questions: Where did all the lost people go? Where are the words for that? Why are the words not important anymore? There wasn't time before his death to tell him that his mute son had hung himself.

The asylum stood at the edge of the bay and was clearly visible even from Nahariyya. Mountains rose from either side of the shore and a desert spread to the east. On the western side loomed oil refineries resembling silver rings on the fingers of Mother Earth. In the distance, where the hilltops and the lowlands of the Nahariyya converged like two rivers, each day was filled with the sounds of people, horses, dogs, cats, wild birds on the cliffs, and music from the restaurants, Raveh's and the Pinguin, and from the garden of the Pension Popper.

At nightfall the songs and music from Raveh's would hover over the seashore and the water tower, which looked like a lighthouse, even with its seven-branched candelabra on the roof. The sounds floated among the clouds which had given no rain for the last eight months. An hour before dusk, a one-engined fighter plane that had been flying along the shore, from Rosh Haniqra, over Nahariyya to Acre, turned above the insane asylum and flew back. The wind carried off the sounds, smells, and songs.

The gulls screamed *Tee ooo terrr . . . Tee eee terrr . . .* from the tops of the cliffs, and the sea roared below.

2

"I'm much more practical now," said Daniela. "I wouldn't trade this for anything. Here I've found everything that I'd lost in Prague—all that no longer exists there for people like me."

"I guess I know what you mean," Kamil Dreisler answered.

She was thinking of the man who, in 1945—six weeks after World War II had ended—spat in the street when he saw her black hair and wondered whether Hitler had not failed in his job. Kamil Dreisler watched the flocks of seagulls. The seashore seemed drowsy as the darkness fell on the water like a thin veil that slowly became thicker as the earth and sky became one.

"No you don't," said Daniela.

"You're pretty." Kamil Dreisler looked at her.

"Why are we what we are?" she asked. "Never two and never one? It's so easy to accept now."

"Everything seems easy," Kamil Dreisler said. "Coming, staying, going."

"When you weren't here and I was alone, I watched the sea. The white caps of waves remind me of men kneeling behind cannons. And the foam sometimes looks like a man approaching. Do we really have to leave? Who or what is telling you to leave?"

"We've discussed that already."

"I won't leave you anymore."

"You left me once."

"Only to come here."

She felt a shiver she did not know, an energy she did not understand. It changed every day, hour, and second of her nineteen years. She now measured this time differently, along with all the places she'd known: Prague, Auschwitz-Birkenau, the big fortress Theresienstadt, Bergen-Belsen, the military camp in which she had trained the Voluntary Jewish Brigade in 1948, and on board the S.S. *Casserta* from Genoa to Nahariyya. They all melted into one. And all languages merged into a single comprehensible language, and many feelings of many countries into a single country. Confused feelings gave way to feelings of new self-confidence, many questions found a single answer, and desire bore closeness. This was her new secret strength. For the first time in her life she felt that the world was at her fingertips, that her dreams, forebodings, and desires were tangible. It was like creating from chaos her own world where she could be happy. But the word happiness scared her a little.

She watched the expression on Kamil Dreisler's face and thought of her own expression. She surrendered to her forthcoming existence like a bird resting its wings on air, like a fish breaking water, or horses running along the shore. Can one forget—even momentarily—that which was, that which one does not want? Maybe. Can one forget humiliations and past worries so easily? Maybe. She smiled.

She felt the pounding of her heart. She smoothed her dress, yellow with big green leaves.

"I would do anything for you to stay," she said.

Her smile denied the anxiety in her alto voice. Daniela's eyes were hazel. She was tanned from the summer sun. As she watched the cradles of the sea, the movements of the waves flowed into one another.

"We'll leave together, as agreed," Kamil Dreisler said.

One of the seagulls dove into the water and grabbed a fish. He flew up with his prey.

"I'll leave but I won't like it. I wouldn't leave with anyone else."

Then she said, "How can Pharaoh Blumen say that family is everything, perhaps more than love, when he's been living all alone as far as anyone can remember? He'll end up in the asylum one day. There are soldiers living in the Pension Popper. The army pays for their lodgings. Most of them are only slightly wounded." Then she said, "Isn't it strange? Since the morning we've been thinking about the same things, but we talk about something else."

"Did they let you keep the gun when you left the army?"

"I had to give it back. But I did it reluctantly."

Kamil Dreisler watched the bay. The wind blew. It mixed with the cries of the birds, the waves, and the music from Raveh's. It was the third time they played "Kiss me, Harry, kiss me . . ." They were lying but now sat up halfway. The sand underneath accommodated them. They leaned on a rock that lay there, like an anchor, smoothed by the waves and covered with mosses and seaweed. The shoreline was long and curved and smelled of dead fish, salt water, and tar. Some pieces of wood drifted ashore; polished like marble by the water, they looked like sculptures of men and women, or children or demons, or water nymphs—crossbreeds of men and animals, water sprites and sea horses, mysterious and innocent, tossed out on the sand.

"Here at the dock, the people from kibbutz Sasa wash their horses. You'll see in the morning. I wouldn't mind working there. I like the horses. They range in colors, all deep, rich as the shades of the sea, the sky or fruit. They're like the color of soil when they run on the shore, in the sand, over the dunes. Mahogany skin, the color of the sand, or blue-black like my hair. Sometimes they have a prettier brash red which the rose cannot approach, the chestnut horses with shoulders the color of sorrel. I like when the sun shines on them and you can still see the ridge of mountains across the waterside." She added, "I already know what I've learned from the horses. A horse wants you to respect him. He's patient. He's big and powerful enough to harm you. The people at the kibbutz told me that a horse will always try you. You must control the horse. Never let him turn his rear to you. Make him turn his head to you, smack his ass. If he turns his head to you, he can't kick you. Anyone who knows horses a little understands this."

"Do they have a lot of horses?"

"I didn't count them. Maybe twenty. Fifty, maybe. The men in charge of the horses claim that the best horse is the one who gets used to one man. For that man the horse will perform. He knows what you expect from him because it is always the one person. That kind of horse is considered best."

She smiled, as if for a hidden reason. "Horses have taught me many things, too. How good it is to give something to someone. With horses it's a cube of sugar or a crisp carrot. There are also horses that will do everything even when they're not being spoiled because they like what they're doing. Horses like that like to please you as a rider. There is generosity in them, kindness; they take their lot as a gift rather than a punishment. These horses tickle your imagination. They're more fun."

"What could they teach me?" asked Kamil Dreisler.

"You can set up a relationship by understanding what he likes, what he wants." She smiled and her eyes smiled also. "You comprehend his nature, his abilities, or his potential. For example, when a horse sheds his coat year round, but more in the spring, he rubs against trees and fence posts to help the shedding, and this feels good to him. You could scratch places where he couldn't get to. There's a fold of skin under his chin that's hard for him to rub. It must be like a caress to a person. As he comes to know you and understand you, he waits for you, whinnying and wondering where you've been."

"How do you know so much about horses?"

"I don't know as much as I know about you," she said, smiling. "But maybe not."

"I have secrets."

"I hope so."

The sea took away their words and reverberations. More pieces of wood floated up.

"Why did old Pharaoh say that ruby is your stone, and that it means passion?" he asked.

"He brought a lot of superstition with him from Poland and from the wars. He also claims that December's stone is turquoise and means unselfishness."

"Which stone means courage? And which one honor?"

Daniela felt his breath.

"Here and now everyone," she answered.

"There is salt in the air," said Kamil Dreisler.

"Wait until it gets completely dark," Daniela said.

"The moon and stars are shining so bright here. How come? It's strange, it's so dark and white."

Daniela also looked at the sea. "It's strange," she said. "Somewhere far away there is a land, a city, or a house and we will be there together. All oaths are useless. All words. I swore that I would stay here and now I know that I won't. Pharaoh Blumen says that will is stronger than love, but that's not true. Why does everybody want to be happy in his own way?

"Hold me," she said. "Just hold me like this."

"Your heart's pounding as if you'd been running," said Kamil Dreisler.

"You know . . ." she whispered. "You must know why."

She kissed him on the lips. Her lips seemed to wince when she let him kiss her back. She didn't want to appear nervous. She clung to him. She let him touch her breasts. The rim of the sun dissolved into the sea. The fiery pillar of the sun reflected in the sea got shorter and sank into the water, and the darkness fell. The moon lit up the sky. Stars shattered and perished into the sea.

"Everything . . . everywhere . . ." she said. And then, "So many stars . . . and each is forever."

On the sandy ridge near Nahariyya grew green oleander bushes covered with red blossoms. Magnolias bloomed beside some of the houses and clumps of grass pushed skyward in the shade. There were tunnels of trodden paths between the bushes. The fences stood shoulder-high, most made of empty gasoline canisters, bleached by the sun and dented, stacked one on top of another with the holders turned inward. In the daytime dogs and cats would lie next to the fence in the sun at a distance from each other; at night the fences were visited by rats in search of food. Occasionally a jackal would turn up.

"Wait until it's dark," said Daniela.

"The moon and the stars are out."

"A little longer," Daniela added. "This is the first place on earth I've come to where I'm not scared of darkness."

"Maybe it wasn't fear, but being careful," he said.

"As a child I feared a lot."

"You're not a child anymore."

Daniela stretched and pulled her hands behind her head. She had shoulder-length shiny black hair.

"My friend Eva was supposed to come," said Daniela. "You can never depend on her. Whenever someone close to her was killed, she went and slept with the first man she met. She has a reputation already. Lying to protect herself from being hurt. Sometimes she lied to herself without realizing it."

Then she said, "The watchman at Solel Boné—his name is Alexander Hermansdorf—promised me that he would let you work his watch in the tool warehouse occasionally, if we'd want. We wouldn't have to be afraid, he'd let you have his revolver for the night. We could use the money while I'm waiting for my papers to be processed."

She turned to him. "Wait. Let me button you up."

She held the edge of his cotton army shirt between her fingers.

"You don't think that I know how to button you up? You think there's something that I don't know or can't fix? I've been too long on my own."

Then her voice changed and her expression changed, and she looked at the sea as if it were a great big window into the world which they would now enter together.

Her heart was pounding so loudly that she knew Kamil Dreisler had to hear it, and she held him tightly around the neck.

Kamil Dreisler carried her in his arms down the sandy path past the oleanders to the small house that was loaned to them by a couple who had been interned by the British on Mauritius for the duration of World War II. It was a wooden shack made out of a crate for moving furniture—they called them lift-vans. Empty yellow ammunition cartridges lay flattened in the sand. Some had been run over by trucks and tractors, and they were still hot from the sun like the white sand the wind swept over them. Kamil Dreisler walked slowly and carefully toward the wooden wall that had the color of baked clay. The moon shed its light on the sea, on the waves of sand, and on the walls of Acre.

Daniela smiled. "I don't understand why my heart is pounding like this. I don't know what's the matter."

Kamil Dreisler stepped in front of the lift-van, which now emerged from the darkness opposite the oleanders, which seemed lighter than before. The packing crate stood there like a hut, a nine-by-twelve-foot structure, supported on two beams. You could see cats prowling between the floor of the lift-van and the beams. On the ocean side the original owner had cut a window. The mover's name had already been obliterated by the salt, last winter's rains, and the beating sun. The window looked out into the darkness through white fringes of a curtain.

Kamil Dreisler opened the door with his shoulder. He put Daniela down on the bed. It was stifling hot. The windblown curtain pressed against the window frame. Old newspapers, belonging to the innkeeper with the Napoleonic bangs, lay on the floor. The innkeeper had also lent them some pans and a mirror. The plates and silverware belonged to the woman from Mauritius.

"If my father were alive, if he'd managed to get here in time, we would have had a better house," said Daniela.

Kamil Dreisler fastened the door with a leather peg made from a belt that old Pharaoh Blumen had given Daniela when she left the army. The pale green leaves of the oleanders gleamed in the moonlight.

He lay on his side next to her, his cheek and eyes next to hers. Daniela yielded to the quiver that told her what would come, although she did not feel ready. Or was she? She had a feeling of closeness as never before.

She looked at the interior of the lift-van and at the oleanders, as if seeing them for the first time. Her expression changed, as had her voice. Her eyes no longer held visions of ravines, funerals, electric barbed-wire fences, trenches, and exploded hand grenades that she had learned to throw. Nor were they filled with strange people, distant lands and foreign tongues, dust, rocks, and sand. In her eyes there was a question and a promise of what she sometimes felt in the evenings looking at Mount Carmel, at the walls of Acre or the refineries of Haifa. She was ready to share her world with Kamil Dreisler, and with it those things she had never experienced before. She touched his soul as Kamil touched her soul with his breathing, looking, and wishing. What was it that was so close, warm, and unknown. For Kamil's sake, she was willing to leave her world and accept and embrace Kamil Dreisler's world, his party, all of his images. All that was far away, yesterday, a year ago, now approached fast, as when you mistakenly look through the wrong end of a telescope.

"Everything," she said.

"Everything," he answered.

She felt his body next to hers. She let him caress her for a long time and then she caressed him. Her lips touched his lips; her palms touched his arms, his palms, his body. She felt his breath. The sparks of an invisible sun ignited her. She felt this fire coming from outside and inside at the same time, and everything was quiet and fast. She thought about a lot of things that had happened. She thought about the innkeeper with the Napoleonic bangs who never had a woman for more than one night. She thought about the members of the Sasa kibbutz and what land and horses meant to them. She thought about people who fought here only a year ago against the British and then fought with the Arabs, with whom they wanted to live in peace, and they had to learn to fight because they'd forgotten how, and they learned to be strong after they had been weak for a long time. And she thought of her nineteen years which had brought her here to this moment, of all the things in life that were connected with killing. She thought about going back to Prague with Kamil to fulfill his devotion to communism, and about how fast her heart was beating. She felt all this disappearing from her mind without really leaving, just stepping behind her and freeing a huge space where something else might enter.

Feeling Kamil's embrace, she embraced him in return. She felt all of her body and all of his body and no longer thought about anything but the meaning of man and woman, about the innkeeper saying that people were like animals entering the ark in pairs, and she thought how different it was for her and why—why it would always be different.

"Everything." She mouthed the word but could no longer whisper. She lay there with half-open lips, eyes closed, and waited.

"Forgive me," Kamil Dreisler said then. "I'm sorry."

The sound of the sea and the wind from the hills, the sand and the night birds on the rocks, mixed with the sultry air. The wood of the crate had a dry smell. Some of the knots in the wood were covered with dried, amber-colored resin that was still fragrant. Their bodies were beaded with perspiration. Although her eyes were closed, something blinded her, diminished her hearing, took away her power of speech. She could no longer find words, even in feigned whispers. Did he hear the pounding of her heart? "Everything" repeated in the back of her mind.

"There's nothing to forgive," she managed hoarsely.

She felt the tension in her throat, her chest, and her hips. She felt the twitching in her underbelly and on the inside of her thighs. She forgot who and where he had been. Everything will start anew, again. Something was coming that reminded her of fire and clear water. All the quivers concentrated in one place, in her blood and in his blood, like light focusing into a cone. With all her awareness she felt his will; it joined with her desire, and she felt the dissolving between slow and fast, between yes and no, between perhaps, maybe, sometime, never. Everything was in her mind. Everything.

"Yes, yes," she said.

She opened her eyes for a second. She saw Kamil Dreisler's shoulders, his throat, his arms, his chest. His hair touched her forehead. She let him do anything he wanted to with her dress. Her naked skin, where the clothes protected her from the sun, was white as milk, and the color contrasted with the wood of the hut.

She whispered, "I waited for you. Come to me."

She caught a glimpse of the curtain, the white sheet, and the sliver of an oleander blossom that the wind had blown in. She saw an earwig crawling across the ceiling near the acetylene lamp and followed it until it reached the edge of the ceiling and touched the white curtain. She felt—and feared—that her blood was on the sheet. Not far from the lift-van, a cat screamed. She felt a movement that came from the depths of the sea, from the warm stream of wind which enveloped the hut, from the friction of sand grains against each other. This stream moved her soul, her legs, her belly, and her hands until she felt she was caught up in a whirlpool that also swallowed up her fear. She heard the echo of the voices of her mother and father, her sister and the dead—who now seemed alive—and she heard their weeping and their song. And then Daniela Klaus heard her own moan mix with the roar of the sea and their bodies. The earth around them wrapped itself in the sky, which was covered with night and the night with stars. She heard the moan of the sea, the pounding of her heart, the crashing of the waves, and the beating of Kamil Dreisler's heart. They heard the birds on the rocks as if far away in the sea: *Tee ooo terr . . . Tee eee terr . . .*

"Is it as you expected?" Daniela whispered. "Are you disappointed?"

Words that she never would have brought herself to say now flowed from her lips like waves of wind, like the hum of the sea and sunlight streaming down.

"Everything? Was it everything?"

It was like horses galloping and churning up sand with their hooves, or birds in flight, or children playing and shouting on the beach. As when she first pulled the trigger and learned to shoot in the army; she was the same as before, yet different, just a minute older, and so much more experienced.

"It's beautiful," whispered Kamil Dreisler.

"It's pain," said Daniela. "Beautiful pain."

"It's everything," he said. "It's for a long time. It's forever."

She kissed him on the lips, full of an unknown passion which was both new and full of self-confidence she could share without losing anything. This passion was different, unlike what her letters revealed or what his answers to her letters revealed. She left the smile on her lips and this smile seemed to turn inward as well.

"Everything," she said again, and let the word echo in her mind.

3

Patches of azure on the horizon seemed to split the sky and change darkness into light. At dawn the sea became brighter. The wilderness and the mountains, beyond which lay the deserts, broke through the twilight in the distance and mixed with the fog. It made the daybreak look like a veil that the day would pull off to reveal its face. The innkeeper at Raveh's turned on the gramophone. Daniela let Kamil kiss her and then she said, "Why aren't we carpenters? We could be hammering nails and singing away and we could be rich and never have to worry."

She had a pleasant, deep alto voice. She looked like a lovely flower that had just bloomed. What she said sounded like the songs taught to her by her grandmother and mother, songs about brides and bridegrooms, about meadows and rivers and about the good and bad fortunes that people are bound to encounter. Life was like a bridge, crossing unbelievable gaps and abysses between men and between lands. Why do we sometimes fear that we might betray something that could actually betray us?

She didn't want to say that it was strange that he hadn't received his papers yet. She was still thinking about what it is that makes the sun warm, what causes the sea to swell in waves, what raises the white wings of the gulls, whose white plumage seems dirty when you see them up close as they fly low. She thought how good it would be if they didn't get the papers and could stay here—it wouldn't be her fault, but it would satisfy her desire to live out her life here and she wouldn't have to say it.

She knew that people love their ideas as if the ideas were people; and that every idea had its own overcoat and cap, its own disguise. Every idea had a personification in someone or some place. This she already knew to be true.

It occurred to her that there is nothing stronger than the idea that old and new sufferings can be healed. An idea that could change the damned world into an acceptable place. An idea that could encompass everything, the whole world, from equator to the pole and from the pole to the equator on the other side, across the starry sky as seen here and by the antipodes, on the surface of oceans and at the foothills of the mountains on the other side of the planet. Is there in every idea a grain of a dream from which one will never wake up?

Kamil Dreisler built a fire in front of the lift-van and boiled water for tea in a cast-iron kettle.

"Burn the letters," said Daniela, handing Kamil Dreisler a bundle of papers and envelopes. She laughed as Kamil stoked the fire with her old correspondence. She was now more self-confident than when he arrived. She felt close to the mountains, the sea, people, including Pharaoh Blumen and the innkeeper with the Napoleonic bangs, the couple from Mauritius and her friends from the army who tried to talk her into joining the nursing corps. Even in the morning the sun looked like a glowing brass gong. Kamil Dreisler threw the letters into the flames. He probably wanted to convince himself that everything was going as planned, even though there were delays. He hadn't been to Raveh's or at the Pinguin for the last two days because his money had run out. Pharaoh Blumen had given Daniela a briefcase for the trip. It was made from the skin of a polar moose and was only a little rotted in some places. Kamil made no comments about that. It was too hot for moose skins.

"Everything you want is good," Daniela said suddenly. "All I want is good. Then why isn't it good if we put it together? I wonder why it isn't good for anyone but ourselves."

"You can't reconcile fire with water," said Kamil Dreisler after a while.

Some dead fish lay in the sand behind the lift-van. The cats must have dragged them there. The wind came in with the tide and carried the ashes from the burned letters into the sea. There the first wave licked them and the returning wave carried them off. The sand was glued together with the tar and the debris. Daniela had removed a ribbon from one of the letters. As the water in the kettle started to boil, she tied her hair with the ribbon.

"It's better now than it was," Daniela said with a smile. "Sometimes I wasn't even sure that I was made of flesh and bones. I felt I was made of ink, distance, promises, and unfulfilled hopes—and absences, too. I felt like a stranger to myself, as though I did not exist."

Then, when they ate, she asked, "Won't you have another piece of fish?"

"That's for you."

"I might think you're afraid I'm going to poison you." She smiled and he looked at her. Her eyes spoke of everything that was good and could be good.

Daniela watched the waves running up the shore and dissolving in the sand. She sat on the orange crates, swinging her legs.

"In the army they issued me size fourteen boots. And the first pants I got were five sizes too big, and the new ones cut me in the crotch. I was given the heaviest German rifle—a Mauser."

"What did that sailor want with Eva?"

"She provokes men, that's all. But otherwise she has a sweet nature. She's different with men. She told the sailor that the salesman in the lingerie shop wanted to sell her a muslin nightgown when she came to buy something with her last lover. She explained that she's not used to going away empty-handed. First she was just playing with them, but now I think it's for real."

"So what did he give her?"

"Don't even ask. We celebrated her twenty-second birthday recently. She doesn't have a lover anymore."

Daniela examined the calluses on her hands and the scratches that had healed. She touched the hot sand with her soles. She liked talking about her friends. It was like giving a vivid picture of them and bringing them close, even when they were far away.

"She dated the captain of a commercial vessel. He was married and wouldn't get a divorce. On Saturdays he stayed with his family. It's hard to live off men here. She told me that the mystery of love is that when a man gets what he wants, he's not interested in the next time. But that's not love. It's only need. Desire to be close to someone. She prefers soldiers. Sometimes to scare men away she tells them she's sick. She had a mailman, but he got locked up for throwing mail into the Gaaton creek so he wouldn't have to deliver it. They won't let him out to do it again."

Where did the two of you meet?"

"In the fortress Theresienstadt. In 1945 just after the war, she stayed in Germany. We were together in Auschwitz-Birkenau in the *Frauenkonzentrazionslager* with Slavs and Hungarian women. She didn't hurry to get home from Bergen-Belsen. She hoped to find an Englishman. She was afraid to return to Prague and not find anyone there. In Germany she learned how to eat, drink, and dance. How to distinguish trees, flowers, and birds. She lied, saying that she was looking for some girl—both of us knew that the girl died a long time ago."

Kamil watched the fire consume a letter that read, "They fell here. There was no place to withdraw." The breeze carried off the slivers of ash.

"Do you like my cooking?" Daniela asked.

"I sure do."

"It's going to be hot."

"It's been hot every day."

"This hot weather will drive people crazy."

"What do you mean?"

"Well, everything just slows down and seems sleepier. It's ninety-nine degrees in Jerusalem today. Here by the seashore it's only ninety-three or ninety-five. Sometimes it gets to a hundred and four degrees. It's like a beautiful hell."

"Even in the mountains?"

"Everywhere."

"And it never rains?"

"When there are clouds there's a storm with thunder and lightning, but it doesn't rain."

The longest letter that Daniela had ever mailed was now burning, all three pages of it. She had written him about her father who went to Auschwitz-Birkenau with the transport in September 1944, in spite of the fact that he worked in the Theresienstadt Jewish Administration with people who had become legends and who had monuments built to them here, whose names appeared on streets, gardens, museums, and some military installations. That way he had hoped to save the lives of her and her sister. Everyone who survived could do so because someone else was killed instead, and she often thought about those who had to go in her place—her father among them. She thought about this once when she was shooting and had become nervous because she did not want to tell anyone about it. She felt proud that her father did not let anyone go in his place, as some of the others in the Council of the Eldest had done. When it is a matter of life and death, man is an absolute egoist. With a few exceptions. Only the very best value their own lives the same way they value the lives of others around them. Her father was one of them. But she sometimes wondered if she wouldn't really have preferred that he wasn't one of them.

She didn't mail the letter because she didn't want to complain, to feel sorry for herself, and she didn't want compassion. But there were moments when she still wasn't sure. As a result, he suspected that she had forgotten him, that she had someone else; because prior to that she had made some remarks about people with whom she spent her nights.

She was almost happy to leave the fortress Theresienstadt. She had lived in an attic next to the fire station. Mice scampered around her head at night. This was the letter in which she wrote, "Come. You will understand why I don't want to go away. I have weighed everything, all the things I want and all that I don't want. I can be happy only if I am free. We were never free, you, I, or the people around us. And I have no illusions about the easy existence of freedom.

I entered the army because I wanted to live, not to die. My father's parents were killed and so were my mother's. Then they killed my father. Mother is dead. . . . This morning I dreamed that you were a sliver of daybreak, a dream spun of lonely nights, dawns, and memories. Your image floats to me across the sea." She was afraid that such a letter would repudiate him.

"What are you thinking about?"

"The same as you," she answered.

He thought about the letters she would get from here and how she would answer them. He wished it would come soon. But it couldn't be done without the papers. She was close to him and he smelled her hair, a fragrance that reminded him of vanilla wine, or maybe just vanilla, but it all mixed with the idea of wine and intoxicated him. He thought about her and the cities where everybody will eat when it's time to eat, and drink when they are thirsty. He thought about sunlit houses for people who come home from work, and about the equal share of silence and noise, smoke and hills for everyone. You don't have to be crazy to have such dreams. It's enough to have experienced three years in concentration camps for having been born of a Jewish mother. It was a dream about a land without fear, where no human cheek will be bruised by barbed wire.

"How do you feel?"

He smiled. He didn't want to say that not having received the papers made him feel like a man on board a ship moving away from the shore it wanted to reach. The members of the Sasa kibbutz washed horses on the dock. The trucks in which the horses were brought stood at the side of the road. They must have gotten up very early, he thought. He drew in the fragrance of Daniela's hair, the smell of vanilla and wine.

"Wouldn't you like to wash first?" Daniela asked.

"I did," said Kamil Dreisler.

"But not with soap. I don't want to get sick like Eva."

And then she added, "Once you told me when we were still in Prague and going to the Wolf Mountain that some woman had compared you to a young horse. Can you tell me why?"

"I was sixteen and you know where it was and why we did it. None of us wanted to leave the fortress Theresienstadt for Auschwitz-Birkenau naive."

"Did it help you in anything?"

"It gave us self-confidence."

"It's simple for men."

"Not in everything."

"I always found it strange that from the beginning you wanted to live with me like an adult, when I wasn't one, although I may have looked it. I can't blame you. Nobody will tell you what a girl should share first—her body or her soul. Aren't you ashamed?" She kept smiling but her eyes were serious.

"No, I may be ashamed that people better than me did not make it."

"Someone else should be ashamed."

"It's always the innocent who feel the most shame."

"I don't want to talk about it."

"Then why do you?"

"And I know who it was," Daniela said and smiled. "You and Eva will get along just fine when she shows up."

Later she said, "For God's sake, bolt the door. You want other things now. Nobody's ever done them with me. But you have done them, haven't you? All right," she whispered, "but wait a little. Only if you do it with me only."

Kamil Dreisler bolted the door of the lift-van with a peg. The tooth of a scavenger fish swung from the end of a rope. It was an amulet given to them by Pharaoh Blumen, the owner of the boat rental place and a small fishing vessel.

Daniela spoke in a whisper then, as if someone could hear them at the dock where the Sasa kibbutzniks washed their horses. "I'll do it to you now," she said.

And later she added, "Why talk about it? . . . Yes, yes, anything you want. Everything. But keep quiet . . ."

TWO

1

The resort town of Nahariyya, which can be seen from Haifa and Acre in the south, and from Rosh Haniqra in the north, grew in the 1930s when people started leaving Germany. The oldest structure in Nahariyya is the cemetery for Austrian soldiers who took part in the first world war and died here before the first immigrant wave arrived. There are white crosses and well-kept graves in that cemetery.

"How many breakfasts have I served you?" Daniela asked.

"Who'd bother counting?" said Kamil Dreisler.

Daniela smiled like someone who is learning patience, but she was anything but patient.

In the morning and in the evening Daniela set the table for them on the tomato crates. The heat wave had lasted for weeks and the radio meteorologists foretold more of the same. In the lowlands by the sea the temperature had reached ninety-nine; in the hills and in Jerusalem it was over a hundred. In Raveh's someone said that such temperatures occur only at the beginning or end of the summer. The local newspapers mentioned that a similar heat wave had occurred only once before, at the end of August 1881, when the temperature in Jerusalem had reached a hundred and eleven, and in Jaffa a hundred and six. It was hard to breathe.

"You can't eat?" Daniela asked.

"It must be the heat," Kamil Dreisler replied.

"You have to drink a lot."

"I drink like a fish."

"You're supposed to drink at least eight times a day."

"Yeah."

"A quart and a half," Daniela added. "I drink almost constantly."

In the morning Pharoah Blumen gave them some fish that he could not sell or eat himself. Letting it spoil would be a sin. He probably thought they would die of hunger without him, so he went fishing more often. Daniela watched the long blue ship with the orange stripe along the hull. It floated on the sea like a resting woman. She was thinking about herself, what it means to be a woman, by day and by night. The innkeeper with the Napoleonic bangs from Raveh's played some European and American pop tunes and then the *Kineret*.

"Why do you think the papers haven't come yet?" Daniela asked.

"I don't want to talk about it all the time," Kamil Dreisler said.

"Do you think I want to?"

"There could be a thousand reasons. The world looks like it's about to fall apart, on the brink of war, and not only here, but from pole to pole, under the sea and in space. Sometimes our personal concerns seem smaller than pinheads to the powers that be and about as important. I realize that for us they are about as important as those from pole to pole. But as I've said, we have to be patient and must not worry so much."

"We don't have to lie to each other," said Daniela. "And certainly not because of someone else who . . . " She did not finish the sentence because he would be on pins and needles after such a remark. But she knew words didn't really mean much. The heart of the matter was not communication—people speak only to assure themselves, or sometimes others. Daniela looked at him the way the innkeeper with the Napoleonic bangs looked at her, as at an idiot.

"Will you take the job that Alexander Hermansdorf offered you? He wants a few days off so he can finally go to the immigrant camp in Hadera to pick out a bride. He has a hard time choosing or finding one quickly enough. He's tried on several occasions. Or maybe none of them want him. He will never tell. He had a girl with him for a couple of days, but she moved out because he counted every slice of salami she ate, told her to close the refrigerator quickly because it uses up too much ice, and finally he just left her salami skins because things had become expensive. I wouldn't stay with such a person. We won't have to feel sorry for him. No one has to feel sorry for anyone here. It's still better than the *Frauenkonzentrazionslager*."

"What did old Pharoah Blumen tell you?"

"The usual: When you have no shoes, think of those who have no feet. The innkeeper from Raveh's offered me a job. And the old lady from the Pension Popper wanted to find me a job in the kitchen. She apologized for the bitter tea—it's not that she's stingy. Once she prepared crayfish for the English naval officers and didn't charge them anything. During the war against the Arabs she cooked potato soup for the soldiers—for free. She used dried mushrooms she'd brought from Europe and had been saving for five years."

"Is that all Pharoah Blumen told you?"

"He wanted to buy sugar from her older sister, who's the mayor's wife, but she didn't want to sell it at black market prices, and she didn't want to lose money either." She was silent for a while. The old man told her that it was always the same story. First utopia, then disappointment; first dreams, then betrayal; first promise, then killing.

Daniela handed Kamil Dreisler a piece of paper that the innkeeper from the Raveh used to charge his guests for food and drink. It read, "Haven't you gone through hell once already, and do you need to make life hell again? There can be no agreement between two dogs and a bone."

"But that isn't the handwriting of Pharoah Blumen."

"No, I just wanted him to advise me on what to do."

"What did he advise you?"

"To throw it away and not make you needlessly mad. To be patient and wait. He said everything will turn out all right, that you will get the papers for me too and that we will be able to leave."

"Can you swear that he did not say anything else?"

"You have to trust somebody," said Daniela.

"Some people maybe, some people never," said Kamil Dreisler. "Who gave it to you? Who wrote it?"

Kamil Dreisler turned red. It was easier to think about the world whose shadow would cover their worries, except for the fact that it was from that world that his papers were not forthcoming. He could guess who had given her that note and who had written those words.

"Did you get it last night?"

"I've been getting them for three weeks. It's not the first one. I've been throwing them away."

Now Daniela turned red, too. A seagull with white wings and a dirty belly circled above the lift-van.

2

The end of July brought hot winds from the East and no one felt any respite from the layer of cold air that had come for the last three days from the Mediterranean and southern Europe. The sultry heat continued. The sun looked like a mirror reflecting broken silver splinters. It was impossible to breathe in the lift-van during the day and unbearable to sleep at night. During the third sleepless night, Daniela sat on the bed, wiped the perspiration from her forehead and neck, and said that staying here was also a revolution. She knew that Kamil Dreisler was not sleeping. He seemed to be on duty, killing cockroaches. Twice a day they had to spray the van, sometimes even at night. The sky gleamed like dark blue porcelain. Daniela wrapped a wet rag around her forehead. The wind brought smells of stale beer, onions, garlic, and garbage from the inn. The innkeeper did not sleep either; he took the chairs out on to the beach and hosed down the dance floor to remove cigarette butts. The stars shone brightly.

Daniela had lost weight. Even Kamil Dreisler had become thinner. They both had tanned.

"Don't think about it," said Kamil Dreisler. "Sleep. You'll be weak as a fly in the morning."

"I've learned how to lose the dead, but I haven't yet learned how to lose the living. It gets on my nerves that someone is constantly making decisions about me. I don't feel like sleeping while you're not sleeping. Aren't you hot? It's hell."

The innkeeper had started playing songs from the time of Palmach. He probably played them just for himself, but they could hear them in the lift-van quite well. Under the stars gleamed the lighted and colored boats, and in the darkness they all seemed the same, like sisters. The boats would go out at night and come back during the day. Kamil Dreisler had been working on the road for three days, and at night he kept watch for Alexander Hermansdorf, who guarded the warehouse highway equipment owned by the Solel Boné company. The boats with their lamps looked like will-o'-the-wisps on the sea. Kamil Dreisler smelled of the asphalt which he and two other men helped spread over the road. He did not sleep long. He dreamed about greyhounds and dachshunds moving in space between heaven and earth. The dogs changed into fish; then into a moth. The moth changed into an aquarium fish, almost an embryo. It streamed down like a capillary or a disappearing meteor.

"My commander once explained to me how to throw a hand grenade, what you have to do so you don't kill your people and yourself. He told me what thoughts are helpful and what thoughts are not. For him a thought was like a parachute when you bail out of a plane. It makes sense only when it opens up, not when you fly and the parachute remains shut. Everybody knows how that ends."

In the middle of the night they heard a warning on the radio that bathers, trying to cool off, should be careful in the water and watch for anything that looks suspicious, including dead fish. Mines sometimes look like beer or soda bottles.

"Do you want to go swimming?" Daniela suggested.

"Well, if you can't sleep," replied Kamil Dreisler.

"How about you?"

"What's the farthest you've ever swum?"

"I only swim as far as I can still see the shore. I don't like jellyfish and I'm afraid of big fish. If I just touch them it sends me into a panic. I swell if I touch a jellyfish or even a bit of one. In the Hachotrim kibbutz there is a man who goes swimming only twice a year, when the khamsin comes. He swims toward the horizon, but never at night."

Then she added, "You don't have to worry about me wanting to drown. I hope you'll never want to drown next to me. Or drown me."

"I dreamed about Eva," Kamil Dreisler said. "She had an affair with an American. They walked arm in arm; they kissed every now and then, but that was all. Then he suggested that they take a shower together. She said why not, but she'd already had an experience with a man who considered showering with a woman to be the maximum he could do with a woman. He preferred to have men in the shower. He watched her, fascinated, and she felt relieved. But he didn't even touch her. He only asked her to marry him. She said that she would have to think it over. At night she dreamed that they were in a meadow with two of his friends. Suddenly all three changed—the American into a grasshopper, the second into a cricket, and the third into a dung beetle. He didn't understand why she gave him the cold shoulder. She needed a man, not a child."

Kamil Dreisler borrowed old Pharaoh Blumen's boat.

"There's a khamsin. In Arabic that means fifty. Fifty times a year the hot wind blows from the desert, carrying with it small grains of sand, like the seeds of a pomegranate. It gives people a headache."

The sea was transparent. The bottom of the sea, when you stood at the shore, looked like a clenched hand—the tissues, the blood vessels and veins, which looked like a body and a plant. Kamil Dreisler rowed the boat alongside cast fishing rods and went past the more remote ones, until they were almost alone in the sea. He already knew about the local goldsmith who was a head shorter than Daniela and whose mother tried to get them to move into their house. He gave Daniela an alarm clock and a business card that read, "Small but yours." Daniela gave the alarm clock to Kamil. When she helped out at the Pension Popper she was accosted on the staircase by a guest who offered to take her with him to Jerusalem. Lying on the dry grass after a night out, an officer of the infantry offered her marriage and was willing to leave his wife and three-year-old daughter. There was also a Piper pilot who was a confectioner by trade, and whose mother liked Daniela very much. He crashed while on a training flight. Now Daniela earned money by stringing beads for the lady from Mauritius. They gave her a copy of the French novel, *La rue du chat qui peche* (The Street of the Fisherman's

Cat). On the cover was a picture of a seated girl who seemed to be about the same age as Daniela when she left Prague with the Voluntary Brigade, wearing a coat that was hurriedly made for her from an American army blanket. Kamil Dreisler wanted Daniela to explain to him why immigrant stories are always so sad. She told him they were only sad in the beginning. She began to undress and folded her dress, placing it in the bottom of the boat. She had on the yellow dress with green leaves. The sides of the boat were cushioned with split tires. She kept only her underwear on.

"I had a dream about you," Daniela said. "They recruited you as a pilot here. You'd like that, wouldn't you? And then the assignment was changed to long-distance transport. They let you drive a truck with a trailer at the Hachotrim kibbutz. The truck was worth a hundred thousand."

"A hundred thousand what?"

"What does it matter? It was only a dream. Wouldn't you like to do that? I mean if it weren't here?"

"You said that once before."

"What have I said before? I don't think you're paying attention to me. You're preoccupied with other things."

The boat was green on the inside, with two oars and a box containing fishing rods and tin cans. On the bottom were hooks and tackle and fishing line wound around big spools. The sky lay on top of the sea and the two were joined in the darkness. The boat had brown sides and a red line around the trim. The old man called her "Freedom." He had christened her with beer and painted the name in big white letters, both in Hebrew and in Latin script. In the box he kept old newspapers and his collection of Dutch beer bottles with a patent seal.

With a quick movement Daniela removed her underwear and jumped into the water. She swam close to the boat. As Kamil Dreisler rowed toward her, she held on the edge of the boat and let the water run out of her hair. Kamil Dreisler gave her a hand and she climbed back into the boat, lay on her back in the bottom, and watched the stars. They were bright and looked like the signals she had known in the army.

"Do you want to tell me something I should know?" Kamil Dreisler asked.

"Maybe the man who is processing our papers doesn't like it that you came to get me. Maybe it isn't just a mistake or a delay. For some people revolution is what they have declared it to be, not what you or I wish for. When they lie to people like you and me, they don't even consider it a lie."

She didn't tell him that he should stay with her if the papers didn't come.

The waves splashed against the boat; the drops of water fell back into the sea and on Daniela, who did not resist them. She no longer showed Kamil Dreisler the anonymous slips of warning that she kept receiving. They opened one of the letters addressed to him at the post office. He was being summoned to get his papers processed himself. She remembered that in the army one noncommissioned officer spoiled her belief in the astrological charts by reminding her that they were not there for admiration but for orientation. The water sprayed against the side of the boat.

Daniela dried herself with a towel and reached for the yellow dress.

"I hope you're not going to get dressed yet," Kamil Dreisler said.

"Why?"

"So that I won't have to undress you again."

"I don't want you to think it's the only thing I can give you."

Night fell toward the earth and into the water. The waves gleamed. Here and there a fish flashed on the surface as the prow of the boat cut lightly through the water.

"You shouldn't spoil it—for me, or for yourself," Daniela added.

He felt that both wanted more, but it eluded them. Her body was the only attainable thing. He suddenly felt incomplete, even though yesterday everything still looked good. He had it and he didn't have it at the same time because it was not connected to the rest of what he wanted. An echo of what Daniela felt, also something unfinished, a sense of incomplete bliss. And again they both felt like a wave in the ocean. Joy and pain. Pleasure with pain. Ambiguity of desire. Desire to possess, yet knowing it could not be.

The warm wind, floating through the night, caressed the sea.

3

Kamil Dreisler and Daniela walked barefoot toward the barrels on the deserted shore, where there was nothing but rocks and sand. Kamil Dreisler pulled the boat up on the dry sand where he could keep it in sight. They spread their clothes on the sand so that they could put their heads on them. There was a black shimmer on the water and the foam looked like scales, like fins, like melted silver coins. The taste of stale beer blew in from Raveh's as cats fought behind the docks. The night floated away like an undiscovered tale of time that had no beginning and no end. From the darkness of the night emerged a ship. It approached slowly and sailed past them like a luminous mirage. As the night and the sea made way for the ship and closed behind it, all that you could see were the lights of the staterooms and the decks. The ship was sharply and softly delineated from the space of the night.

"It's lovely here," said Daniela.

"Why are you crying?" asked Kamil Dreisler.

"We could live here together."

The ship sailed into the night, carrying away its lights, far into the distance, until it became smaller and finally disappeared.

"Don't cry," Kamil Dreisler said again.

"What is the meaning of love, loving, promising and commitment?" asked Daniela. "I have never said this to anyone. I love you for the rest of my life. Just as I wrote it on the wall of our little house. It will still be true even after I'm gone."

Five minutes later she asked, "Give me your hand."

For a few seconds she held Kamil Dreisler's palm on her belly. He immediately understood.

"No one in the world knows it—only you and I."

"How do you know? Did you see a doctor?"

"I don't have to go to a doctor." And then she added, "So it happened. That first Sunday evening. On the twenty-fourth, when you carried me into the house. It only takes a fraction of a second."

He looked at her. There was a question in her eyes, and a reply, together with tears and a smile. Her expression changed. Her eyes, clear and somewhat nervous, reflected yesterday's and tomorrow's truth. Her truth, that she had to make him see. Her eyes explained why she didn't have to ask anyone, and it was as clear as the turning earth, the rising and setting of the sun, the seagulls sitting on their nests. It was as clear as night following day and day following night, like the flight of seagulls from the rocks behind Rosh Haniqra and as clear as their crimes. She smelled of the sea and of vanilla wine.

Kamil Dreisler suddenly felt older and more mature. He felt very proud but also tricked. His throat was dry. He caressed Daniela's temples, her hair, her lips.

The feathery tall grasses waved in the warm breeze.

"The second week in September we'll have better weather," said Daniela. "According to Pharaoh Blumen, the weather always gets better when the Nile floods. Very few people lie about the weather, even at Raveh's."

THREE

1

As Pharaoh Blumen left the shack and brought the evening mail, he watched the old freighter. Kamil Dreisler threw a paper back into the garbage can. It contained his hair—Daniela had just given him a haircut. Pharaoh Blumen stood there in the light of the full moon. His tanned and wrinkled cheeks looked like pulp, like the bottom of the boat, like a layer of tar, hardened and baked by the sun and scarred by the sand and pebbles on the shore. He pulled out the boat over land every day, and the sun had burned his skin.

Pharaoh Blumen brought Daniela a fishing line so she could hang her laundry, along with a monster of a fish that could last them until New Year's. He told them that some new immigrants arrived in Nahariyya on the freighter, but these were not nervous millionaires from Borneo.

"Maybe in this life I'm not supposed to have what normal people everywhere can have," Daniela said. "I can only dream of having my own bed."

Kamil Dreisler turned to the sea and watched the tall waves.

When no one said anything, Pharaoh Blumen volunteered, "Strong waves can split a freighter in two. The waves create a sort of cavern into which the ships fall. If the ship hits a wall of water in a certain place, it will split in two and sink. Of course, it's usually the wind that turns a wave into a strong one."

And then he added, "But it has to be between the tides. From low tide to high tide early in the afternoon, between noon and one o'clock, and from high tide to low tide early in the evening, between five and six. But I'd better be off now. Good night."

The wind made the door creak. One could feel the saturated breeze of late summer. Leather rotted and wood dried up.

"Good night," said Kamil Dreisler.

"There's life everywhere," said Daniela. "You can live everywhere if you want to and have two healthy arms. For God's sake, it's not a jungle here either."

Pharaoh Blumen took one last look at the two of them as he turned to the old freighter. He walked away slowly, barefoot, in cut-off corduroy pants, the calves of his legs covered with a web of blue varicose veins. Sailing above the sea, the seagulls flapped their wings.

"Good night," Kamil Dreisler said again.

Daniela was silent. At night, Kamil Dreisler had a dream that he threw himself into the sea and swam behind the dock, where they occasionally fished out an unexploded mine. He swam in the direction of the night waves, beyond the Pension Popper, all the way to the rock at Rosh Haniqra where the seagulls came from. He probably had a fever. He dreamed that someone was looking for the water that was spilled by the oxen in the children's rhyme, which every little kid in Bohemia knows. Then he dreamed about Eva. He was lying under a dirty blanket when she came to tell him she got a job at the Pension Popper and that she made the blind and wounded happy. She was slight, flat-chested, and had uneven teeth, and wore a gaudy green dress and white sandals and a very large vinyl bag over her arm in which she carried all of her belongings. As she removed the blanket, he suddenly felt her lips, shuddered, and thrust his fingers into her greasy hair, which was full of sand.

"You're not sleeping?" Daniela asked. "What should one do when the best things become the worst? Why do you want me to feel like a widow?"

Kamil Dreisler had given the money that he had received that evening at last from Solel Boné to Daniela. He had been keeping nightwatch for Alexander Hermansdorf, who came empty-handed from Hadera for the third time. When Kamil Dreisler returned the pistol to him, he did not even wait for Kamil to be far enough away before he shot himself. Nobody blinked. The innkeeper with the Napoleonic bangs served beer on tap and said that in the cemetery in Godera a big chunk of clay was reserved for suicides.

"Are you so cold that you are shaking?" asked Daniela.

"Something probably bit me."

"Don't you want to undress? Shall I undress you?"

2

On the beach, last season's hit, "Kiss me, Harry, kiss me..." blared out from Raveh's. It seemed to catch on in the last days of summer and in the last days of fall. The experts at the Pinguin and the Pension Popper predicted that the tune would keep its popularity at least until the next season. The gramophone needle got dull over the summer. The innkeeper with the Napoleonic bangs decided to add some wicker chairs and tables, and also introduced two brands of beer.

In the autumn the beach was deserted as the summer guests departed and the children went back to school. Only the die-hard swimmers showed up for a dip in the sea during the afternoon and evening. Someone had thrown a hand grenade into the water in hopes of quickly catching a lot of fish. Now thousands of dead fish floated on the surface, and the sand smelled of the dead fish that the sea churned up every day. There was a stone sidewalk leading from the mouth of the Gaston, and because of the construction there everybody had to make detours around piles of stone, cement, and wood. This went on until November. On Friday the eighteenth, it finally sprinkled a little. For the last two nights, Wednesday and Thursday, Kamil Dreisler could walk to the barrels buried in the sand without disturbing the surveyors who spear-headed the mayor's plans. He watched the seaweed, the morning sky, the horizon, and the stars at dawn.

The sparse sand grasses, the clumps spit out by the sea, and the sun-bleached stones, even at night and in the silver dusk and mist, resembled anything he wanted. They reminded him of the skeletons of big ships, wrecks of vessels washed up on shore, or exhausted swimmers whom the waters had thrown high on the beach. In the morning the tide carried most of it all back into the sea. Yesterday, Pharaoh Blumen had said that those who make decisions must suffer. Toward morning, the hours between night and dawn became silent. The light dissolved the nights more slowly, like the sea melts salt. At dawn, Kamil Dreisler would look toward the rocks at Rosh Haniqra or at the walls by the insane asylum in Acre and at the oil refinery. The morning arrived slowly, although sooner than the shadows and the sunrise, and wrapped the landscape, the sea, the sand, and the hills in gentler colors. Beads of dew glistened on the reeds. Between the stones covered with mosses and slime teemed aquatic life: newly born aphids replacing those that died yesterday, crabs, worms, and crayfish. The light dispersed the phantoms of the night and the mists; and the dock and the two barrels in the sand resumed their previous forms.

Kamil Dreisler watched the boat rental and the stalls where they had begun selling turkey cutlets. It occurred to him that a man can be good for the world but bad for himself, good for one person but bad for another, that he can be both good and bad, and that only some things are within his power. All the wise sayings of Pharaoh Blumen were short. Is a man tougher for having gone through what Daniela, or he himself, went through, or is it just the opposite? If a man has two dreams, can he give up one and lose both of them? Kamil Dreisler watched the morning buses at the stop in front of Pension Popper. When they carried wounded soldiers you could hear singing, and the buses would stand there with their lights on.

Finally Kamil Dreisler went to see if Daniela was up yet. He walked by the sea that spewed out all sorts of sediment, oil slicks, and splinters, as in the film about the destroyed submarine. The smell of tar filled the air. A white horse from the Sasa kibbutz stared with large eyes at the sea. The horse stood listlessly in the shallow water by the jetty near the dock. It was a little gray and moldy on the hips. The motions of the man who brushed the horse showed both carelessness and strength. The animal waited patiently for the kibbutznik to finish. The man was in no hurry. Kamil Dreisler presented his cheek to the morning wind. The air was humid and cool, the sand wet from the rain. Kamil Dreisler wore the red sweater with a rolled collar that Daniela had knitted for him.

3

"How did you sleep?"

"Good, and you?"

"I went to look at the sea."

"What is this future you are preparing for us? An empty crate in which you can hide everything? Do you still think that a person can do it like turning a light switch on and off?"

The clouds became heavy and again it looked like rain. The waves gathered at the line of the horizon and found their way through tides to make the shore. Again they looked to her like men bent over cannons, or sprinters on their marks before dashing out. Soon the waves began running in the opposite direction. Daniela looked at her tracks in the sand. The sky stretched away from the land and the sea, and they were replaced by fog, clouds, and a wave of cold air. Flocks of egrets found refuge on the other side of the dock which was protected by the wind. She thought about courage, about shame, about strength; as an echo came the reverberations of hope and hopelessness.

"You're bound to reproach yourself," said Daniela. "You will disappoint so many people, not only here. You're making me ashamed."

She felt that she couldn't breathe, as if it were only a second since the end of World War II and she were still in Germany, in Bergen-Belsen, in Auschwitz-Birkenau. She could not speak. Or did she not want to? Why? So many other things happened. It was the same face, faces. What is it, what makes life a lie? Old Pharaoh Blumen once said that the biggest lie of man was pride. Or, maybe love is the biggest lie? People do lie to life and life lies back to people. She could not speak, nor did she want to speak, for a long while. Now she restrained a voice that was ready to say, Why? Why? Why? She covered her mouth with her hand. She only wanted to add that she would be happy knowing that only the sea lay between his conscience and his will. She felt her heart pounding as if she'd been running.

"I never wanted anything from you," she said at last. "But now I do. Don't go. Write to them that you do not have a passport, that I threw it into the sea. Tell them that I'm sick and that you can't leave me here. Or throw your shirt and passport into the sea so they'll think you've drowned. We can begin a new life."

As the wind chased the gray waves toward the shore, they broke against the rocks, covered the sand, and then silently returned to the sea from which they again came roaring back. The sea made sounds like the crashing of crumbling rocks. The rocks at Rosh Haniqra loomed white as though they had come bubbling out of the water.

Farther away in the sand, a dying cat lay with its belly up and its legs outstretched near the pile of driftwood, tar stuck to its wet fur. A dried blot of blood on its side was covered with sand. The seagulls took no notice of the cat. Again trucks came from the Sasa kibbutz with the rest of the horses that were driven to the sea and run across the road and the railroad tracks. A colt ran alongside the gray mare.

Daniela watched the manes of the running horses. In the distance she saw the outlines of Haifa, the refinery, and the hills of Carmel. When she was nervous or depressed she would look toward the asylum at Acre and close her eyes until an image of the legendary, silent old man came to her. But now, she would force a better mood and think, instead, of the child. She wanted a boy, but she wasn't sure why. Perhaps because boys can protect their mothers. She would consider names. All those that occurred to her were biblical, names of fighting people with great devotion.

She turned to the sea. Why did old Pharaoh Blumen speak of love and endurance in the same breath? Why didn't he say that they were only rarely found together? She thought about the superior forces that make a woman give in, even if she had the right and the strength of ten men. Is it love? Maybe. God? She felt the absurdity of her life, of their lives: The feeling that comes when life is miserable; that she didn't know what to do, what not to do; that life had become a mockery of everything entrusted to man between his birth and his death, such as beauty, meaning, and endurance; the feeling that her life was a lie; that the abnormal had become normal; that life had become sheer punishment, and harbored no rewards. Yes? Maybe? No? Why? She could project phantoms of herself, backward and forward. Everything. What should a woman do to be happy?

She looked at the horses, at the lift-van, and at the sea.

Sometimes the world seems to be a place for fools, some in asylums, some almost free.

"It's raining," she said.

4

The echo of the ship's horn mixed with the low, almost animallike mooing sound of the wind. On the other side, at the entrance to Nahariyya, the November wind lashed at the signs which on one side read, "We welcome you and wish you success," and on the other side "Bon voyage and better hopes."

Whole islands of seaweed floated on the surface, all intertwined, forming sorts of families. The water close to the shore smelled, as it always did in the fall, probably because of the dead fish.

"There was a brief shower at five this morning," said Kamil Dreisler.

Daniela looked at him the way she did yesterday before she'd asked him if he'd at least enjoyed himself a little. But she said something else. "That woman from Mauritius who loaned us the lift-van told me that her husband wants to cover the roof with linoleum so the sand and mud won't leak inside over the winter. . . . I think the innkeeper from Raveh's had a woman in the house last night. I saw her leaving at six o'clock. Maybe he will love her from a distance," Daniela said. "I don't think she turned once, she just smiled."

Daniela said nothing more. She thought about the woman from Mauritius. She and her husband had left Germany and wanted to get here during World War II, but the British wouldn't let them in, as if this place belonged to them. They separated wives from husbands and children from parents. They were like the Germans. They sank their ships and beat them. When the woman bit the boatman they knocked her teeth out. Some people lost their teeth in Dachau, some here. How can one come to terms with such a world? Daniela felt ashamed to appeal to the testimony of the woman from Mauritius with the knocked-out teeth. She should have known all this beforehand.

The sun slipped out from behind the clouds and the light changed. It seemed to Kamil Dreisler that Daniela had a strand of gray hair at the temple.

"I'm sick to my stomach," she said.

"You should squeeze an orange for yourself."

"My belly aches. As if someone were ripping me apart."

She already knew what he wanted to do.

"You'll come and join me," said Kamil Dreisler. "I'll send you tickets for the boat or plane."

"What will you do if you don't succeed? If you don't get it even after a year?"

"Everything." It was a different "everything" than her thoughts remembered.

"Everything?" she echoed.

"Yes. Everything," he answered.

She tried not to look nervous. She remembered that the Nazis sold the living and the dead abroad, sold them truth and lies, took away people's jobs and citizenship, closed the borders and made people behave like scurvy dogs. Pharaoh Blumen knew that it all came from somewhere and did not evaporate like morning vapors over the sea. It was in the air. Should she remind Kamil Dreisler of that and make him mad again? Does he want to exchange an idea for himself, himself for her, her for an idea? She looked at the water touching her ankles and realized that it was thick and salty, like phlegm. She looked sideways at the white crosses blistered from the summer's heat.

"Does it hurt that much?" asked Kamil Dreisler.

He half closed his gray-green eyes. It started to rain. The land became quiet, and the silvery gray meadow of the sea heaved up and down. The water along the shore became muddy. Further out the waves broke in small hillocks with white foamy caps.

"Maybe you'll come back before I'm old, and not only to me," Daniela said. "While I'm still young and unwrinkled."

Grains of sandy dust and drops of rain settled on her eyebrows. The crystals of sand and the rain looked like needle points. Kamil Dreisler saw her watching his lips to see if his reply would be better or worse than she expected. The innkeeper from Raveh's played the gramophone as he always did when a ship left. He played the *Kineret*.

A little while later, all that remained was the content of her words and the dusk of her alto voice. The ship rocked on the open sea. Kamil Dreisler looked toward the shore. Did he see clearly? There was Daniela Klaus, beautiful and proud like a dark red gladiola, walking toward the barrels in the sand. The wind tousled her hair. She stopped and looked at the sea, her eyes following the ship.

She stood with her back to the red oleanders. The flowers were cuddled inside the tufts of leaves, silent and hidden from the sea. Daniela used to believe that the oleanders, in the morning, looked like cradled children; at noon like young, blushing women; and at night like brides and grooms. But that was before the winds began blowing through the bushes on those sleepless nights. The sea's breath flowed through the bush, creating a pleasant hum that blossomed into a gentle voice. It was a beautiful voice that spoke to her, telling her good things; but bad things, too, and the terrible things it came to say made her afraid of the red blossoms.

She stood between the oleander bush and the sea; her lips parted as if to speak, as if to interrupt the wind.

Kamil Dreisler imagined the questions that could not be answered. The sea, the sky, and the wind now spoke their language, as did the birds and the waves. The voice of the earth and the voice of the sea joined with the wind that carried them away. He heard questions for which he had no answers.

At the other end of the shore, but not clearly visible from the ship, stood old Pharaoh Blumen with his yellow straw panama hat. He leaned on his boat, which had been pulled out of the water and looked like a rotting seashell, turned over on its side, with the oars lying in the sand. Somebody else was coming: the woman from Mauritius. For her, land was like a flask and the rest of the world the place where one gets mail.

As long as the shore could be seen from the ship, Daniela stood there alone. Kamil Dreisler could still see the edge of the white bay at Rosh Haniqra toward the bay in Acre, and saw the long boat with the orange trim. Nahariyya became smaller and smaller. From the distance, the land at the edge of the sea and the sky looked like a bluish memory somewhere in the future, seeming clearer and clearer, and already lost at the same time. The oleanders looked desolate. Only the rocks jutted into the sky, and then they began to disappear, too.

Occasionally a flash of lightning cleaved the waters, and in the darkness at midday the drops of seawater glistened like tears. The white precipices would open for a moment, over and over, like a chasm, and then everything closed again like the ravines of all times, and the surface of the water was joined again by the golden rays of the sun. The depths of the sea, where everything was blind, would show up for a second.

At times the sea, the waves, and the land resembled eyes. And the eyes of the sea, the eyes of the land, and the eyes of the waves resembled the eyes of the madman from the asylum in Acre, who watched the sea and the world from his cell before dying, and this world floated away even though it was near at hand. He saw things that had already been forgotten or would be remembered differently by the next generation.

From the northern border, guarded by the old fighter plane, to the bay at Acre, the sea formed an alternate line of straight shore and shallow inlets, except for the deeper bay at Haifa. In the evening the sea rose with the tide and fell again through the night and morning. In autumn and winter, when the storm and rains came, the sea turned gray and black. When the days were calmer at the beginning of spring and in the summer, the waters would become quiet, and the surface would have a blue-gray tinge. In summer the sea had a calming effect, but in winter it was deadening.

During all seasons, little wild birds would leave their nests on the rocks deep in the sea. They would sail past the hulls of ships with hungry eyes, competing only with seagulls, ospreys, or cormorants. They waited for the live prey appearing in the rays on the foamy water, and they cried, *Tee ooo terrr . . . Tee eee terrr . . .*

The sea roared on.